Praise for
The Drum Made from the Skin of My Sisters

"Written with sensitivity, *The Drum Made from the Skin of my Sisters* unmasks the brutal face of tribal Afghan and Iranian societies, where numerous citizens are enslaved, ignorant of their own potential or afraid to express it. Two young girls, considered women by their tribal societies, narrowly escape death. They gain strength and hope from a widow, still recovering from her own loss. Eveline Horelle Dailey's courageous book captivates the heart, enriches the mind, and etches the soul."

— Ellen L. Buikema, M.Ed.
Author of *Parenting . . . A Work in Progress*

"Eveline Horelle Dailey has created a story of immense value, helping us to understand the plight of young women from distant and different cultures. The book is written in a personal and intimate way that goes far beyond describing the lives of two young girls from the Middle East. This author invites us to compare our lives with those of Saadia and Leila, as she intertwines the feelings of the widow from Maine who adopted them. This story does not stop with despair but instead shows the power of the human spirit. A must read."

— Rose Winters
The Foundation for Living Medicine

The Drum Made from the Skin of My Sisters

Big Change   Equal Rights   New Mindset   Free Women

Other books by Eveline Horelle Dailey:

Lessons from the Lakeside—
  A Journey Toward Self Discovery

The Canvas—A Secret from the Holocaust

The Drum Made from the Skin of My Sisters

Eveline Horelle Dailey

Two Cats Press
Sun City West, AZ

The Drum Made from the Skin of My Sisters

Published by Two Cats Press
13836 W. Terra Vista Drive, Sun City West, AZ 85375
(623) 810-5044
www.TwoCatsPress.com

First Edition

ISBN-13: 978-1-937083-52-6
ISBN-10: 1-937083-52-7

LCCN: 2043219689

Edited and designed by Gale Leach
Cover design by C. A. Wilke

Dedication

Leila and Saadia found breath in the stories that were given to me. It is to the young girls and the women who remain nameless that this book is dedicated. The flames they ignited and fanned continue to burn in my heart.

Contents

Foreword

Almost all women and girls living in countries ruled by religious dictatorship go through systematic abuse and violent discrimination. Women are treated cruelly with regard to their health, their psychology, and their livelihoods.

They are deprived of fair education, work opportunities, and, most importantly, from being free human beings who can decide the course of their lives on their own.

It is our duty as conscious people in the free world to help these women break the cycle of abuse and backwardness in their societies by promoting Human Rights Provisions and insisting on necessary changes in the legal systems of those countries.

Only by these changes will the children of tomorrow not face stoning, gang rape, acid attack, forced marriage, honor killing, and genital mutilation as happens now in some Muslim countries.

A society that ensures freedom and education for its women will have healthier future generations.

I am honored to share my views for this exquisitely written masterpiece, and many thanks to my dear Eveline for tackling this sensitive and covert subject.

Love and peace to all,

Dr. Siamak Rafi-Zadeh
Vancouver, Canada

Preface

When we think of the societies that brought us alphabets, the concepts of numbers, which we use to calculate our values, or the area of the world where the first banking system was formulated, our knowledge of world history travels more than 3,000 years and takes us to the Persian/Mesopotamian regions of the globe. When we think of the first enforceable laws regarding human rights, we must look at the Zoroastrians of Iran. Today, it is difficult to think of these teachings and principles and think of the same areas.

This project did not arrive by means of an angelic tap on the shoulder. My mind, soul, and heart became engaged when a man from that region asked me to write an article about the abuse of young women and girls in the areas mentioned. Being a global citizen of good conscience, a fire was fueled, and I began to hear the drums. The music had passion, and at times the passion was nothing but pain. Every time the hands of the master struck the drums, I heard the voices. They were clear. They told me stories of pain. I could feel the heat on the skin and the flesh tightening around the wood, and the beatings did not stop. I heard the stories of men exercising reproachable behaviors toward women and girls. I decided to uncover veils of tears. It was time to be engaged.

The tears of my sisters whet my desire to acknowledge the songs.

Soon, unexpected events followed, and through the eyes of technology, I witnessed the stoning of a young girl. Her death opened a door wide, and her red blood marked a dark spot in the world I knew. I promised my sister her short life would not be in vain. I may not have known her name, but I gave her honor because she is one of my sisters, and no one deserves to be stoned to death, raped, or battered in any way. Not for honor, not for country, and not for belief.

It is through my inspired lenses that this novel comes to you. You will read fictionalized stories of two girls rescued from horrific endings.

Is societal victimization of females, their oppression and abuse, a form of ignorance seemingly primed soon after birth and continuously nourished after the passage from the womb? Does it take large and long amounts of time to indoctrinate such sociopathic behavior? What permits a father to cast the first stone aimed to kill his daughter?

Have we lost the sacredness of the female? Have we lost the one responsible for our lives?

Extremists do not want their women educated, because then they can pass their knowledge to their children. In some societies, fundamentalism is a tool used to establish total control by means of fear and cruelty under the guise of religion.

What happens to a society that inflicts fear, distress, and even violent death upon its own? Where has dignity, respect, and hope gone?

While the children play, older men recruit with their eyes the young girls who would be more profitable in a marriage intended to promote their self-satisfaction and gratification. In certain areas where the rules of decency were abandoned, the male child is also without education. He does not know how to be decent or compassionate. He does not know how to be a man who is respectful of a young girl. He does not know these things, because he is also a victim of his environment and the society that brought him into the world.

Acknowledgements

If I wrote volumes to thank all the people who fanned the fire that blew into my heart, they would not be sufficient to repay my debt of gratitude to those mentioned here and those remaining unnamed.

During the penning of this novel, I learned about the differences that separate many of us. I also learned that acceptance knows no boundaries, and taking chances comes with noble rewards.

When Dr. Siamak Rafi-Zadeh took a chance and asked me to write an article with him, neither of us knew that the hands of the great muse would pour fuel onto an unseen fire. Thank you, Siamak!

My esteemed friend, Rose Winters, read the first few raw pages and gave me the title of the book. She fanned the fire with her strong words.

Authors and critics from the West Valley Writers Workshop, without a whisper, became the sources of incalculable encouragement. I thank each of you Inkslingers!

I felt the winds of Iran and of Sweden as they blew a unique direction to my prose. Thank you, Sara Sarifi.

I appreciate the comments, edits, and suggestions from my dear and special friend, Serge Corvington. He exposed my prose and gave my thoughts a patriarchal perspective.

No words I know can express the honor I feel or the strength of Khaled Hishma's poem. A simple thank you for allowing me to include of his words in my book does not suffice, yet I know no other way to express my gratitude to this educator and activist from Jordan. It is upon reading his words that you will understand the texture of his work.

I thank my children, Daphne and Rachel, and my husband, Donald Dailey for their watchful eyes and the space they gave me when I was penning this work.

Thank you, Christopher Wilke, for reading my mind and producing the beautiful cover art and design.

To Gale Leach at Two Cats Press, I tip my hat as I give her an accolade. What you find under your eyes is the product of a manuscript handled with confidence and direct probing by an editor unafraid to ask the questions I left unanswered. It is because of her tenacious editing that my prose found its clarity. Thank you, Gale.

I am grateful to Ken Johnson at YourEbookBuilder. com for making my words available on e-readers everywhere. Many thanks, Ken, for bringing my work to these 21st-century devices!

CHAPTER 1

Julienne Returns Home

Dusk—all was dark. Above my head, the stars. These jewels of the night were my crown. My curls were free, no one was around to tell me to cover my head, and that felt good. Born in France and now a resident of Maine, my home in the United States, I was inspired to travel from Asia to the Middle East. I made it back home in one piece. Home! My home!

A different soil welcomed me. I was home! I made my approach to the newly built driveway and garage, driving slowly—very slowly. Every four feet, dim twinkles of Malibu lights the contractor installed presented me their sparkling heads. I was not certain about his idea, but now, driving to the cadence of a moving turtle, I liked the white glow. My long, winding driveway had taken on a new character. It took a while, but now I believed Maine to be the most beautiful state in the continental United States. This place had become home!

Headlights off, slower than minutes before, with the car's windows down, my nearly motionless ride continued. Nothing disturbed the nocturnal symphony. Animals and plants in unison sang me their songs. They were all out to welcome me. I could hear them all. I was home.

The repairs to the road brought me a seamless ride, with no bumps, no holes. The contractor had done a good job while I was gone. The sea breeze of the harbor stroked my senses and awakened in me the sensation of a peaceful lover's embrace. A few deep breaths brought me various scents I had not realized I missed during my absence. The lushness of this environment was different from the parts of the Middle East I left a few days before. The route I traveled caused me to feel a deep sense of appreciation for many things. All around me the sounds of familiar refrains: night creatures chanting, waves of the Atlantic in full force to orchestrate the music. Again, I was reminded that I was home. Something elegant was happening.

There was a satisfying feeling that came with returning home. This drive was not like my first time on this driveway. I felt no apprehension about what I would find. I had no fear this time, only contentment. Frank, my deceased husband, purchased the property many years ago, and this house was now my refuge. Still missing his presence, I was no longer brought to tears every time I experienced something new. Numerous times, he told me he was complete. Finally, I knew Frank used these words to prepare me for what I would not face. His illness ravaged the distinguished American in Paris I married.

Cancer took him from me before he could teach me how to speak English. I have plenty of memories to cherish, but wishing he was by my side is a continual happening. He suggested that I experience the things we did not have time to do together. This journey was one of them, and while his presence was missed, there was solace. I made it back home in one piece.

Whoosh, whoosh. Almost imperceptible, I recognized the sound of my resident owl. She must have been hunting, or she was welcoming me home. The first time I heard the faint sound of her wings, I called her Adeline, but I still did not know if my owl was female or male. In and out of the tall trees, I could almost trace her flight and then nothing else. She rested, not a sound, watching me—I was sure of it. A few more feet, at the curve, I perceived the outline of new granite boulders. I wanted the entrance to this home to feel more like the one I grew up in. Alas, it was not yet spring to smell and see the wildflowers. Anticipating my own bed was the bonus to this night. Home! I was home!

One more curve, and the new garage door's light came on—magic!—but I had no key or device to open the door. I parked the car a few feet away in front of the garage and walked toward the house. The light by the new side door came on as I approached. I did not want my garage seen from the front of the house. As prearranged, the key was under a pot beside the new mat. The contractor had mentioned something about motion-detecting lights, and now I understood as they worked well. Once inside, I found all was in order. A note taped to the wall read, "Press button to open or close the garage door," and an arrow pointed to a small black button. I pushed and magic again! The enormous door rolled up to the ceiling, lights came on, and my new garage, now painted white, had a multitude of cabinets on both sides of it, and all looked great. When I told the contractor I needed a place to store my Christmas decorations, for some reason, my request caught him off guard, but he delivered! He did not know I had drawn plans, but I soon brought them to him. When I created the plans, I gave emphasis to the long front porch and the blue spruces on the terraced part of the yard on either side of the porch. They created a semi-circle following the drive to the stairs that led to the house. My two rocking chairs would stand centered and protected. At the middle of this, lower than porch and drive, would be a bench, one I would find sooner rather than later. All this would be done to have various levels of view of the harbor. In Maine, the winter's snow came too often and in large amounts. My colored lights on the trees would bring life to the environment. I was excited that my drawing would soon become a reality.

He did a great job. All was clean around this giant garage. On a counter by the door, I noticed a screwdriver and a small hammer tied with a bright red ribbon. Nice man—he could not know that I already had a screwdriver and a hammer. Once more, I walked toward my car, feeling pleased about lighting in all the right places and the fact that this old car delivered me to my door. I continued my inspection. On what I gathered was a workbench empty of tools, I found two garage door openers and an invoice. I smiled. I was one driver, had one car, and now a two-car garage and two openers were all mine. The universe may have been playing with me.

All looked almost in order. I closed the door. The poor car that was stored for two months in a parking garage at the airport in Bangor, Maine, was covered with dust. Now tucked away in her new home, the car would wait a few more days to be washed. As I looked at what was once my shiny, black car, I was reminded of the dusty black *burkas* I saw not such a long time ago. I made a mental note to find other arrangements next time: washing this car was going to take me hours. There were no car washing businesses in my little town. Now, an experienced globetrotter, I traveled only with essentials. I removed my small suitcase from the trunk and went inside the house.

Taking this trip and exploring a world I knew nothing about had been both exhilarating and frightening, and it had been many years in the making. My aunt Ursula said it took a certain gumption. Suzannah, her younger sister, who taught me about the gentle side of my Jewish roots, would have chosen a different word. She was subtle in her teaching, but the resonance of her words was permanently etched in my mind. I will remember Suzannah always. She was my nanny when I was a youngster and my friend later on, as I grew into adulthood. Before her death, I found out she was my mother. Life circumstances did not permit her to inform me before she was gone. Ursula was different in character but looked just like Suzannah. I did not know her prior to my arrival in Maine. The way she spoke was more a staccato, and I often wondered why they were so enormously different. Ursula was blunt; Suzannah was softness itself. Regardless of their differences, it felt good to have a relative around.

My husband, Frank, dreamed of exploring other than the Judeo-Christian societies we came from. His life was cut short. I was not yet fully recovered from his death, when the time to travel and explore came upon me. When going through a series of pictures Frank had of Iran and Afghanistan, I was not expecting anything of the kind. Compelled, I had to fulfill not only his dream but my own. Taking a trip to regions of the world I did not know turned out to invigorate and have a profound effect on me.

The trip began in North Africa. I had to visit Morocco one more time. My excuse was that I needed some saffron from the market in Fez. At one point in my life, I must have decided that I needed reasons for what I did—possibly because, when I acted without a reason, the results were always disastrous. The call of the pyramids was strong. I had to stand in front of the great giants. This time, I felt small, with a deeper feeling of awe. Somehow, as if they talked to me, the Pyramids gave me the permission to continue on with my journey.

Frank often told me, when opportunity knocked, and I had the means to do something, I was to do all that I could and seize those openings. Thanking my father and also Frank for the fortune left me, I had no excuse, once fear was set aside.

During this voyage, I not only discovered new places but also was particularly touched by some. I fell in love with Afghanistan. Its topography seemed to sing to me; yet, looking back, my feelings did not come from the beauty of great buildings and various museums. The place was mostly destroyed—desolate in many areas, with the rubble of past wars scattered everywhere I looked. Bits and pieces of various war machines littered the landscape. In the rural areas, a sort of awakening and transformation came upon me. The jagged stones mixed with sand had a pink tint and, at times, all looked menacing. Often, the colors changed. The pink took on deep brown and red tones. I felt as if I were looking at dried blood. I was sure it would be many years before I could assimilate all that I observed. The farther landscape was not pink but almost a pale yellow, and I was sure that, too, would present me with some speculation. When I went to their marketplace, I felt sadness in many eyes—too many to make it comfortable to stay long, and too many to ignore. The women did not wear western clothes. A land of sharp despair and rugged beauty was all around me.

Regrettably, like all things, this phase of my travel had to end, and this time I again crossed the same countries I had been in, but the route was different.

The well-tendered gardens of Iran and those of Turkey will stay with me always. Some I sketched, with the idea of duplicating them somewhere on my own property. The finished product would have a different effect, because Maine is so green, but that did not matter. If not in a garden, my sketches would make it to some of my paintings. The scents of the flowers were still all around me, yet looking at snow-covered mountains made the feeling almost supernatural.

The trees, the parks, the fragrances of flowers

Eveline Horelle Dailey

I could not name, the spices, and the fresh-brewed tea—I knew would carry the people of Teheran with me for a long while. It was in and around this capital city that I saw a marriage of parallel civilizations. In Teheran, I saw women in western clothes walking the streets and women with their heads covered. I was surprised. Numbers of women wore traditional Islamic clothes, yet most men in the capital wore western suits. I never saw a Middle Eastern or Arab man in shorts, and none looked like Omar Sharif. Overall, varieties of traditional clothes were apparent. I assumed the financial status of a person dictated the attire.

I met shopkeepers, and they offered me tea. This was a custom that left me smiling often. The cultural richness of many of these places captured my soul. Many of my experiences would take a long time to digest. Through the exchange of friendship, I was invited to a wedding—the marriage of the daughter of the innkeeper. She looked particularly young to be getting married. They felt I must be their guest at the party since I was already a guest at their inn. At the last minute, I decided to claim an illness and did not attend the celebration.

While in each country, many times I held my breath. The sites I saw demanded no motion at all and complete silence. I missed Frank a great deal every time. My feet conquered no mountains of Pakistan. It was explained to me that a woman alone could not do such a thing. For reasons made clear to me, I could not ignore the advice. To look at the mountains from my hotel room window would have to satisfy any curiosity I had. Surprised and somewhat angry, I knew enough to keep my feelings to myself. I was in a foreign country, and with its patriarchal rules, the gauge I often used to judge or evaluate a place did not apply in such settings. I was not inspired to take chances. The people I met in Pakistan were distantly polite to me. Their food, however, enraptured my palate. It was the thought of Frank that caused this reaction, I was sure of it, for when he was alive, we shared flavors of India and Pakistan.

The innkeeper in Pakistan made it clear that I could not walk the busy streets of Islamabad by myself. Too many things I could not do alone made it necessary to hire a porter to escort me around town. I did not feel comfortable with him. I felt something ominous in the air I breathed. My stay in Pakistan did not take me to Karachi, which had been my ultimate destination in that country, and the Arabian Sea would not touch my feet. Disappointed, still I felt right about going elsewhere.

CHAPTER 2

The Crossing

As I traveled these regions of the globe, something I could not describe haunted me. The people, their foods, and their music felt vibrant. Colors, textures, and sounds touched my soul—yet accompanying these feelings too often were eyes that told me stories I did not understand or want to know. Beautiful, wide eyes of young girls, too young to have experienced life, gazed at me without wonder. The women I saw had eyes filled with sadness and no sparks of hope. They looked at me without giving a sense of seeing me. Something I could not grasp, something caustic, collided with a part of me I had not recognized, and the feeling was uneasy.

As I was reconstructing my trip, a cup of tea from my own kitchen brought back the memories of being in Pakistan. Wanting to see Afghanistan, the crossing to Peshawar was the most logical place from my location. I had seen picturesque sites of the place on posters, and these preoccupied me as much as the eyes that penetrated my soul. There were some flights from Islamabad to Kabul, but I wanted something more exotic, more dangerous! If we drove, I would see the mountains I hoped to experience at close range. My travel agent and advisor regarding the cultures and their differences from my own arranged the crossing. My silk scarf had a way of rolling off my head, and he explained to me more than once that it was culturally unacceptable to show off my curls. I was being disrespectful to my host country and its people.

He had the good grace to plan and arrange the journey from one country to the next. My strong feeling was that he wanted to get rid of me. I was to be with a guide and his wife and a guard hired to protect me. None of them spoke English. One sip of tea, and I remembered the road, if it could be called that. Covered with dust, we trucked on in a Toyota pickup that had lost its outer color and any remnant of shock absorbers it may have had. When the door opened for me to get in between the man and his wife, I discovered the Toyota was once green.

Though there were only three of us in the pickup, between my traveling companions, I felt like a sardine in a can. The man was small in stature, I am a medium size woman, and his wife made up for the weight we both carried. She was huge. He must have been about my age, or perhaps slightly older. He spoke nonstop in a tongue I did not understand. He wore a traditional costume, but I could not tell from which country, as the men from Pakistan and Afghanistan wore similar clothing. If there were differences, I could not see them. The trousers were not made with the same cut as western pants. Most were white or gray and in need of cleaning. On all counts, they were covered with a long shirt I believe was called a *shalwar kameez*.

My driver wore a vest with magnificent and colorful embroidery. His teeth were almost brown, and when he stood next to me, we looked eye to eye—his were green and mine are brown. As he drove, he pointed toward beautiful and rugged mountains, but his wife never spoke. At best, it was a difficult crossing, and I did not know when we left one country and entered another. There had been tattered signs, but none were international, so, again, there was nothing to understand.

Many times during this trip, I questioned my sanity. My apprehension about these places and some of the people was not entirely unfounded. I had the distinct feeling of being with a greater part of humanity I knew nothing about. Not understanding their words, many feelings remained unspoken, with only a hint of clarity. With a gaze or a movement of the head, we began to understand one another. The wife wore a long, black, chemise-type dress, and her head was covered with a black cover I cannot exactly describe. It was not a scarf, but it managed to envelop her head, making her face look like an egg. The travel agent told me this type of head cover was called a *hijab*. Her eyes were amber; her hands looked worn out. During this trip, she made sure that my head was always covered. At every stop, she made us some tea. She was a magician at finding the smallest sticks of wood to make her fire. Her husband never helped. I attempted to pick up small dried branches. She smiled but made it clear that I did not have the knack of finding the right twig. I did not speak any of the languages of the region, yet I communicated with signs, pointing a lot, and smiles. Most of the time, I was able to get all that I needed. Given more time with this particular family, I would have learned enough to be able connect with my new acquaintances.

During one of our tea breaks, I decided to show them pictures of my home that I had with me. Based on the sounds they made, I trusted they approved. The lady liked my trees and my flowers. With their body language and their fingers pointing, they asked about my rocking chairs. They became hysterical when, with my body movement, I gave them descriptions of a chair that could rock. It was good to see that it was fine to be made fun of. Over tea, we laughed a lot.

The approach to Kabul came with something serious in the air. Making certain that my head was covered at all times, the lady tightened the scarf around my neck, nearly choking me. We were in a different country, and the protocol had changed. Men loitering in various places gave me the appearance of quiet desperation. They all had very long beards and did not give the appearance of being clean. They had large firearms, and some had goods to sell. It was clear to me that women were banned from the scene.

My driver/husband/guide stopped many times to speak to roadside merchants. They spoke to him, ignoring the lady and me always. We were insignificant. The feeling was distinct, but we were not threatened in any way. A while later, on less tattered roads, my

13

driver friend pointed for the last time as he parked in front of my hotel. Compliments of various wars, during this drive I saw walls with holes larger than the Toyota. Again, I questioned my sanity: my plan was to spend two nights there.

Once the Toyota stopped, my guard took my suitcase and headed to the entrance. Some luxurious items were in the lobby, including incredibly beautiful handmade rugs of wool and silk. There was an uneasy feeling because, prior to entering the hotel, I had seen the signature of war all around me. I felt uneasy. I pointed to the lobby so my friends would come with me. I wanted to buy them dinner, but they did not accept my offer. I wanted to hug them, and I knew that, too, would not be acceptable. Tears of gratitude fell freely on my face. The lady, whose name I never knew, took my hands and pressed them against her heart, and that I understood. She appreciated and accepted my gesture when my one extra scarf, tucked away in my bag, became hers. I took her hands and pressed them against my heart.

CHAPTER 3

The Invitation

After the long and sometimes difficult trip from the Middle East, arriving at the New York airport to find a plane in disrepair was not part of my plans. At least this arrival did not turn me into a panic-stricken young woman unable to understand the language. Although Frank spoke French to me when we were married, I was delighted by the fact that I had now learned English. This time, I knew where I was and where I was going: HOME! No map was needed, nor did I need to look for names of streets or numbers of houses. Something penetrating told me I had taken the changes in my life for granted.

Owl's Head had become my home while I must not have been looking. I took all of its oddities as normal and charming. They were part of me now, a very new me. Thanks to the new heating system in the house, I handled the winters almost like a native. No longer missing Paris or the opera, which for a long time was my second home,

I recalled the lecture halls at the Sorbonne as vague memories.

Suzannah would have liked this place, but not my mother.

There is something soothing about this home that Frank purchased for us. I still miss him after so many years. My life here is good, but I miss talking to him, I miss his voice. I miss his embraces. The feelings when he sang songs I had never heard have not left me. His singing voice became weak as he lay dying, but the intensity of his love never faltered. The few dinner parties of today bring me some joy, but there is always something missing. New friends depart; satisfied with food and company, they go to their homes. My bed remains cold.

My mind traveled to and fro the entire night.

Once I parked the car, I carried my small suitcase to the kitchen. The first time I entered this room, tears swelled and dropped uncontrollably, but on this occasion, they stayed where memories are meant to stay.

I sat by the window, still too dark to see the harbor across the street, although my mind traveled of its own volition, tracing a route I wanted to take, but not alone. Not absent-minded, yet not focusing on what I was doing, I sifted through the mountain of mail I carried from the mailbox by the street. One more day away, and there would not have been room for a hair.

My mind continued to jump from one subject to the next, something that drove Suzannah and Frank nuts. As I looked through the mail, the cup of tea I made like an automaton flavored my senses.

My two rocking chairs were safe in the living room to be taken out when I woke up, whenever that would be, but not now.

My comfortable shoes were still on my feet. I walked to go to my bedroom, smiling as I saw my reflection in the mirror in the hallway. My stance was much like that of Suzannah. My clothes looked a lot like what she often wore. Smiling, I thought of that incredible woman who kept her promise and did not tell me she was my mother until her death. My heart felt warm. I went back to the kitchen for more tea.

HOME! I was tired, but I needed to unwind, so I continued to look at the mail. Before I realized it, the sun was bright. The best thing to do was to take a walk. Another seashell would find its way to my growing collection. Under my cold bare feet as I walked the beach, every grain of sand held me in a sort of love lost. Soon I felt I had become part of the ocean's voice.

Shoes back on, the morning walk on my long driveway reminded me that life, as I had left it, had not changed at all and had returned to the pace I left only two months ago. I returned home, dusted every piece of furniture, and brought my two rocking chairs onto my long porch. I sat and burst into laughter, as I remembered my traveling companion laughing at my explanation of the motion of a rocking chair. All my plants had been taken care of by my new neighbors on the next property, south of me. The fragrance of wet soil, mixed with a breeze from the sea, brought a smile. All was in order.

Since I had not dealt with all the mail, I began to separate the envelopes containing bills. Too many advertisements for things I did not need or use began a pile on the floor next me. A few envelopes from France, two from Germany, and one from an address nearby; curious, I opened that one first. It was a handwritten invitation.

How odd that an invitation to meet a group of women from a global symposium would be awaiting my arrival. The mail, the mail—it never goes on vacation!

My trip was symbolic enough, but now the air I breathed felt pleasant. Perhaps a change of season was in the air, or perhaps it was simply that I was home. How did these people know of me? I did not recognize the name on the return address. The few friends I had made in Owl's Head never mentioned belonging to any group. What drove a person to send me an invitation? To what, was more the question? Nevertheless, my curiosity was on full alert as I examined the envelope that had no particular markings. When I opened it, I found a note attached, signed by Mr. Rand, the French teacher at the local school. The letter to me was from a woman.

Dear Mrs. Fairchild,

Your aunt gave me your name and address. She told me of a trip you were taking in the Middle East and parts of Asia. I think you will be interested in being part of our group.

At that point I decided a cup of tea was in order.

I am Zelda Swartz and I wish to extend an invitation to you. We are a group of women, though there are some men in our organization. We have been looking into the wrongful sexual abuse of young girls and women, primarily in the regions you visited. We are aware that this abuse happens in the capitals or large cities, but the vast majority of these abuses happen in the immense rural areas. I grew up in these regions, and after going back to what once was home, I became an advocate for a cause.

I pray that you will be able to join us.

The note continued with the time, address, and a telephone number. There was not much about the true purpose of this meeting. I held the note a while, recapturing something I noticed when traveling the region. I had sensed something ominous in many pairs of eyes that looked at me. As I read this woman's note, that feeling was inescapable—I was back there, attempting to understand what was behind the beautiful yet sad eyes that looked my way. I got up and went to the telephone.

After a long conversation, I went back to the porch. The temperature was perfect. My newly planted blue spruces sang with the winds, and songbirds joined the chorus. The sea breeze caressed my neck and, unpreventable as it was, I thought of Frank. I met him purely by accident, yet it was not—it felt more like a meeting orchestrated by forces beyond our understanding or control, and in an instant we became inseparable. We did not wonder what awaited us along the route we would take. An awareness of something greater could not explain something palpable. When I read the note, and during the telephone conversation with Zelda, I had á type of premonition, I could sense something I could not explain.

On the given day, and for the formality of it all, I arrived on time with a bouquet of flowers for the hostess I did not know and to a meeting that would change the course of my life. There were seven women already there. One of them was my Aunt Ursula and also two men. One was Mr. Rand, a teacher at the local school, whom I had met some years back when I was invited to speak to the children about languages. An American woman spoke with two very young women in a dialect I did not recognize. Her name was Gale, and she was from Connecticut. At first glance, I guessed one of the girls was from Iran, the other from Afghanistan. They appeared scared, with their heads covered and their eyes cast downward.

The meeting took place around a long rustic table. I pulled out a chair, sat, and introduced myself, but they already knew who I was. The two young girls smiled at me but did not say anything. Their eyes went downward again. Timid, I surmised, but feeling something more, I could tell they were not comfortable around this table.

"Julienne, this is Saadia. She is from Afghanistan, and this is Leila from Iran."

I smiled, wondering how I had known where they came from.

We talked and socialized, but nothing of great importance was said. The girls never uttered a sound. They drank tea, and so did I.

As the afternoon ended, a suggestion was made to find a home for the next meeting, and I offered mine. We agreed on a time and date. Soon after, we got into our cars and drove off. The two young women left with Gale, who was their temporary host.

Puzzled by the meeting, but satisfied to have met new people, I waited until evening and called Ursula. I asked her what the meeting was really all about.

"My dear, we wanted to meet and greet you, so all of us of the same mind could get to know one another on a social basis first."

"Are you helping to organize whatever this is, or are you like me — a guest who shows up when invited?"

"Julienne, I am one of the organizers. I am passionate about women, girls, and female children being abused by men who are not able to understand the damage they do. I feel all women who are free to think for themselves should find conscience, sympathy, or the will to help those who cannot help themselves because they do not know anything different. That is why I am involved. Like the two girls you met, they do not know how to stand up against abuse and develop their full potential as human beings."

I was surprised by her remarks. I had never seen Ursula so animated. "You are so passionate. I did not expect to see this side of you, I like it. There is so much I must learn about you and you about me. Being my mother's sister does not make up for all that we missed when we did not know the existence of the other. But this may not be the right time. We will have to spend time together, to get to know one another."

"Yes, that is a good idea, but you're right: now is not the time. Since you offered your home for the next meeting, I am hoping you will join the group. We need help. The people being abused need voices to tell their stories, the children such as the two girls you met today need attention."

Across the telephone line, I could almost feel Ursula patting my head, as she had done many times before.

"I have a very early day tomorrow. Let's talk more about this in the late afternoon. We have a lot to talk about. I love you very much, Julienne. You remind me so much of my sister. But do me a favor: don't take trips to any more war zones. No one needs that in their lives."

I smiled. "I know you are busy right now, so call me when you are free. I cannot say why, but I have more than a passing interest in the welfare of these gals. I want to know more about all this—like who decided to bring these girls into the U.S.A.? Are they some kind of war trophy?" I had a lot of unanswered questions. I sat back in my chair and wondered what I was getting into. "Ursula, this is the way my life has always been. I feel with my heart while my head gets tangled in details and logistics. My gut tells me to listen to the whole story. I can't say why I am interested, but I am."

"You're a woman, aren't you? That should be reason enough! I'll talk to you tomorrow."

As a true German, she was done with the conversation and the phone went dead. Pondering what possibly lay ahead and still puzzled, I looked for something Frank had written years before he met me. He had read it to me, and I vaguely remembered the paper was yellow, so it would not be too hard to find among the thousands of pages of his notes. Soon enough, I found what I was looking for.

It was one of Frank's many such papers, never published. Remembering that Frank wanted to know more about the laws regulating the growth patterns and the movements of women in the Middle East, I felt compelled to read on.

As was my custom, I made myself yet another cup of tea. These days, my numerous cups came from the various countries I had visited. A friend once told me tea was the language of my thoughts.

I found Frank's note and on the first page, hand written with various pens. My eyes fell upon, "They need our help and understanding, so they can learn to understand themselves and find the courage to free themselves from their oppressors. This may take centuries." Based on these words alone, I knew whatever discovery I was to make would not be digested in one day.

Frank had been deceased over three years, but he was still very much part of my life. There was so much we did not have time to explore. A few tears could not be held. They escaped and fell onto the paper I had been reading, Frank's variety of inks formed a psychedelic rainbow.

CHAPTER 4

The Second Meeting

The meeting on Saturday afternoon was going to be perfect. The day before, I went to Ursula's bakery and store. I ordered some of her delicious pâté, with slices of dark breads, and I also ordered cookies to have with tea. Ursula would bring everything when she came to the meeting. I got some cheese, enough greens, tomatoes, and cucumbers to make a salad. I had some recipes to make lentils with vegetables; I felt the girls needed to have something reminding them of home, even if I did not have all the right spices.

A few hours before the meeting, I cooked the lentils and the rice according to my palate. Rice from India made this portion of the meal regional. In both countries, they ate similar foods, and I prayed that my herbs from Provence would not be offensive to the girls' taste buds.

Early in the morning, I woke up to a bright, sun-shining day. In my delicate coffee cup with blue and gold design from Limoges, the best aromatic brew from Arabia was ready for me. Life felt good. My favorite rocking chair was also waiting for me. It was the one closest to the entry door, because it offered the best view of the harbor. Today everything appeared clearer than usual. A good omen, Frank would have said.

Promptly at one o'clock, everyone showed up. After so many years, I was still taken aback that Americans were rather punctual. So far, I had not mastered this habit with any degree of success. I found so many subtle things to be different from culture to culture... so while I told people around one o'clock, I did not expect them at one o'clock. While time established by the sun did not change, the cultural concept of time was different from one country to the other.

Saadia entered first, dressed in a colorful, long, blue skirt with ribbons and some sequins adorning the edge. She wore a long-sleeved blouse she must have gotten in the U.S. Over the blouse, she wore a magnificent, multicolored vest, embellished with silk threads of brilliant primary yellow, blue, and green. She looked regal. In the custom of her religion, her head was completely covered with a yellow and blue scarf. I welcomed her with a smile, and she responded with a timid one.

A full head taller than Saadia, Leila followed. At the first meeting, I had not noticed the height difference between the two. She wore western clothes: a long, brown skirt, the type Suzannah would have worn, and a pink cotton shirt with long sleeves. It was a very light pink, and that surprised me, as I had not seen pastel

25

colors in any of the countries I had recently visited. Her head was uncovered, and her beautiful hair was a shiny, heavy black tied back with a bright pink bow. Her beauty unspoiled by a scarf was striking. Almost black, her eyes were framed by the longest eyelashes I had ever seen. Saadia's eyes were green, yet at times her eyes showed off some purple and amber, too. Though different, they were each very beautiful. They wore no makeup and were stunning in their simplicity. Leila, comfortable with her attire, seemed somewhat westernized. Saadia kept her ethnic stance.

The presence of two young people among a group of forty plus women and men felt good and bought life to the house. My aunt Ursula must have been in her late seventies, perhaps more. She never spoke about her age, and I could only speculate about that of the girls.

They had been in the house fewer than fifteen minutes, and the ladies and the two gentlemen wanted a tour of the house. It turned out they all knew its history. They told me stories about it and the fact that, for generations, no one took care of it. One hundred years of age explained a lot to me. Now I understood why I had to repair so many things.

Ursula led them to the library — she called it a den — and they all saw the picture of Frank on the fireplace mantle. She was a good tour guide. Next she led them to the first guest bedroom facing the harbor, where I had an open easel showing a canvas I was working on. It was an oil — a seascape almost finished. I noticed Saadia looking at it intently. She was analyzing it, but of course she said nothing — she did not speak English. No one noticed her, and they continued across to the bedroom facing the back garden, not yet awakened from its winter slumber. Ursula showed everyone the bathroom I had improved with a mural of ferns and butterflies. The existing tub had been moved at an enormous cost, but now it took center stage in the room. The sink and vanity were new but looked adequately old to blend with the tub and its clawed feet.

Ursula asked me if she could also show them my bedroom. I did not mind, as all was neat and clean, although I had not expected people taking a tour of my home and certainly not my bedroom with its lavender and gray colors. They were pleased with the new modern bathroom with French doors leading to a private, walled garden. They came back down the hallway and I took over, suggesting we adjourn to the dining room.

We were eight around my dining table—Gale with the two girls, Ursula, Zelda, Bob, and Mr. Rand (and I do not know why everyone called him Mr. Rand, since his name was Jack). I took the chair closest to the kitchen.

Gale, a take-charge person, had some papers for us to read, all clipped with our names affixed to the first pages. She gave each of us a set. Since reading would be involved, I got up and made some tea to go with the cookies Ursula brought. My tea was from Persia, and I noticed Leila's smile when the aroma traveled to the dining room.

The girls were delighted with the bounty in front of them. In mid-stream, I remembered that I should have had the customary nuts. Alas, I had none, but I had lots of flowers around the house.

I kept referring to them as the girls. Gale reminded me, by virtue of the fact that they had been married, they were more than girls—they were women! Gale was efficient and took care of every detail. Shades of gray were probably not part of her life. According to her, the "women" were twelve and fourteen. To me they were girls!

The pile of papers in front of each of us described their individual rescues. Saadia's papers were on top, and I began there. She was born and raised near Kabul. For reasons she did not know, her family moved to a rural area of the country, where they were to help plant trees. She knew the people planting the trees were from another country. One of them spoke Pashto, but she was not allowed near any of them. They were Christians. She reported that sometimes they gave sweets to her father to bring to his family. She said the village was near the town called Jalal Abad on the Afghanistan side of the border. She did not know the name of the place. She was about seven or eight when they moved there. The descriptions of the surroundings read like a travelogue, but nothing of consequence was said. Important details were somehow missing.

Her mother died shortly after the birth of a boy, and he died soon after her. The notes indicated that all the other children died soon after they were born. I got the distinct feeling that no one knew the birthdate or place of this girl. If I understood correctly, Saadia was the oldest of an undetermined number of children, and she was the only one alive. "It must have been the wish of the merciful" was noted twice on the pages. What surprised me most was to see nothing about missing her mother or siblings. There was nothing explaining how her mother had died or the death of the other children, all of whom were girls. I made a mental note to ask my questions, but this was not the time. Still thinking about her life circumstances, next I read that soon after the mother's death, her father decided it would be better if Saadia were married. He could cook his own meals and make his own tea. He would not have to feed her, and he had to find another wife—he wanted to have sons. He had no use for her.

The material we were reading demanded that I stop a moment. Looking around, I saw that we had all paused our reading. Nothing was said about how many years or how many children were born after Saadia. Looking at this lost child, I would say she was less than twelve years old. She did not know her age, because no one had birth records where she came from. The papers in front of us had no indication of the dates of events. This child had no human status or value. For a split second, I became aware of the work it would take to bring her to this century.

Soon after the mother's death, her father went to prayers every day. He said he needed to talk to the *mullah*. One day, he came back to the house with a man about his own age. This man was fat and had a long beard. Her father made arrangements for Saadia to be his wife. This man was in a rush because his wife was dead and he needed another. He offered a handsome amount for Saadia because she was very pretty and young.

The material we were reading contained only parts of interviews with Saadia that were recorded immediately after her rescue. As of this meeting in my home, I was told she had yet to talk about her rescue, her wedding, and, for that matter, the wedding night. We were reading what someone else had composed based on interviews with her. Nothing in what I read addressed the nature of Saadia's rescue. The information was presented as an inventory of events, with no compassion or emotional input. As I read on, I wondered how a bureaucrat with a computer could render such a wonderful and humane act so cold and heartless.

Without the loss of tempo, the bureaucrat went on. Saadia became pregnant a year or so after the wedding. The young girl eating a cookie in front of me had been impregnated before the age of eleven. The birth produced a stillborn baby boy. Her husband, or should I say rapist, did not accept this and blamed Saadia for the death of his son.

I found this difficult to absorb, yet I was aware that, according to his customs and the fact that he was probably ignorant and indoctrinated to his way of thinking, he could only act as he did. He gave her a beating that left her almost dead. According to rules no one could point out to me, his wife had shamed him, and he therefore found it necessary to send her back to her father, since she was not able to produce live sons for him. As I listened to the women around me, I felt sorrow. I was hearing firsthand about a way of life that had existed for millennia. I was reading about a society that cared nothing about the value of one human being.

I kept hoping for a more humane feeling as I read about Saadia walking a long, hard, mountainous road. No names of towns were mentioned. There were descriptions of what I could only presume were Russian tanks and other vehicles that had been left behind. American soldiers handled the actual rescue, and not much was said beyond that.

The document was not always in chronological order. It mentioned that she walked most of the time. Her guide put her on a mule when she started bleeding too much. Again, I assumed she was bleeding because she had just had that baby. The husband was not with them. Many times she said she wished she were dead. The description of how she got to Pakistan was not in the pages I read. There was a long sentence describing how her father was going to receive her. She had shamed him, and she would therefore be stoned to death.

I looked at her, got up again, poured her some more tea, and put a special cookie in front of her. That was our communication of day. She smiled, and this time, for a split second, she looked me in the eyes before lowering hers. Since I was still standing next to her, I touched her shoulders as a sign of affection. She froze. It was clear to me this young girl had never received any affection. Realizing I would serve her best with greater distance between us, I went back to my seat.

The next paragraph informed us that we were to make this girl feel safe and comfortable. Wondering how we were to accomplish this, I read on. There was no possible communication. She spoke Pashto and only Pashto. I smiled at her again and felt ridiculous. Despair was what I sensed from her. Her eyes looked distant and without focus. Could she have been reviewing her recent past or a future she could not understand?

Looking at her again, I realized I was meeting emotions I had not experienced before. A deep breath took me to the center of her heart. Realizing it would have been impossible for me to endure what she had, not at any age, again I paused. The thought of Suzannah came to me, and then the words of a dear friend: "Within impossible, the word possible exists." The point was clear: it would be up to me to bring comfort to this girl. Not knowing how I would accomplish this, I knew I would have to find the means to rise to this task. In an instant, I decided to do all I could to help her become more than she presently was. With balance of heart, I looked around the table and realized if I helped one, I had to help both.

Safety and comfort had to become priority if I was to have them in my home. Inwardly, I felt I was about to enter an arena I had not bargained for. I remembered when I did not speak English, I felt lost, but because I had never been abused, I did not fear others. I was certain this was not the case for these young girls. It did not take armies to teach languages, and based on stories I had heard from Suzannah, with her first-hand knowledge and experience, she knew armies did not necessarily make people feel safe. She also told me more than once, "People make people feel safe, not armies." So we were to make them feel safe, people to people. Suzannah never bothered telling me how. I was on my own.

Looking around the table, I decided that the feeling in my home would be one of safety. I knew I was approaching a world with subjects as obscure to me as the Rolling Stones were famous.

Without pause, after we had read the pages in front of us, Gale spoke. "These young women and many more like them need us. They need homes. They need to learn the language. They need to understand how we live, what we eat, what we think. In other words, they need to be immersed in our society, not to become who we are, but certainly to become greater than the women they were. They were rejected by their own. Remember that when dealing with them."

Ursula turned her head to look at me. "Julienne, I was so glad when you offered your home for this meeting. As always, I will be blunt: we have no time to waste. I am too old to take on such a project. Julienne, you have the room. English is not your native language, but you managed to learn it, and you are not doing too badly with the American culture." One corner of her mouth turned up as she said, "So you do not eat American cheeses—we will forgive you, I don't either, a ramadur with the smell you hate is what I like. Forget cheeses, what do you say we take a vote and have you become the host home for Saadia and Leila? Because you learned the language later in life, you are the one most equipped to teach them. We will all assist as best we can. We will help you teach them all we know."

I opened my mouth, but nothing came out. I was spellbound and certainly unprepared. I took a deep breath. I remembered Frank and Suzannah telling me that, when opportunity knocked, I was to be ready. I took another breath. Ready or not, I had to say something.

"I can do this. I have the rooms, I have the resources, the only obstacle is that I have no idea how I will do it.

I have no children or sisters. I have no models to draw from. With the assistance and guidance of each of you, I will be able to be what they need at least for a while. I will be a sort of friend. When will they move here?"

Without a pause, Zelda suggested the following Wednesday.

This part of our meeting was over, and we all felt somewhat less tense. Ursula made a joke about being old enough to be the grandmother. Bob and Mr. Rand would not be hosting anyone, so they headed toward the kitchen to help with the food.

Leila looked in disbelief, and Saadia, looking back, made a very slight movement with her head, as if to say this must be the way they do things here. No one else noticed, but I did. I knew that men did not get up to help women in kitchen in the villages of Afghanistan or Iran. They actually did not even eat with them. Around my dining table, we were about to share a meal that two men were serving. One day, I would attempt to explain to them this simple yet gigantic difference between western and eastern men. They did not understand that western males did not feel less than a man because they did these things. It was obvious the girls had never seen anything of the kind.

Gale told Leila and Saadia they would be living with me. I kept looking for a clue of approval from them, but there was none. The only reaction I saw was when Leila took a spoon of lentils. Her face told me the taste was not what she had expected. When she noticed me looking at her, she smiled and continued to eat.

CHAPTER 5

What Is a Choice?

All along, Gale translated for the girls so they would get the gist of our conversations. She was amazing, speaking Pashto one second and Farsi the next. She used a different language for each girl, turning from side to side, never missing a beat. As we went on and ate, it was evident that both girls appeared more relaxed, almost pleased. I suggested that they decide who would have the room with the view of the harbor and who would get the room with a small veranda to sit and enjoy the garden.

When Gale informed them that their first act in this home would be to choose which room each would occupy, they appeared surprised. Neither understood the matter of making up one's own mind. In their countries, they had no voice and never made their own choices.

Gale suggested they look at the rooms again and decide who would get which. They spoke to Gale as they walked around the house again. After some deliberation,

Leila chose the garden room, and Saadia was overtly happy with the harbor room. No one knew how they arrived at their decisions, but I was pleased they had chosen what felt good to them.

It was evident that they had exercised their first right of choice. Something as simple as choosing a room was a much bigger event than I would have believed possible. I also think this action gave them some sense of themselves: they were now people with rights.

I asked if there was anything at all they wanted in their rooms, and almost immediately, I realized I was asking too much. A room of their own was more than they ever had before, and my question demanded of them something they were not yet capable of assimilating.

Small talk was followed by hugs, and soon everyone was ready to go home. I gave the girls a hug, they were less rigid this time. I knew it would take time for them to receive or give a hug without this unbending fear of strangers.

After they left, I made myself another cup of tea, remembering it was Suzannah who got me to drink tea all day long, and I went to the living room. There, I drank my tea, daydreaming and wondering how often my life had changed drastically since my birth. Thinking a great deal about Leila and Saadia that afternoon, I became cognizant that theirs were experiences few human beings ever encountered. Ursula had sensed that I would be capable of handling this unparalleled experience.

I was scared and anxious, but I wanted their lives to become better than what they had known thus far. Ursula's suggestion that Leila and Saadia move in with me was an act of compassion, not only for them, but also for me. I felt humbled and honored. I wished Suzannah were around. To talk with her about my feelings would have been glorious. She would witness my tears of gratitude, and she, too, would have felt gratitude—after all, I was the product of years of her nurturing. She would also have detected and understood the fears this venture brought to the surface.

Decisively, I got up, went to the Harbor room, and removed the easel. I brought it to the library, which had a small window, so I could see the harbor. One day I would have a larger window installed—I now had a reason. For the moment, I was only attempting to anticipate what two girls foreign to western culture could want or need.

They arrived with Gale and Ursula with very few clothes and no words to express their thoughts. Gale then informed me that Saadia was not literate. She waited until the girls were in their rooms to let me know, as if they would understand.

Immediately after the women left, I began to point. "Bed. Night table. Lamp. Chair. Closet. Door. Window. Bathroom. Towels. Soap. Toothbrush." I repeated the words, pointing each time. I realized after a while that these words would not help them survive or truly communicate, I started all over. Pointing to the bed, I said, "I am tired," and I rubbed my eyes. "I am going to sleep." I went with them all over the house, making gestures and lots of words.

I knew I needed to get dictionaries for Farsi/English and Pashto/English, but in Maine the chance of that was one in a million. I did not know where to begin.

One could not read at all; the other could, but we did not share an alphabet. I was alone with two people who were unable to communicate. Suddenly, I felt panic. What was I to do? I could only continue with my litany of words again and again.

When Ursula visited only two days later, I asked her where I might find the dictionaries I was looking for. Once more she came to the rescue. "Did you learn how to speak with a dictionary under your arm? Look—they are repeating your silly words; they are getting the hang of what you are doing. Talk to them, girl, just talk. That's how mothers teach their children. Just talk! It is called immersion!" As usual, once she said what she had to, she dismissed me. She gave each girl a hug, but not before giving each a present. She left without saying anything more.

I remembered my own learning process and also my own sense of isolation and frustration. These girls were from a completely different culture. Not one person nearby was a native of their lands. My heart bled for them. I promised myself that I would do all I could to alleviate their loneliness. How I was to accomplish this was a great unknown.

The notes from Gale included no time line regarding their arrival in the USA, and I could not ask them. I showed them the map on the third page of the document, and I wrote their names according to their country.

Wednesday arrived, and I found myself alone with the girls. I could appreciate why Saadia could not look at a person directly. She believed she carried the shame her society had harnessed to her. For me, it was impossible to understand how the loss of her male child could be a cause for shame, yet Saadia was to be stoned. It was clear I faced cultural differences no one had explained to me.

I felt an electric surge, decisive in thought, if not yet in action. I was not only to help and teach them to communicate—I was going to make strong women out of them. They were already courageous.

My mind was flooded with bits and pieces of information. I recalled when Gale told us Saadia was still bleeding from the birth. Not having had any children, this was another idea foreign to me, but I knew I had to handle the matter of blood immediately.

I got up, took them by the hands, and opened the door to the garage, all the while talking, telling them what I was doing. We drove to a drug store. We needed the right supplies so the blood would not flow without protection. Once there, I began a march, showing them all sorts of things. Down the wide middle aisle, we saw combs and brushes in rainbow colors. I did not know if they had any, and they did not understand my offer to get them some. The colors were enticing. Even if they had some, they were about to have more. They kept looking at me as if I were a lunatic. My basket was no longer empty.

Next we moved to a display area with hundreds of nail polishes and lipsticks. The best way to break the ice for the girls was a demonstration: I chose a lipstick and tried it on. My lips turned bright red, and they did not know if to laugh or pretend they had not seen. I made a

39

face of disapproval, found some tissues, and I took it off the best I could. Choosing another color, I repeated the process saying, lipstick, lips, hand, fingers, and on and on. The words and the pointing toward things never stopped. They got the idea. Each chose a lipstick and did as I had. Facial expressions coupled with sounds gave them the understanding of approval, and the "yuk" told them I did not like the color. A mirror made this experience great fun for them. Prior to being rescued, they had never seen a mirror; perhaps they were too young when they were sold. It was important that they relax a bit. We continued up and down various aisles, and by the time we got to the sanitary napkins, we were at ease.

Roommates had never entered my mind, and now having two felt overwhelming. Because they could not communicate, I had to think for them. Feeling my own emotional turmoil, I decided I would learn courage from them. The idea of being their teacher and guide had not yet penetrated.

Without a word, they were changing my world, and I was to rebuild theirs with words. The importance of something as simple as communication became immense. I felt it creeping up my spine, but that feeling was not the answer I was anticipating.

We were back from the drugstore, and I had given a lesson in using sanitary pads. An embarrassing moment it was; yet, when it was all said and done, a bonding of sort had taken place. Perhaps they now felt they could trust me. We were able to look at each other. From sheer nervousness, I burst into hysterical laughter. They saw my humanity, and they laughed, too.

Basmati rice and vegetables came to the rescue, along with lentils, to which I added copious amount of spices like cumin, coriander, turmeric, and curry. Everything looked great and smelled good, but it was not what I was accustomed to. I went in the kitchen, pointed, and asked them if they wanted some. They made it clear that they did. This time I also took them to my spices and opened a few. They got the idea. Leila added some pepper, Saadia more coriander and salt. I showed them how to turn the stove on, and soon enough the food was warm, I showed them where I kept the dishes, and, to my surprise, Leila took out three medium-sized bowls. I opened the drawer of eating utensils, and, without hesitation, Saadia took three spoons.

At all levels, our cultures were obviously different. We ate with different tools. It was evident that a fork was not their preference, but they made do because I used one. We ate different foods. Theirs were spicy; mine were creamy and rich. We dressed differently, and I did not cover my head. While I felt comfortable with a chair and a table, they apparently preferred the floor. We had a myriad of things to explore. I did not know how I would understand or anticipate their needs. Not prepared for any of this, I only knew I would do my very best. The journey would be laborious for the three of us. While I neither liked nor disliked them, I felt a sort of kindness and a great deal of compassion for both of them.

It was not long ago that Ursula, in her blunt and direct manner, suggested that both young women would be well served around me. Now, looking at the girls and myself, I knew the benefit would not be theirs only. I was alone, and Ursula may have felt their company would be good for me. I could teach them English, hopefully without an accent, she said. When she questioned my French accent, I reminded her that her Germanic accent had not taken a holiday, either.

I had an internal dialogue going on without order, but it was not chaotic either. We ate quietly, but we could not communicate. For me, that made the spicy meal difficult. They, however, appeared perfectly at ease without saying a word, and the hot spices did not seem too strong for their palates. The only difficulties were with the fork and I did not know what their particular customs where regarding either a fork or a spoon. I got up from the table and immediately realized they did not know what to do. Telling them that it was all right not to follow me to the kitchen was meaningless. I held Leila's shoulders, turned her back to the table, and told her with gesture and voice to eat. Saadia seemed to be a docile person; she followed Leila back into the dining room and sat. They relaxed and smiled when I brought them some tea.

Would we ever be able to communicate? How will I bring them from the dark into the light they needed to see?

Zelda had suggested we meet again in a week or two. I felt I had one week to make some progress. It had not yet been twelve hours.

When we were done, I took my bowl to the kitchen and washed my dish and utensils in the sink. Reminding myself of the hard time the girls had earlier with the fork, I understood why they chose to use spoons. I knew eventually they would be at home with forks and knives. I dried my things and put them away. They each did exactly the same. I smiled and said thank you. They both smiled back. They understood that. The cups were still on the table, and I poured some more tea. As had been my ritual, I took my cup and went out to the long patio with still only two rocking chairs, and I pointed to them. Leila nearly burned herself—she had never been near a rocking chair and was not prepared for the motion when she sat. I pulled some chairs outside from the dining room. I used my rocking chair, and they watched. A while later, Saadia sat on the floor.

Rugs and cushions instead of more chairs . . . items to be purchased in the very near future.

They talked a while and often looked at me. I soon realized it was no easier for them than it was for me.

From the rocking chair, I got up and pointed toward the harbor, suggesting with words and movement that it was still light enough, and we could go for a walk. My gesture toward the harbor somehow instilled fear in both. It was palpably visible, yet I could not understand why. The best way was not to insist. In our own way, we were beginning to communicate.

Only moments after, Saadia almost dozed off. I took her hand and brought her to her bedroom. I pulled the covers down and told her to go to sleep. Leila followed and went to her room. From the hallway, I said, "Good night" to them and, to my delight, I heard, "Good night," not once but twice! They each had a voice!

CHAPTER 6

Must Talk, Must Paint

Giggles from the kitchen woke me up. A good omen! Still in my nightgown, I went to the kitchen to see what was going on. The girls were attempting with difficulty to make their tea using the stove, but at the sight of me in a nightgown, they nearly fainted. So accustomed to walking around my home like that, I did not think to cover up.

When an opportunity presents itself, Suzannah and Frank were never too far from my consciousness. Without too much display, I pointed to my breast, my breast, and your breast. I do not think I had ever seen faces so red, but laughter was my ally. My body, your body. I went on, while I also showed them how to turn the stove on and off. They took a journey from the head all the way down to the toes. We counted fingers and toes, and I told them about left and right. Most times, they repeated the words. Some had to be repeated numerous times. We were not communicating, but we were making attempts and making sounds.

They were having fun with my methods, even if they were not at ease with my nightgown. A while later, when there was a lull in our conversation, I told them I was going to my room, and I would come back with a robe on. They were being exposed to new words at every opportunity. I never stopped talking and showing.

When I reappeared in the kitchen in my red satin robe, they both smiled as a method of giving me some approval. Since they were in the kitchen and already dressed, I opened the refrigerator and pointed inside, offering whatever was there. My dozen eggs in a box amazed Saadia. To lighten the mood, I made my best rendition of a chicken, and again they became hysterical. They joined in, first with their chicken sounds and, of course, the rooster. During this transaction, it occurred to me that the chickens of each country made slightly different sounds. Not so odd, because American chickens did not sound like the French ones I knew. To explain this to them, I had to go to my dictionary and show them the various flags, naming the country and its flag and making the sounds of its chickens.

The lessons and their accompanying laughter allowed a sort of transition from fear of the unknowns they were constantly facing to an air of pleasurable, upcoming normalcy. I could not ask them what they were thinking, but I felt confident that they regarded me as a local nutcase, and that was not offensive to them.

The refrigerator opened. I had some pita bread and some jam. Leila looked at the eggs and also the jar of apricot jam. I gave them the option of pita or English muffins. They both had trouble making choices. This was the least of my concern; I knew in no time at all they would learn and master the art of choosing. My intention was not to make feminists out of them, but rather strong women able to stand their ground.

Prepared with a little help from me, we soon cooked a meal together. Scrambled eggs. I realized they did not know about toasting things. I got the jam out, and we toasted pita and English muffins. My variety of cheese did not entice them. It took me very little time to begin a list of essentials. *Yogurt. They do not drink milk.*

Without being told, Saadia got three dishes for me to serve everyone. Progress had begun! I spread butter and an abundant quantity of jam on my muffin. I added salt and pepper to my eggs, picked up my fork, and began to eat. It was time to show them the best way to use a fork. They were fast studies. In no time at all, they were eating properly with a fork and knife.

From that point on, every time I used their names, I reminded them that Julienne was mine. They both learned it well.

They were learning English words, and when we went to the supermarket, it was not only a treat to them but also a place of amusement. They marveled at the foods in those places. More lessons continued.

It became clear to me that the people from the town knew about the foreign girls living with me. I found this amusing, since not too long before, I was the subject of pointed fingers and small talk. A local farmer, who received produce from farms I believed were from the south and southwest of the U.S., soon became my best ally. The most important thing about this man was that his wife was a refugee from Pakistan. They had spices I had never heard of or tasted. The girls recognized their scents.

My girls were no longer alone. Malika was older than they were, but the kinship was instantaneous. Often she came to the house with special delicacies from the Middle East. The sadness was that Malika and her husband were in the U.S. for only two years, with only six months left to go. Before leaving, she must have talked to every person she ever encountered about the girls and their need to learn the language of the land.

Learning English became a town's project. No matter where we went, someone or sometimes a few people would approach us and begin a conversation. Little by little, Leila and Saadia recognized some of the words. It was clear to me that my girls were willing and eager, and before long, words began to flow.

CHAPTER 7

Discoveries and Hope

We woke up with snow on the ground, and according to the news, the whole of New England had been blanketed with white. Winter was giving us one last blast, and this area did not have a battery of equipment to clean snow on streets and certainly not my driveway. We were prisoners! We had been cold enough. Now acclimated because of my strolls, every walk to the harbor's beach required us to wear coats, gloves, hats, and scarves. The girls actually enjoyed the treasures they found. I had purchased plenty of winter clothes for them, and I bet they were happy not to wear their cotton clothes. I felt we were all ready and wanted to change wardrobe.

They had been with me for a while now, and aside from language, it was safe to say they were easy to live with. Perhaps, unlike me, they did not know the words to complain. They learned to use all the appliances in record time. They were thrilled by the wonders of the washing machine and the dryer.

There was not much to do on this day with more snow on the ground, and conversation was not exactly easy. I was racking my brain to attempt anything to entertain them. Sometimes they ventured on the porch, I believe to experience some fresh air or the sea breeze. They were not comfortable going near the beach. I wondered why, but I could not ask. The ocean was, after all, a large body of many unknowns.

On such days, I painted, and they came into my room and sat on the floor, quietly observing. They each had the ability to be wordless and motionless for hours, something I had not mastered. When I lived alone, I even talked to myself.

They had helped me pick out small rugs from antique stores and yard sales, which proved to be a huge success. They enjoyed the treasures they saw, but most of all they loved meeting people living in Bar Harbor. When the weather permitted, we became adventurous and traveled often to other nearby towns. Each rug came with a story from its owner. When I painted at the foot of my bed, they each had their rugs. I had no prayer rugs, but they did not seem to need them.

To help this white, snowy day pass, I decided to teach them how to mix pigments. I lined up tubes of paint, mixed a few colors, and asked if they wanted to do the same. It was obvious that Leila had no interest, but with plenty of gestures and few words, Saadia let me know she wanted to have a canvas. Luckily I had a blank one. It was about 24 by 16 inches, and when I pointed to it, her immediate broad smile made it clear to me she wanted it. I removed my canvas and installed the new one on the easel. I showed her a variety of brushes, linseed oil, and tubes of paint. She smiled from ear to ear. I was curious about her excitement because no one told me she painted.

"Thank you very much."

She said the words clearly and with resolve. I had no idea she could say a word of English. When I asked where she learned, she was again lost for words. I responded with a hug and kissed both her cheeks. By this time, she was accustomed to my extravagant displays of affection. She patted me on the head as I took her place on the floor. Deliberating and knowing I would be more comfortable on a chair or my bed, I decided to oblige and observe as she had done so many times when I painted. I soon discovered that, unless one was groomed to be on a rug or a pillow or, for that matter, a hard wood floor, one found no comfort.

Saadia was no longer a prisoner due to the weather outside. In moments, she mixed some Prussian blue, white, and a minute amount of yellow ochre and began a sky like I had never seen before. Her brush was a mixture of a Matisse and a Renoir all in one. I was dumbfounded. She was an artist. When I asked if she had ever painted before, she said no. I also realized that she understood a lot more of my English jabber than she let on.

As she painted, Saadia entered a world of her own. She and the paint found an amazing union. She no longer knew we were watching her. "Outside I want."

I got up, but before going outside, I went to the kitchen. Leila followed and helped me taste a new batch

50

of tea. It was very cold outside. The artist was at work and would emerge when she was ready.

We each carried our hot cup of tea and walked to the porch. Somehow the wind had cleared the snow away — the steps were clean. Leila walked down to what once was a grassy area. With her bare hands, she busied herself sweeping the snow from the ground. No one told me what this exercise was about.

I was freezing. I went in to get us some heavier jackets. When I returned, she had exposed two fairly large rocks. Bending down to give her a jacket and the cup of tea left on the first step, I noticed she was crying. Tears were rolling down freely on her apricot-colored cheeks. Was this a way to wash away the troubles of her previous life? I did not know.

"Leila, what is going on? Why are you crying?" I touched her tears so she would understand.

She showed me a blade of grass. Obviously, this poor blade of grass, like me, was waiting for spring to arrive. Why a person would cry because she saw a first blade of grass making its yearly appearance to announce the arrival of Spring, I could not understand. When I told her I did not know why she was in tears, she explained.

"Soon, Julienne, *Nowruz.*" With that, another flood of tears came. She was inconsolable, and I did not understand.

"Leila, what is *Nowruz?*"

Like a gazelle being chased out of a forest, she ran to her room. I followed and went into the kitchen, the warmest room in the house. Leaving her bedroom, Leila came to the kitchen where I had a calendar. She took

51

it off the wall, turning pages as fast as she could. She pointed to March 21st.

"Ha, your birthday? I will have a party for you."

"No! *Nowruz!*"

By this time, her tears had become uncontrollable sobs.

.

CHAPTER 8

Prisoners with Hope

The girls came to live with me toward the last days of a hot, damp summer. Fall, though beautiful with colors was nasty, with almost daily rains, and winter was not much better. One good thing happened: the girls were learning to speak English, but with a different alphabet. Leila had nothing to draw from, and Saadia, with no schooling at all, had even less. Every time they learned something new, I could see a ray of hope and a smile. No matter how difficult, I knew all would fall into place.

Leila kept crying, repeating *Nowruz,* again and again. Attempting to console her, I held her in my arms. It was not easy for either of us. I did not know what to do. To my way of understanding, women only cried that way because of a great loss. There had been no new loss or trauma that I knew of. I did not know enough of her story, and the tears could not be explained. I felt these were not tears from the past. I knew her husband had sexually abused her, but my feelings told me she was crying about something else. I did not ask if it was on March 21st that her husband raped her—I did not know what words to use, and describing such a scene was not my preference. She kept repeating *Nowruz*—a word with no meaning to me. The library was closed, and I could not think of anyone to ask about *Nowruz*. I felt the problem might be related to snow, but still there was nothing for me to do. I consoled her as best I could, praying the snow would melt. At one point, she put her head on my lap, but the desperate tears did not stop. I was only grateful to be inside by then.

We did not have enough words, but I asked her again and again to explain what March 21st was. I was trying to help, and I believed she understood that, but the frustration kept growing with everything I asked. She got up and went to her room again.

I stayed in the kitchen. Moments later, she came back from her bedroom with a torn picture I could not identify, nor did I know where it came from. I could tell it was from a magazine. It showed a tabletop, and on it was a bowl with some grass. Perhaps I was looking at a clue. Could she have wanted a bowl to put two blades of grass in? The picture showed some fruits, some seeds I could not identify, candles, cups, and other unrelated items—even a mirror. All looked luxurious, but I still did not understand.

Leila took my hand and started opening the spice cabinet. She opened some of the containers, and sometimes she would sniff, but she kept saying, "No." I obviously did not have the right spices. I told her we would get whatever she was looking for and promised, as soon as I could drive, we would go to the grocery store. First we would stop at Malika's—she would help. At the sound of her name, Leila's face lit up. Malika's parents were from the region, so she perhaps would have an idea about this *Nowruz* thing. She stopped crying but continued to look for things I did not know about or have.

She went into the closet where I kept the linens and pulled out an embroidered tablecloth. It was linen from Ireland, and the white, silky thread made the embroidery spectacular. It had not been used since my mother was alive. I told her I would iron it for her. She liked that I allowed her to choose it.

Continuing to walk around the house, she went into my room, and there she took a medium-sized mirror I had on a side table. Strangely enough, when Frank was alive, we purchased it at a flea market in France. We were told it was Persian—and perhaps it really was, because she did not take the mirror made in England. The one she chose was free-standing and made of silver. The very ornate work created by a method the French called *repousser* was exquisite. We were told the craftsman hammered out the designs. It was a magnificent piece to have. Who would have known one day a girl would stop crying because of it?

Leila showed me the picture again. There seemed to be a bowl with a fish floating in what I assumed was clear water. We went into the dining room. Since she was using heirlooms, I got her a crystal bowl. I quickly drew a fish on a piece of colored paper and put it in. My girl was now laughing. She took the rest of the paper from me, and made a sort of a circle and went to my room where Saadia was painting and helped herself to some paint. Using her finger as a brush, she dabbed her index finger into yellow ochre paint. She immediately smeared the paper, following the circle she had drawn. I was looking at what might represent an orange, an apricot, or even a sun.

As quickly as she did this, she left the room. Like a sheep, I continued to follow her. Leila entered Saadia's room. Temporarily startled by our intrusion, Saadia continued to paint. Leila gave me only seconds to look at a masterful piece of art in the making. Back to the dining room we went, and she asked me for another bowl. While she was doing this, she also picked up my mother's candle holders, as there was a similar one in the picture.

Leila had a plan and a reason for what she was doing. I, on the other hand, was not privy to any of it, nor did I understand what she was doing.

Her eyes were bright now, and she smiled as she went to and fro, looking for treasures to create something that made no sense to me. I had ordered a dictionary from New York—the only place I could find a bookstore carrying one for Farsi and English. They told me it would take a few weeks, as the book would be coming from a warehouse in California. No one was counting on the sudden snow on the ground. My old French dictionary had no words resembling what she was saying. Noruz, nourous, no russ—nothing came close. March had no correlation to the things she was collecting, although I thought of the solstice. She gave no inclination of a relation there, either.

Completely lost, I went along with her collection of odd objects seemingly unrelated to one another.

Leila went into the kitchen, opened the container where I kept lentils, and took some. She also took kidney and navy beans. From each container, she took less than a handful and carefully placed each bean at the bottom of the large crystal bowl. She added enough water to cover the beans.

Maybe she wanted to have a garden, but why take my crystal bowl to sprout beans?

She got some vinegar and put some of in it into a small bowl. From the refrigerator, she took an apple. Wondering about how apple cider vinegar was made, I did not ask her what she was doing.

A corner of the kitchen counter had become a repository of unlike objects and foods, and I felt soon the corner would not suffice. Only the various beans bore some family relationship. The tablecloth lay there also, serving no purpose, at least to me.

Hours had passed since the sobbing. Now radiant, Leila wanted to iron the tablecloth.

It amazed me how we could communicate with so few words, yet she could not explain to me the reason for the event of the day.

Leila was a person with an even temper, sufficiently patient most of the time; she never showed frustration because she did not know the words she was looking for. Yet today, the trauma that came from a blade of grass continued to make no sense to me.

It was getting close to suppertime. We never had lunch, and I guess they did not mind. My original intention was to take them to visit Ursula, but with roads and driveway covered with a thick blanket of snow, they would have to wait for German food some other time. No phone service made communication impossible with anyone. We were prisoners of the weather. In some countries, they would have said we had been bad, and therefore we had been cursed.

Perplexed by the quick glance I had of the painting, I went to check on Saadia. Her canvas, though not finished, was a scene from Afghanistan, I was sure of it. The mountains she created looked like the ones near Pakistan. She captured how menacing a terrain it was, and there was not much vegetation in her painting. Dead center, she had an entry to what was conceivably a dwelling within the bowel of a mountain. A cave turned into a home, perhaps, but I was not sure, as this part of the painting was not advanced enough to tell. Not much farther to the right of her scene, I was looking at some soldiers, fully armed.

"Where is that, Saadia?"

She only smiled at me and continued to paint. One day, perhaps she will tell me the story of the cave and the people who lived there, or she may choose to tell me about the soldiers. Even if she was not yet ready to speak of it, the fact that she took the initiative to paint something from memory seemed to me to be psychological progress.

No longer able to postpone supper, I went back to the kitchen. Leila had taken over a lot of space, arranging things in a way only she could visualize. It was getting dark, and I did not want these girls to have my poor habits of not eating regularly. Before cooking, I opened the ironing board and plugged in the iron. Leila wanted to do this herself. A blessing that was, because I once ironed this tablecloth and it took me hours. She was thoroughly astonished—the iron was magically getting hot! The tablecloth might be burned, but I prayed she would not burn herself. During this quick conversation with God, I wondered, should the conversation have been with Allah? One day, we would discuss the differences of religious words and perceptions.

In the kitchen, preparing something to eat today would not come with Middle-Eastern flavors. The weather was conducive to soup, and I was getting tired of lentils. I prepared a potato soup, and to it I added leeks, carrots, and celery. My recipe was based on what I had on hand, along with plenty of garlic, some salt, and lots of butter. The girls had gotten used to some good bread with butter that would make this the perfect dish for this kind of weather. Just in case, despite their trouble with my cheeses, I brought some out.

One frozen baguette replaced the flatbread because I had none. In no time at all, the meal was ready, and so was I, but the painter and the steam presser were both hard at work. My soup was not interesting to them. I added more garlic to bring the aroma to their nostrils.

Nothing happened. They were engaged in their own lives, doing what they wanted to do, and Leila was no longer crying. The best I could do was to have a bowl of soup and let them be.

There was something wonderful about seeing how they were learning to make simple decisions. They soon discovered this new life of theirs, no matter how challenging, came with a certain freedom they knew nothing about. In many ways, they displayed what they felt. My observation said they were feeling safe, and the environment suited them well.

Both were learning they were no longer slaves to men abusing them for their self-gratification. It took a short time for them to grasp the idea of what I called freedom. They could not talk about it, but I could tell that they would never again give up the newly discovered ability to act freely. One day, I was certain, because I would see to it, they would discover freedom of speech. Working on it was challenging, but not impossible. They had not yet discovered their own sense of confidence. I knew that, too, would take time. They were not yet independent—they were too young and in need of education—but I felt, with time, the progression of their growth would not stop. They were determined people.

I ate my soup feeling content, realizing what a privilege it was to witness their development and mine as well.

I was deep in thought when Leila came to me and pointed to the driveway. A man was walking toward us carrying a flashlight and a bag. Only his footsteps were illuminated, so we could not tell who he was. My Malibu lights were not working and would not have helped me see his face. We had to wait until he got much closer. His stance was not a menacing one, but Leila's face showed extreme fear. I had never seen her so scared. She held the iron as a shield or a weapon. A few more steps, and one of the outside lights went on. It was Mr. Rand.

A sigh, a laugh, and Leila released whatever fear she had. I gave her a hug, reassuring her we were safe. A passing thought in relation to our security had come to mind, but we had more pressing things to handle. We were as secure as anyone else.

Mr. Rand came in, and his were clothes nearly frozen. We had no men's clothes in this house. Today, the fireplace would come in handy. The girls gathered wood from the pile on the porch and started a fire. The fireplace had not been used in a while, but it seemed like the thing to do. Saadia was an expert, and in no time she had the fire going. Mr. Rand was drying out while enjoying some hot chocolate.

He pointed to the floor near the front door. A black, cloth duffle bag lay waiting for the girls. As usual, they dashed toward it. By now, they were accustomed to his visit, usually with a grocery bag containing everything from nuts to dried fruits and whatever else he could locate that was not found around the corner. The bag was filled with delicacies from the Middle East; he had been to New York. The girls' eyes were big, and their mouths were watering. Leila picked out some cookies and brought them to her stockpile in the kitchen.

Mr. Rand's fisherman's sweater was not going to dry anytime soon, and I did not want the man the catch anything. I had saved some of Frank's sweaters in a box, including three sweatshirts, so I decided to go fetch one. Mr. Rand's Irish wool sweater would dry in due time. I knew enough not to put it in the dryer. I suggested he use my bathroom to change. I did not know how the girls would react to a man in their bathroom.

CHAPTER 9

Tell Us About Nowruz

"*Nowruz,* Mr. Rand! You tell."

Mr. Rand told me he had not only read up on *Nowruz,* he had once celebrated it. Surprised but grateful that he knew something about this mysterious word, I suggested he needed to educate me. The timing for his visit was impeccable.

He was telling the girls about some Belgian chocolate in the bag, because he felt bad weather and chocolate went hand in hand. When I asked him how he got here and where he got the care package, he told me he had gone to New York and shopped for things not available to us. He never told me how he got to my house from his home miles away from mine.

He had dried apricots from Afghanistan, and Saadia recognized them instantly. Leila opened the Turkish delights. "Mmmm, Julienne, good. Try. Eat."

Mr. Rand could not believe the girls had acclimated

themselves so fast and were actually able to make conversations with very few words. "And they are speaking! How are you teaching them? This is something remarkable! I must tell the other teachers!"

"Calm down. They can express simple thoughts. They are not yet able to think in their languages and translate to English, but I feel they will be able to transit from one language to the other in no time. They are both very intelligent people."

He showed excitement about their progress, as he had not seen them in three or four months. Leila left us in the living room and went to the kitchen. She returned with one of her treasures: a silver tray purchased at the local thrift store, polished enough so we could see our reflections. She balanced cups of tea for everyone and on a small dish, also silver, and there were four cookies from her stash.

Since we were about to eat, I invited him. The tablecloth had been ironed, and Leila had no idea what to do with it. First she needed help to fold it. We went into my bedroom, and I showed her how to use two hangers so nothing would drag on the floor. When she realized I was going to hang it in my closet, she was horrified.

"No, no, Julienne." With her arms, she indicated I had too many clothes. We went to her bedroom. When she opened her closet, I made a mental note—*buy more clothes for them*.

Leila may not have been a painter, but she knew how to iron linen. She did it from the backside, making the embroidery pop. It was brilliant—as beautiful as I remembered it on my mother's table. The sight of it reminded me of my home when I was her age, but this was not the time for sentimentality.

"Let's go, Leila. We have a guest."

"A guest, what that?

"A guest is a person who comes to visit. Mr. Rand is our guest today. He is visiting us. You can also say Mr. Rand is a visitor."

As we were about to walk out of her room, we saw Saadia taking Mr. Rand to my bedroom. She wanted him to see her painting.

"Oh, my goodness! Did she paint this? Did you help her? This looks like a Renoir!"

"Yes," Saadia's soft voice answered. She was pleased and soon she was attempting to explain the sky of Afghanistan. To do this, she showed us the various tubes of paint she mixed. She was adorable with no head cover—just a beautiful head of shiny hair now mixed with a little yellow and also some blue. Almost touching the wet paint with her finger, she traced the mountains. Her gesture was almost sensual over the canvas. Her finger stopped at the entrance of the cave. It was more than a cave—we all felt it. She had created a wall of large stones around a paved pathway and proceeded to show us the stones.

"Home," she said, her face becoming somber. We could not pry because she did not have the words to tell us more. To my hug, this time she responded with her arms around me, and tears welled up in her eyes, but she did not cry.

"Mr. Rand, soup?" Leila was a take-charge person, and this was the signal for all of us to go to the dining room. Once there, she took some bowls and began to serve us. I reminded Leila that I had already had a bowl and wanted very little. She served us and afterward served Saadia and herself. Both sat on the floor to eat in the kitchen. I knew this was customary for tribal women in their respective countries.

"No, no," I said, coaxing them up from the floor. "We all eat around the table. No more eating in the kitchen on the floor when we have a guest."

My girls were confused about this business of a man in the home. They enjoyed what he brought back from his trips, and they no longer felt necessary to cover their heads because of his presence, yet eating with him was a different story. On this snowy day, we were all around the same table. I made sure they understood it was all safe and acceptable. I suddenly understood why they had appeared so uncomfortable the day of our second meeting. The men around my table were not husbands or family.

While they were learning a language, I was learning the tribal customs of a world I knew nothing about. I felt there were explosions of ideas, concepts, and customs I did not understand. In retrospect, I am sure it was the same for them.

We talked about many things while sharing a meal.

"I wanted to bring you this bag of goodies because I knew, in this weather, you all could use the treats. A buddy of mine, who is making attempts at clearing the main road with his tractor, dropped me off, and he will be back soon, I think."

"Will he honk? I do not think we will hear him."

"No, he said he will make a path for you and your gals to walk out from the porch, at least. You will not be able to drive out of here until the snow melts in a couple of days, but the temperature is predicted to get higher."

"At this rate, see you in July! The weathermen are wrong 98% of the time."

Leila knew the names of the months in English.

"March *Nowruz,* Mr. Rand."

"I know, Leila. Many years ago, I had a foreign exchange student. He was from Iran, too. We celebrated *Nowruz.*"

I knew she could not possibly have understood most of the words he spoke, but she was perceptive, and she could read his demeanor.

"Mr. Rand, you need to use small sentences. Make them simple, and talk a little slower."

"*Nowruz,* YES!" Leila said again. "You tell all. Julienne not know."

"Yes, I can do this. Leila, when my student lived with me. I got most of the things he needed to celebrate the Spring Solstice. I still have some stuff. So now you know another word, the one we use, but we do not celebrate *Nowruz.* It's like Christmas. We celebrate that holiday, and you do not. We did not have a beautiful silver tray or dishes like you have here. We made do with what I had in my kitchen. My cups for the tea were mugs, but we drank Persian tea. I collected my cups from many places. I still have some of the spices at home. I will bring them for you. I saw what you had in the kitchen. I think you will have everything you need. I will get you a goldfish or two. By March, the supermarket will have oranges.

Make sure you do not eat all the cookies. I know Julienne will not find them here, and your aunt Ursula does not make them like a Persian baker. "

He got up from the table and went to the bag, as he continued to talk to us.

"I brought a dictionary for the house. I found this secondhand Farsi-English one. Leila, I know you will find it useful."

I was ecstatic. "Now, that is a present Leila can use. She will be able find the words she is looking for and get their meanings. You have saved me hours of explaining." I picked it up, gave him a thank you hug, and then we continued to eat. I left sorry for Saadia, who did not know how to read but was learning fast. They were both like sponges.

It broke my heart to see what affectionate people they both were with me, and yet they could not hug Mr. Rand because of some distorted teachings. Leila turned toward Saadia and, with both hands, held her head. That was affection at its best. They were learning to express.

"*Nowruz*, Saadia!"

They both smiled. I knew they were not accustomed to show the feelings they had, at least not to a man. I knew, one day, they would discover that it was fine to express emotions toward men.

A warm baguette and plenty of butter complemented the soup well. The girls were slowly getting used to the foods I ate. After dinner, Leila began to speak to Mr. Rand.

"*Nowruz*, yes! Tell Julienne about happy time."

She was amazing. She used the words she knew

and, along with her hands and facial expressions, as if she were Italian, she told him what she needed. Her communication was getting better.

We cleared the table, and Mr. Rand began to tell me more about this ancient ritual of celebrating spring as the beginning of a year. Up to this conversation, I had not realized the differences in calendar. Three thousand years definitely made a difference.

CHAPTER 10

More About Nowruz

"First, you need to know that *Nowruz* means "new day."
It is the day of the vernal equinox, when winter is over
and spring begins. It is like our new year. This event
happens on the 21st or the 22nd of March every year.
It is a celebration that I believe all Persians celebrate.
It represents what is good and what is not so good in
the world. It brings people to nature and together for
celebrations that last for days. I believe it is celebrated in
Afghanistan, too. Saadia—do you know about *Nowruz*?"

"Yes, me know." Saadia was not a talker. She was
the younger of the two and possibly too close to the abuse
she had suffered. Aside from her newly found outlet with
a paintbrush, she had not yet come out of her shell. Mr.
Rand was happy to give me and also the girls a great deal
of information we did not know.

"The feast is celebrated wherever people have
been influenced by the Persians. This means Iran, Iraq,

Tajikistan, Uzbekistan, Azerbaijan, India, Pakistan, and Turkey. Even in Canada and in the United States, some people celebrate *Nowruz*. It is a holiday that dates back to the Zoroastrians. *Nowruz* is almost a spiritual holiday, and I think, this year more than ever, it is important. Both of you will celebrate it, and it can become the party for a new beginning. I will help as best I can."

"Leila, how much do you know about Nowruz?" I asked. "Tell me."

She went to the kitchen, came back with the calendar, and brought the things she had collected, one after the other. The dining room table took on a mysterious glow with the mirror candelabra. She had the ironed tablecloth folded in her arm. In no time, she explained through her own brand of body language where every thing should go.

"Julienne, look." Leila stood by each chair and named the people she knew who were here during the second visit with her. She also named Malika and her husband, John.

"Julienne, people come for *Nowruz*. Here, yes. Cebration, Julienne. People, sweet food, many food, much cebration, yes."

"No, not cebration: celebration."

"Oh, yes. Ce-le-bra-tion, yes?"

"Yes."

I looked at Mr. Rand. "This is how we have been doing it. They are learning, and I have no idea what the results will be."

"Amazing and easy, and based on what I am seeing. This method may not take more effort than what is standard, and it is fun and effective, proving it is better than going to school for a few hours. It takes attentiveness, and you are giving them that. To tell you the truth, I had no idea how you were going to do this. You are doing very well. They are learning language, our customs, and yet you are affording them theirs as well. Two very lucky girls! Bravo!"

"Thank you. I believe, when possible, immersion is a great method to learn a language quickly. It becomes a way to survive. Learning the customs and the language of the host country is the only way to understand or at least accept other people. "

"Look, Julienne." As Leila pointed to March 21st, Saadia took the calendar and examined it. She was learning from the alphabet onward.

"Girls, see—March 21st. In Europe, people say the 21st of March. You say *Nowruz*. In the U.S., just say March 21st. It is all the same day telling us it is solstice, when the day is the longest of the year. No more winter! It is an important day in many cultures. We all call things by different names, but they are all the same. What do you think?"

"*Nowruz*," they said in unison.

"Yes," Leila said. "Now explain us spice, Mr. Rand?"

"Yes Leila, I will bring the sumac the next time I visit you. Julienne, it is crushed berries or something. It is the spice of life. I also have some dried lotus fruits, for love and affection. I may not have everything but I'll get close."

Both girls were beaming. They could see he was explaining something to me, and I understood.

Leila went to the kitchen and brought back some apple cider vinegar. Mr. Rand said it was for patience. Looking at me, he repeated the word for patience in Farsi, and the girls thought it was hysterical. They were having fun.

Saadia came back from the refrigerator with an apple. "Beautiful, good."

"Yes." Leila knew about the apple as well.

"It is for health and beauty," Mr. Rand said.

"Do you have any pudding or cream of wheat, or something like that?"

"Yes. I have vanilla pudding in a box. I got it when I moved to the U.S. I will have to get a new box."

"Well, it's not exactly right, but it will do for now. Leila, do you know how to make *samanu*?"

My soft Saadia answered, "Yes."

Leila got the bowl with the beans, but nothing was sprouting yet. Mr. Rand explained to me that it represented the renewal of nature.

Leila took her yellow circle, and immediately Mr. Rand knew what it was.

"An orange in a bowl of water. It represents the earth."

She picked up the fish she had drawn and put it in a bowl. To this, Mr. Rand said I needed a goldfish. He suggested I get two—one for each girl.

"They are the perfect symbol for new life—their new life."

Leila put my mother's candelabra on the table, as well as the mirror. "Julienne, *Nowruz* table like that."

"With the things you have here and what Mr. Rand

72

can bring to us, I think we will have a good *Nowruz*."

Saadia pointed to the window and the calendar. She counted 13 days and indicated somehow that the holidays were over.

"No *Nowruz*."

"On the 13th day, we will have a picnic," Mr. Rand said. "We will have to go to the park. They have a small pond, and there we will release the two fish and also the grass or sprouted lentil and beans."

"Wow, this holiday takes thirteen days, plus the days the grass needs for growing." I looked at the girls. "Leila and Saadia, we are going to have *Nowruz!*"

We all hugged as we heard the sound of a tractor. Mr. Rand had become part of the pack.

CHAPTER 11

Talk. Conversation. Confusing.

After an evening with Mr. Rand, learning about *Nowruz*, and watching his friend clear our driveway of snow, I woke up to a beautiful, warm, sunny day. A white sweater, similar to the one Mr. Rand left here to dry, fell out of my closet. It once was Frank's—I kept all his sweaters. Too large and too long did not matter. Wearing it felt great just the same, cozy and warm.

With the sweater down to my knees, I walked to where Leila had been the day before. The melted snow exposed the blade of grass that made Leila cry the day before. Now multiplied by many like it, green was the order of the day. From the white of twenty-four hours past, shades of emerald, lime, bottle green, and more came out to greet a new season. The brown of the earth was lush, and the aroma was alluring. Something comforting was happening. It was about the arrival of a spring that would be celebrated with my girls. I understood *Nowruz*.

It was time to wake Leila and Saadia to share this with them. Looking at something as simple as grass growing impacted me a great deal because transformation was in the air. Now all I had to do was to impart the message to the girls.

I wanted to show them what gifts we had received with the passage of a few hours. Saadia joined me outside, and I gave her a cup of tea.

"Good morning, Julienne. I smiling. Leila slow come next."

"Good morning, Saadia. I am happy that you are smiling. You look very pretty. Do you want to go for a walk? The beach looks so good."

"No like beach. Sand wet. Wait Leila come."

"Well, of course it is wet. The waves are always coming and going. You should try to paint the waves and the sky, or maybe a bird. Later, when Leila comes to join us, we can talk and have tea but not walk the beach. We can have lunch with Ursula and go to an art gallery and look at some paintings. Great artists are there. They paint beautiful waves and skies, too. The paintings are called seascapes. Would you like to see some?"

She was in deep thought, or perhaps she did not understand me. "Julienne, what is art gallery? Seascapes, too. Me want sea."

"An art gallery is a place where people go to buy art. Art is what you are painting. Art is this vest you are wearing. Many things people make are called art.

Museums are places where people go, and they look at art. You do not buy art from a museum."

"Confusing. Art, gallery, sea and scape, museum scape, too? Much confusing."

"What is confusing you?"

"Why store call gallery?"

"Because they sell art."

I was confusing her with my explanations.

"Complicated! Saadia home make no art."

"Let's go get Leila, and we will visit an art gallery or two today. Afterward, we will visit Ursula and have lunch."

"Yes, me like. Me like this, too."

We were turning around to go back to the house, when we noticed Leila coming toward us, a cup of tea in hand. Leila was already having one more cup of tea, and this was no different.

"Leila, no tea. Go art gallery."

"What is art gallery? Saadia, you know?"

"Yes, Julienne tell me store, sell art. We go now."

First, I made sure to show Leila the grass. She sat on a step and just looked. Her face was radiant. A change of shoes and I was ready. I took my pocketbook and to the garage we all went. Leila too a second look and said,

"Julienne, you no go to art store with this cloth, too big."

"You are right Leila, my old, oversized sweater is not appropriate for an art gallery visit. I will be right back." In the house, I took the sweater off and put a blazer on. With my skirt, it was perfect. This was going to be a great day, I could tell. The snow was completely melted, and the road was not wet.

76

When I returned, Leila asked, "Julienne, why guest is visitor?"

"Because, Leila, there are many ways of saying the same thing in English. Maybe in Farsi, too."

"Farsi not confusing. English confusing."

"Let me confuse you a little more. You should say: 'Farsi is not confusing, and English is very confusing.' See how 'is' makes the words sound better, the words flow? When you know more English words, you will begin to think in English."

"Why! I no think, Julienne. Saadia no think. Girls no think. Only men think."

I was again taken aback by their way of thinking. "Who told you this nonsense? Women *do* think! They are the ones teaching their children. They are the ones taking care of sick people. Women *must* think! They are scientists, they are artists, and they are religious leaders. They give birth. They construct the very fiber of our lives. Women are important. When there are wars, especially in the areas where you came from, it is the women who clean up what the men destroy. Those men are bent on destruction, and they like people to fear them. The families! The villages! The towns! The women put them back together. A woman is a baby's first teacher! Remember, it is not a bunch of buildings that make towns or communities. It is the women! This is why women must be well educated."

Saadia looked upset. "Julienne talk too fast. Slow please. No mad please."

"Sorry. I am not mad at you—only outraged at what has been told to you and many women. Let me try again. Girls and women must think because they must teach what they know to their children. Most times, women take care of sick people. This is another one of the many reasons women must think. Women learn to become doctors. They know about numbers, they know about religions, and they are artists, like you, Saadia. Women are important, and this is why education must begin with girls."

"Artist make art?" Saadia asked.

"Yes, they do. You are an artist and a very good one. With education in the arts, you will become a great artist."

"Not good, Julienne. I not be artist, not good."

"Saadia, you can be anything you want to be. You will learn many things, just like you are learning English now. You will paint many canvases, I know that!"

"Julienne, I can be paint. You teach me read?"

"Yes, Saadia, you can be an artist, and you will paint a lot. I will teach how to read well. It is taking time, but you are doing well."

"I like women take care of children and women, not men," Saadia said.

"One of these days, I am going to take you to a hospital. You will see women who are nurses and doctors. They take care of sick children, sick mothers, sick daughters, sick sons, sick boys, and sick men. In the same hospital, you will see men doing exactly the same."

"Woman doctor fix men? No."

"Yes, Saadia, they do. Just because you are a woman does not mean you cannot touch a man. If you are a doctor, certainly you can touch the bodies of men, women, and children. And you know what? A man doctor can also touch the body of a woman or a girl or another man. We are all beings, some male some female. You see, when you learn to think for yourself, you also know how to make choices, and you will know you can do almost all of the things that a man can do."

"No choice, Julienne," Leila said. "Husbands make wife sick, hurt wife with stick, with hands and feet, too, and other ways. You know."

"Yes, Leila, this is why you are here. No husband will ever hurt you again."

Both girls smiled, and Saadia went on. "Husbands bad, they hurt, give pain. Husband make bleed a lot. Husband feels no pain, only wife. Mother not teach boy. Mmmmmmm enough, yes?"

"Yes, mothers cannot teach what they do not know. This is why girls must be educated so when they become women and have their children, they will teach their sons how to be men and their daughters not to become victims."

"Julienne, husband give pain to you?" Saadia asked.

"No, he was a very gentle man. I felt pain only when he died. I felt a lot of pain. That is a different kind of pain."

"Did father choose husband?

"No, I chose. My father was dead when I met Frank."

"No uncle choose for you?"

"No uncle chose for me. There is no shame in choosing the man you want to be with. This is the way in most western societies."

"Julienne, confusing yes. You like husband? You choice husband. Husband not hurt you... so confusing," Leila said.

"I loved my husband very much, and I liked him very much, also. We chose each other. He chose me, I chose him. That was important."

"Beautiful, Julienne."

"Yes Leila, it was very beautiful. And for the rest of my life, when I think about my husband, I will smile and I will miss him."

"Beoutiful," Saadia said.

" No, not 'beoutiful'— the word is 'beautiful.' Saadia try to repeat it: 'beautiful.'"

"Beautiful."

We were ready to begin a new adventure. We chatted about all sorts of things but nothing too serious.

"Ladies, look: we are in front of the art gallery. I am going to park the car, and we will go in."

"Thank you, Julienne," Saadia said.

"You are welcome. I hope they have lots of sky and seas with lots of waves for you to look at."

"Seascape!"

"Yes! Seascapes!"

CHAPTER 12

Not Alike, We Build a Bridge

We journeyed many times to the surrounding towns. The weather got better every day, and stores that were closed during the winter opened their doors. Leila and Saadia could not believe that people left their villages to come to our shores, yet once they started trekking from store to store, they understood why.

Their thinking process was fascinating. Nothing in their immediate background permitted them to understand that many young people traveled on their own, with no men accompanying them. When we walked the beach and people we did not know spoke to us, if they were female, the girls were more or less accepting. When a man spoke to us, their first apparent reaction was fear. My hope was that they would not take a long time to realize there was no danger in talking to a man. Mr. Rand, who had become some sort of a grandfather to them, cautioned me about being street smart, but he forgot the abuse these girls experienced did not come from strangers. Fathers and husbands were the perpetrators. Restored faith in family could not possibly be an avenue I would pursue. I was not the one to indulge them in matters of patriarchal endearing or caring. Their experiences with the men in their lives left me with only disdain and certainly no respect.

The learning curve was not only theirs—I was learning, too. We needed to bridge the differences between our societies in order to connect at a deep level. To accomplish this, I had to provide the safety they needed. As a trio, we had to accept codes, beliefs, and opinions not always understood by the others. At the core, our thinking processes were at opposite poles, but while our views of ourselves came from a different stance, we walked and advanced toward a bridge that would take us to the desired destination.

Frank and Suzannah were often on my mind. I know they would have been engaged with this endeavor. I sorely missed the assistance and wisdom they could not give me. At times, I felt very alone with the best interests of two young people at heart. With no practical experience, I often felt the task to be overwhelming. There was no one to ask how I was faring. I could only rely on how I felt and also how they looked to me.

Our group met once a month to evaluate the girls and their progress. Though no one said it, I believe they wanted to know how I was doing with them. Those were interesting visits. My guests found satisfaction when they noted the girls were well fed and dressed. No one asked Leila or Saadia how they felt. Often I had the feeling that asking questions of them might be met with answers they did not want to hear. It was clear the girls were becoming mine, and mine alone.

The support group showed up like clockwork on the first Monday of every month. We chatted a while, we ate, and they left. Ursula and Mr. Rand were the only sources of support we received. What was not monotonous was the progress Leila and Saadia were making on a daily basis. The girls were learning fast. They could converse with others and be understood. Saadia had learned the alphabet, and she was beginning to read well, yet her passion was a brush and some paints. She was a prolific artist. We had twelve canvases, the majority of which were seascapes, with a couple of landscapes to break the monotony. I began to get her art books. She absorbed and understood the work of the great masters. It was awe inspiring to watch her, as she turned pages and observed the paintings. It never failed: often she traced with her hand something I could not see—a brush stroke, a color she could not explain . . ..

One day, when we went to buy some more art supplies for her, I suggested that I would take one or two of Saadia's paintings to show to a gallery owner. I wanted other people to see the art this young, untrained artist was creating. I had only one expectation: to give Saadia a greater sense of herself and her potential. She was a gifted artist and had not a clue.

It was not long before when the three of us went to get the art supplies she needed, including more canvasses.

I suggested that Saadia pick two or three paintings to take with us. I explained the concept of consignment to her, but also that sometimes gallery owners might refuse to look at the art brought to them. It took a while to explain the idea that difference in taste did not mean her art was not good. My objective was to be as realistic as I could, but I had to make sure she would not feel rejected.

Our ritual stop by Ursula's for tea and cookies did not change that day. After a short time with me, both Leila and Saadia became comfortable walking around stores and looking at the treasure trove surrounding their new world.

Something magical followed those two. If nothing else, their respective rescue was miracle enough, but the fact that they were acclimating themselves so fast was a social phenomenon I enjoyed. The people in town, most likely because of Ursula, often talked to my girls, and in their broken English they were beginning to answer. We were on the right track!

Able to watch the pedestrians by the window, they had tea and cookies, while Ursula and I had strong cups of coffee. Ursula told me about the gallery owner she knew. Back from his winter hiatus, he was anxious to see Saadia's work.

Once done with their snack, I went to the car and returned with the three pieces of art. Two were 16″x20″ and the other was a 24″x36″. Despite the fact that I wanted the large one in my living room, Saadia chose it to go to the gallery. She was learning to stick to her guns. This whole affair was about them and not me. My living room could wait for another Saadia original.

We each carried a piece of art as we walked the two short blocks to the gallery.

Tall, with blue eyes, wearing jeans and a red plaid shirt, the owner looked like an old version of a lumberjack, yet somehow he was very well groomed. His shirt and his jeans were pressed. He stood on a ladder, hanging a seascape that was nowhere near the level of mastery Saadia's work offered. He did not notice us when we walked in.

Leila pointed to a vase with seashells. "Like you, Julienne."

Hearing us speaking, the man descended and walked toward us. "Good afternoon, ladies. What have we here? I am Paul, the owner, and also the one who sweeps the sidewalk and does everything else around here. You must be Ursula's niece. And these are your foreign roommates?"

I extended my hand to shake his, and Leila followed with the same. Saadia was not ready to touch the hand of any man.

"Where could we put these for you to look at them?"

"Let's go to the counter. I can prop them up and admire them there. I can already see that they are well-executed seascapes. How long as she been painting?"

I did not answer. With all three pieces well propped on the counter, he took a few steps backward, and then a few more steps, until he was almost by the front door. He walked back to the ladder, climbed, and took down the piece of art he had hung moments before. Nearly sliding, he came down, picked up the larger piece of Saadia's work, and up the ladder he went. Once it was secured, he came back down and walked toward the front door.

"What do you think? People will see it as they walk in. I like them all. She is very good, but you know that! Do you have a price in mind, or—I tell you what. I would much rather have them on consignment. I can spend money having them photographed and, if you do not mind, what about giving me a biography I could print for people to read? We can write a contract for three months or more—whatever makes you comfortable will work for me. I want these and more."

Saadia was bright red when he took her hand. He noticed she was not comfortable and had the grace to take a step backward and release her hand. His age may have helped him understand her distressed look.

"Does she have more that she could show now? Even two or three more pieces? I would open my doors at the end of the month or early next month for a one-woman or girl show! She is a very good artist! Unable to contain his enthusiasm, he walked up to Saadia and gave her a friendly hug. This time, she nearly fainted.

"Saadia, he likes your work." Almost inaudibly, I told her that some men liked to give hugs when they were happy, and that it was okay. "He wants your work here. Do you want to have the canvases that you painted here at this gallery? He can sell them and give you the money afterward. That is what 'consignment' is. We will have to talk more to know how much he will pay you."

"Come back tomorrow," Saadia said. With that, she was done and started to walk out. The hug did not have the desired effect. I explained the cultural matter to Paul, who apologized.

He did bring one thing to my attention: she was focused enough to see waves and clouds, skillful enough to interpret them on canvas, and assertive enough to walk out when she was not comfortable. He felt certain that, within an equally a short span of time, she would master our culture. "Either you are a good teacher, or she was born like this. She will be okay."

We arrived at a price for each piece. He wrote something to the effect of a contract between his gallery and me as the guardian of Saadia. While we were talking and calculating, Leila left to be with Saadia.

While this had been a successful day, I felt drained. We walked toward the car and I drove home.

CHAPTER 13

Learning Brings Freedom

We all took a nap—there was a lot to process. When I woke up, I found them with books, dictionaries, paper, and pens. They wanted to learn all that there was, and they were beginning to understand what freedom could mean to them.

I took the calendar from the kitchen and showed them with a circle Saturday April 18, 2009—the day the gallery would open with Saadia's art. It took a while, but I was able to explain what a reception was and also about an art opening.

"Like a wedding?" Saadia asked.

"Not exactly. It is a party, but not for a bride to be given to a man. It is a party so many people can see what you did. Some may want to buy one or two of your paintings. It is an honor to be hung in a gallery.

Leila felt great about this party. She wanted to experience everything about her sister's successes.

Saadia, seeing her jubilation, felt more at ease. I felt like a proud peacock.

"How about if the two of you start to think about wearing a new dress for the party? I have a lot of dresses, and I do not need to get a new one. I even have clothes I purchased in Afghanistan. We can go to my closet and see what I have that you may want, or we can go to a store find something new. Do you want to see what I have? You can try what you like."

"We can choice?"

"You can choose. You make a choice."

"We make choice! No shame, no punishment. Many happy."

"That is right, you choose what you want. There is no shame to making a choice, and there is no punishment for choosing. How do you feel about all this? You speak better now, and I think you understand, too. You are the same people, but you have changed a lot. What do you feel about all that?"

Their physiognomy changed instantly. They understood my questions and knew we were entering a territory they had not visited before.

"What if I tell you how I feel about you? About the art that you are making, about the books Leila is reading, and her garden, too."

"Yes," came the choir in unison.

"When you came here, I was very scared. I did not speak Farsi or Pashto. I was afraid I would not understand you, and you would not understand me. I wanted both of you to be happy in my home. I wanted this to be your home, too. I did not know how to do this. I do not have children."

"Not scare like us, Julienne."

"Saadia, you are a very strong person. It is okay to be scared, and it is okay to cry, but it is never okay to be abused. I do not know everything that happened to you, but I know enough to realize it was not good. One day, when we are all comfortable, we will talk about it. For now, you must know that no one will abuse you, and I will not give you away to a man—any man—not even your father."

"Julienne, you strong, you scare and cry, like me. I do that."

"Of course I get scared, and I cry sometimes, but I know that I will be all right. I know how to take care of myself, and I want to teach you that."

"No man you give Leila and me, too?"

"That is right—no man, unless you want one. You do not have to have a man in your life. Look at Ursula. She was never married, and she is happy. She has her store, she helps people, and she has friends. She takes care of herself. You will also, if that is want you want. Look at me—my husband is dead, and I miss him, but I can be alone."

Leila turned the pages of her dictionary and looked at me with a broad smile. "Remarkable!"

"Yes, it is remarkable, and you can do it, too."

Saadia looked quite serious. "Julienne, when you marry, your husband hurt you a lot?"

We were entering that zone everyone had managed to ignore. "When a young woman is in love, and her husband is also in love, there is a lot of passion. Our body works in a way so that even if something is uncomfortable, it does not hurt."

"No hurt? What is passion?"

"For me, passion was wanting to be with Frank more than anything in the world. I wanted to give myself to him."

"You give? He not take?"

"No, he did not take or force himself on me. That is love. That is passion. It is also very beautiful."

"Remarkable," Leila said again.

We all laughed with Leila and her new word. I opened the closet door and told them to look. "If you do not like anything, we will go to get something new for each of you. Now I am going to cook supper."

I left them and went to the kitchen. Today, I was making them some Americanized French food. They did not particularly like my variety of cheeses, so today would be a filet mignon for each with a mushroom and a wine sauce. I made some mashed potatoes with garlic and an enormous salad with all sorts of greens.

A burst of laughter caught me off-guard, and I went to see what was going on. They were coming out of my room. Leila wore my backless red dress with gold shoes. For some reason, I had not realized we were the same size.

Saadia wore a white peasant blouse and a black velvet skirt. I never realized how high the slit in the front went up. Over the blouse, she wore an Afghani shawl purchased during my trip. The embroidery with silk thread looked good on her. Neither girl covered her head.

Though the clothes they wore were not age appropriate, they both looked stunning.

"Ladies, you look beautiful. Now we need to talk about what is *appropriate* (a new word.) It means you

91

should wear what is comfortable to you but also right for the occasion. "When a person is your age, to be dressed with too much skin showing is not appropriate. It is better to look like a lady with good manners.

With a severe look, Saadia turned toward me and said, "Like Taliban say?"

"No, you do not have to cover yourself from head to toe because men are afraid to look at a woman here. You do, however, have to put the right clothes on for the right occasion."

"Prostitute," Leila commented, after searching through the dictionary.

"Yes, you do not want to look like a prostitute. You see, I wore this red dress when I was married to Frank. We were going to a ball and, because I was with my husband, it was fine to wear it. If I were alone and wearing it, the impression would be different."

"Prostitute?"

"Well, Leila, some people could get such a message." I approached the closet and started pointing to other clothes. "Did you see any other clothes you liked?"

"Yes, Julienne, all clothes, but not know which one. Hard to choosing. Saadia can you choosing?"

"You two just gave me an idea. Saadia, and Leila, I am going to take you to Boston for three days. We will go shopping and you will each get a new dress. How does that sound? "

Leila looked puzzled. "Where Boston? Saadia, you know?"

"Girls, Boston is in Massachusetts. Let me get the map that I have in the car. We will look it up on the map."

Brightening, Leila said, "A map! Saadia, Julienne have map in the car. She driving alone, long way, far away, yes? I get map, where, in box glove?"

"Leila, the map is in the glove compartment."

"I get map, and you showing Boston to Saadia and me, too. One minute, yes!"

I took Saadia to the kitchen, cleared the table, and we waited for Leila. She came back with several maps one of which was of the northeastern portion of the United States.

"Thank you, Leila, for getting the map. As I opened the folds, I decided to make this adventure another lesson. Leila, you may have to move some of your stuff from the dining room table, this table is too small. I want to show you where Boston is, how far and how long it will take to get there."

"So much preparing, Leila is slob," Saadia said. "I learn word on television."

"I am not a slob! These things all important for *Nowruz*."

I intervened and said, "Leila, move your things to the side so I can open the map." She did, and I thanked her and spread the map open. "Look here on the side. See that little box? It shows you the length of the miles. If you measure from this length to that one, you know you must drive 30 miles. From that same length to this one a little further, you have 60 miles. Then if you take the length and add it again and again along the road, you will know how many miles you have to drive. See Bar Harbor where we are now? Leila, look for Boston, south of us."

"South—where is south?"

"When you are reading a map, up is north, down is south. That is the way it works with all maps. The sun wakes up in the east—that is on the right side of the map. The sun goes to bed in the west, on the left side of the map."

"I know!" Saadia said. "When I make painting, I look for sun, in my head. Now I know east. Yes! Make color bright and light, too."

"That is right. Saadia, you know these things instinctively because you are an artist, and you know where to put the shadows. That makes you a very good artist. Now, let's look at the road on the map, and we will know how to get to Boston. I think it will take five to six hours. We do not have to rush; we can stop wherever we want. Saadia, let me have a marker. We can mark the map with it and follow the road."

"Julienne, I want drive," Leila said.

I smiled. "You have to wait a few more years, but I have an idea for both of you. You can take turns being my copilot."

"What is copilot?" Leila asked.

"Do you remember, when you flew here in the airplane, a man piloted the plane—like a driver, like me in the car? Other people were there with him. One was a copilot. Like you, Leila—a copilot and an engineer, too. Saadia, that will be you when Leila is the copilot. You'll take turns with Saadia, and you'll each follow the road and tell me where to turn and when to stop."

"Difficult, Julienne. I look at trees. I want to paint trees. Leila be copilot."

"Okay, Saadia. You watch the scenery, I'll drive, and Leila will tell me about the road. So, what do you say we get up very early tomorrow and drive to Boston? We can spend the weekend there, and you can find the dresses you want for the reception."

They were both smiling, not knowing what to do with my spontaneity.

"We will stop a few times and enjoy ourselves with what we find on the road. There are little stores all around that I am sure you will enjoy. We will arrive early enough to have a great dinner, and the next day we can go shopping. Boston has a wonderful museum and many things you will enjoy."

"Julienne, American village have no broken tanks, like Afghanistan?"

"No Saadia, we do not have places like that here. We call them states, not villages, and we have not had a war here in a very long time. When we did, it was because those who came to America wanted the new land—'the new world,' they called it. Every time humans want something from other humans or something from the land, many people die. That war for independence is how America became the United States."

"Complicated. Leila and me do not like war, do not like men. I like you. Good to us. Thank you."

"Thank you, Saadia, I appreciate that."

"Julienne, we eat, we sleep we go Boston, we see art, yes? We happy, yes!"

"Yes!"

"Julienne, I like you."

"I like you too, Saadia, and you, too, Leila."

"Julienne, thank you, no *hijab*. Thank you for art. Taliban say no art, no books, no painting, only *burka*, black window, no go outside alone. Not good for happy."

"If you want to wear a *hijab*, that is okay with me. Now that you know your alphabet and you are reading about the great masters of the arts, you may want to read also about Islam. I like your beautiful hair, but only you can decide what you will wear on your head." I hugged them, one after the other, and headed to the kitchen. Our supper was ready.

Saadia followed me, and Leila was not far behind. "No *burka*, no *hijab*, many books, many art I make. What you think, Leila?"

"I want learn many things. I want to be lawyer. Read about laws. Read about laws everywhere. I want help other girls like us."

Sometimes I still found it hard to believe the incredible progress these girls were making so fast. We sat and ate our meal, and when we had carried our plates to the sink, I washed while Saadia dried, and Leila put everything away. When we left the kitchen, all was clean, cleared, and ready for the next meal.

"When we return from our trip, I will call Mr. Rand and ask him how to register you as students in the school where he is a teacher. You are both ready for school. I will have to call the state department and find out about your refugee status."

"Julienne, what is 'refugee status'? Leila, you know?"

"No, Julienne tell us."

"Girls, *this* I believe is complicated! You arrived

in the United States under different hospices. You were each rescued by American soldiers, and you are both sponsored by an American."

"What is hospice? What is sponsored, what is rescued?"

"Ladies, remember these questions. It is now very late. Let's go to bed. We will have all the time we need tomorrow in the car. Write the words you want to learn, and I will do my best to explain while I drive."

CHAPTER 14

The Road to Boston

I woke up at 5:00 A.M., made some tea, and gathered some almonds and dried apricots so we would have snacks during the drive. I packed some clothes and was ready.

Saadia appeared and handed me a piece of paper that read, "How no pain husband? What is rescue? Leila gave me only time to read the note and handed me hers: What is a sponsor? Dictionary is not clear. Are you sponsor?" My girls were growing and learning.

They looked at my bag left on the floor by the kitchen and ran to their rooms. It felt like seconds later, they reappeared with the luggage I had purchased from them.

"You may want to take your pillows. It is a long drive, and you might get tired and want to take a nap."

Off they went, back to their rooms, and got their pillows. In record time, they were ready, and I was driving. Saadia, usually absorbed by the scenery, began to talk.

"Julienne, when you married, you say husband Frank not hurt. Explain please."

That was hysterical to me! They did not know that, before Frank, I had been with other men. I decided to let such details alone. "When Frank and I were together the first time, we were not yet married."

"Oh no!" Saadia said. "Not good, Julienne. *Fatwa* not good. You die! You tell her, Leila."

"Have no fear. *Fatwa* does not apply in the society I grew up in. It is not always a good idea to sleep with people before a marriage is pronounced, but both Frank and I were in agreement. We wanted to make love to one another. It felt right for us. Saadia, you asked me, so I am being honest."

"No, you talk," Leila said. "We hear you. Tell make love, not hurt, confusing, nice too. Talk now."

"So, here is the story. After we met and walked for what seemed to be a hundred miles, Frank took me to his apartment in Paris. Before that, we had a glass of wine and some cheese and bread, too. He was not French, but he did many things like French people do. Once we were inside his small place, he showed me a chair, and I sat. He got on his knees so we were about the same height. Frank was a tall man. We talked like that for a while. I liked the way he looked at me. I liked his laughter, and a few times he caressed my face. He had soft hands. He was very gentle."

Telling them about my first encounter with Frank was not difficult, but talking about him, I felt the pain of his absence. There was something about the texture of his soul that left a hole in me. I missed that look of his, the curling of his lips when he did not know he was doing it. I could tell when he was in deep thought. I missed him—the human being he was.

I stopped daydreaming and continued. "He took my hands and kissed them, one after the other. The way he touched me was very gentle. He held my head, and I felt his eyes. I liked the way he looked at me. In them, I could see joy, and I could see pain. I sensed he was a strong man, yet he had a soft side. I felt very warm inside. He kissed me gently on the forehead. He was patient with me, because I was not ready."

"Julienne, Frank waited, how, how, he not hit you if you not ready?"

"No, Leila, making love is something that happens between two people. It is gentle, it is deliberate, and it is passionate. It is strong, it is soft, but it does not hurt. If a man feels that he must possess his mate with force, it is not an act of love—it is abusive. I call this rape. The man is not making love to his mate or with her. He is abusing her. He is using her like he uses a chair to sit on.

"Some men are giving of themselves, and some only take. Some men are considerate and some are not. I think the men in your lives were not considerate, and they were not giving, because all they wanted was to take from you. I believe the men in both your lives did not know differently because that is the way they were raised. They came from abuse, and that is all they knew. I find that very sad, because both men and women in such cases miss the joy and pleasure of lovemaking. Your husbands raped you—at least this is what I say. How old were you, Leila, when you got married?"

"I lived in small town name Ahvaz in Iran. I born in another village. My grandfather has a man in the other house next to him house. My father married me to this man. They said he a good man. He was 44, me 11. That married came after my mother dead maybe, I do not know about my mother, I do not know what age for sure.

"He brutal. I learn this word in dictionary yesterday. After wedding party, he take me to his house, far away different village. He has another wife also, older not like me, sixteen maybe. I am not know for age, no papers, Julienne. He pushed her in stomach, she get away. She pregnant, he told her to go to sleep with goats in the back of room. I feel sorry for her. He came where I was sitting on the floor, he take my wedding shawl off. I had it tied under my neck and maybe he was to cut my head off. He screamed to me to get up. I did, he ripped my clothes off. I naked and crying a lot.

"He says to me, it be all right, he my husband and he can see me like that, he touch me, in not good place. He say he want do to me. It is the will. He push me on the rug, I fall, and before I get up, he on top of me. He held my legs like a chicken, and opened them real wide. I scream. He hit my face—the tooth on side of mouth come off. Now, in your house with mirrors, all time I look at my face and see the missing tooth I see of him and what he did to me. He beat me up like I am a drum. My skin hurt, my legs hurt, everything hurt, part not seen bleed. He hurting me with his body. I want to die. He pushed me, he hit me more, my body his drum. My skin tight. He smile, he laugh, he touch again. He say he can do to me. He say he feel good. I want dying."

Still driving, I took her arm, reached to her hand, and kissed it gently. She felt like a rag doll I once had. I told her she would be fine, she was no longer alone. Along with the assurance I was giving her, I also I kept wondering how could anyone be restored after such an ordeal? I had no preparation to assist this girl. I had never encountered such human trauma—not even in a bad book. Would she be affected for the rest of her life? Are such experiences ever . . .

Leila broke my train of thought when she spoke again. "He big man, Julienne. He put his peis between my legs and pushed self hard. I screamed. He hit me again. I feel something break inside, he tearing my body with peis. It hurt so much, Julienne, he was like a dog, and I saw many dogs doing this. The girl dog not cry. No tooth come off. He made a lot of noise and after a while he stopped. Got up and went to the door, he told me to get him a cup of tea.

"I was hurting a lot, between my legs, my ribs here, my mouth, my face too was hurting. I knew if I did not get the tea he would hurt me again. I put my *roopoosh* back on, the front was broken. He take my satin pantaloons' to clean him. They had my blood color, I learn this word yesterday. I crying a lot, his other wife gave me a cup with tea, I bring to him. I still crying and he smoking pipe outside the door. Smell terrible.

"The moon big full after I gave him his tea, I walk to the trees. I walk, I feel blood between my legs, but I no can see what he do to me. He call me, like a sheep. I go back where he is, I so scared, and I tell him I bleeding.

"He scream at me. He never talk, he scream only. He laugh at me, he told me it was the will of the merciful one. I his wife and I to be good, obedient, it is the way. He said he pay good money to my grandfather and *mullah*, he gave three goats to grandfather. He laughed again and grabbed my arm. He was so fast, he had me on the ground this time, not even a rug anymore. He put his hand on my mouth so no hear me scream. He mounted me as if I was a horse. My skin was tight again, like drum again, tight—he beat with big body. He did three times before he was too tired. I want to dead, and I cried, no one me telling, no one me asking. I prayed Allah that I should be dead."

She became silent, and from the corner of my eye, I saw tears flowing slowly. Because she attempted to stop them, she was silent. Leila was not alone this time—we were all crying tears of anguish. This was not part of a bad movie. Leila had told us about her wedding night. This young girl had exposed herself and her memories to me and also to Saadia. She may have broken an involuntary inner vow never to tell, never to be vulnerable. She did not know it yet, but I knew that soon enough Leila would realize she was on the way toward achieving personal freedom. She was disengaging herself from her burden.

We were silent for a long time, feeling angry, resigned, accepting, but also forgiving. From my stance in life, I felt strongly that it would take a lot of forgiveness to walk this child through a valley of spring flowers.

Leila broke the silence again. "I woke up when one of the goat touch my face. There was no mirror, but I know the side of my face was swollen. When I went to pee, there was more blood, a lot blood. Julienne, I very small, I a little girl. He very big. I glad he dead. I am very glad he dead."

It was not the time to correct her. It was the time to slowly digest a feeling that enraged me. At least in appearance, I had to remain detached from the story she told. We all were silent a while. I had a lot to process. The girls must have sensed it—they knew when to give me the space I needed to think, to be. Our cultures were so far removed from one another that I had no tools except the content of my heart to use for healing, for repairing what I could not fathom. Saadia understood a lot more than I could, because her life had a lot of similarities.

Leila's tears were still flowing as she said, "That is the way for girls like me. After first night, I never feel him again. When he beat me I try not crying, it did not matter what he did to me, it did not matter . . ."

Leila was inconsolable. I did not stop the car because I believed she needed to get the story out—that doing so would be cathartic, and perhaps she would find some healing in the release. I was glad she was in front with me so I could touch her, pat her hand. There is something healing about letting these things out, but I did not know much about how to help her. I had driven almost to Bangor when I decided we needed to stop— maybe to walk around a park or some other place suited for us. To our right was a small coffee shop. I parked the car away from the few others and suggested we could walk a little before going in for tea, if they had any.

After she got out of the car, Leila's tears flowed freely, as if to water the flowers on her blouse. She walked toward me and gave me a hug—one like I have never experienced before. She told me she was glad she told me. Saadia already knew. She told me how much she appreciated me.

A hundred yards or so from where we stood, I noticed a path to the woods, and we followed that way. There were more tears to restore her broken soul, yet I could not even tell her everything would be all right, because I did not know that it ever would be. Fueled by frustration, ignorance, and self-gratification, a man had wounded the spirit and the body of this young girl. I walked . . . I walked, holding the hands of two young girls, knowing they were not the only ones.

It was not compassion I felt that day—it was rage.

And we walked. There was nothing more to say. Each step we took became a covenant. We became one, not because of a secret, but because a secret was no longer a cause for shame. I felt gratitude, because in my life I had experienced great love.

Saadia pointed us toward three large boulders forming a sort of triangle. Without words, we walked toward them. We each took a boulder and sat, our knees touching, and with our hands we held each other in a space to heal. We sat, and the hard surface of the boulders gave us strength. Holding hands, we became a circle—unbreakable.

We did not have our watches on, so I don't know how long we were there. I do know that something happened to each of us that morning. No words were necessary to explain. We were family.

Leila got up, breaking the circle, and we followed her back to the car. This time she opened the back door for herself. That is when I told them the word was not "peis" but "penis." They both laughed. Soon after, Leila fell into a deep sleep. I drove, and Saadia sat next to me now, admiring the scenery.

Because of our various stops, we arrived at our hotel later than I had planned. We had a suite, and for that I was very happy. This was not a night to be separated by doors. A trip of any length can be tiring, but this one was different. We were processing something none of us had anticipated.

In the room, we cleaned up and went a block away from the hotel where the concierge had suggested a small restaurant. The girls had never eaten Italian food.

Once seated, a waiter arrived with bread and olive oil mixed with basil and Parmesan cheese. The girls and I did not drink sodas, so I ordered a bottle of Pellegrino. Franco, the waiter, told us of the daily specials and asked what I and my daughters would like. I felt honored to be taken to be their mother.

For a split second, I thought I should adopt them.

CHAPTER 15

Shoes, Clothes, and More

It was a bright Saturday. I woke up before they did. Along with the bible in the drawer of the nightstand, I also found a telephone book.

There was no reason to spend only three days in this glorious place. I had a plan, and I was looking for a dentist. I found a few close to the hotel. Too early to call, I copied names and numbers.

My customary list had the important entries: take girls to breakfast—call a dentist about a tooth replacement—go to some art galleries—go to a museum. Get clothes and shoes for the art opening.

The old cathedral not too far from the hotel let me know it was 6:00 A.M. Another addition to my note: take the girls to see this cathedral. Since they usually woke up around eight o'clock, I went back to my bed.

It was during this period of neither wake nor sleep that I began to think about the future of these two girls.

It was evident that, in order to flourish in this or any other society, they needed to be prepared. They needed to go to school. To advance better and faster, a private tutor would be my solution. They had to be brought to grade level. Children being cruel the world over, I did not want them persecuted in school because they looked different, or because they did not speak English perfectly, and so on. Their short lives had been peppered with enough traumas to maim a hundred people. Their wounds were too deep to take chances.

How best to serve them was my dilemma. Based on their horrific experiences, I thought a psychologist might help them along in order to process the memories and the traumas. Perhaps Ursula or Mr. Rand could assist. For certain, Mr. Rand could help with the matter of a good tutor. On that thought, I wrote another note and put it on the nightstand to be retrieved later on.

"Good Morning, Julienne. What you doing?"

"Good Morning, Saadia. Did you sleep well?"

"Yes, no, me think many lot."

"Do you want to tell me what you were thinking about?"

Her amber eyes lit up. She was a little girl with an important story to tell. Moments like that reminded me of when I was about that age. I would run to Suzannah with my latest revelation. My stories were most urgent and important. This day, I moved over a bit, giving Saadia space to join me in the bed. Another story was important today and needed to be told. It was not mine but Saadia's.

"Julienne, Taliban say no books, no art, no music, no dancing. I like when you have radio, you dance.

Make for smiling, I like when you take books for answer question for me. I like when I paint, one day I learn to dance too. No Taliban here, yes? I think Taliban afraid of girl who can read. I want education; it is dark when Saadia not know anything. Shame, Julienne. That come to me shame. I like read. Thank you for alphabet."

"Saadia, you missed a lot, but I can assure you, you will be educated. You will catch up and exceed all that you can now dream of. You will do your art because you are an artist. Please never feel shame. You have desire, and you have discipline. If you believe in the Merciful, you know he spared your life for a good reason, and that is to become all that you were born to be. You are taking a risk every time you pick up your brush or your pencil, but the risk is that you are pushing yourself to be better than you were before. No one can tell you what to do or not to do. Only you know what is good for you. You are an artist, and that is a gift! You have the character to be true to yourself. You have the courage to take your life to places you have not yet experienced. I am going to help you with self-confidence."

"I want be strong and nice, too, like you. You teach me, Julienne, good, I learn good. What is confidence?"

"Sweetheart, this is something we develop as we grow. First we go to school, we learn many things. It is a while after that knowledge, wisdom, and awareness come, and I think, after that, we develop self-confidence. The process begins when we are young. Because of the conditions in Afghanistan, there was no way for you to know these things. I know you are a very strong person, and you will do all that you set your mind to."

"The mind is not dark much. The painting take me to more nice place inside my head."

"I like that. It is not dark anymore because you have vision, you have clarity. I am only helping you toward the things that will illuminate you. You see, you have a brilliant mind; you simply were never given the opportunity to use it. Now you have your entire life to explore your world. You will make fantastic discoveries as you grow. You belong to yourself, and as you are exposed to more things, you will find that you change—you will know more and understand better who you are. You will want more out of your life."

"Saadia belong to Saadia, not husband, yes!"

"Yes, you belong to yourself and no one else. Even if later on you get married or are in a relationship other than marriage, please remember, you belong to yourself always."

"No husband, too much pain. No want husband."

"You do not have to be married. Many women are not married. That, too, is fine."

"How you know about Frank? How you know he is okay to love?"

"Saadia, let's explore this. When you have a canvas, and you are going to paint something wonderful, you work hard at it. A marriage is almost like that. You know you like the person, you know you can love him, and from that point on, you do all you can to make him and you happy. Like painting a canvas. You have to work at it."

"Like my painting."

"Exactly!"

"I like you, Julienne. You strong, you know how to put a little of paint in the canvas. You know how to be freedom."

"To be free you must start in your head. Your mind must be engaged. As you learn more English, you will know when to use 'free' and also 'freedom.' They are almost the same, but they are not. People are free, and they exercise their freedom." I could tell Saadia didn't really understand what I was saying. "I am having difficulty explaining this one to you. Wait, I think I have it. You are free to ask me anything you want to ask, and I have the freedom to answer you or not."

She burst in a hardy laughter. In the process, Leila woke up.

"You said I no say to be freedom, now you say you have the freedom... I confused, so confused."

"I know how to explain," Leila said. "Saadia, you are free, but you *have* freedom. I speak English very good!"

"Yes, Leila, you speak English very *well!*"

Leila shook her head smiling. "So many words the same, I get confused."

"One day, you will forget you were confused about these things. You are both doing very well. I have the same problems."

"That is because you talk a lot, Julienne. That is good for us."

"I guess so, Leila, I like to speak to both of you. Now, let's get ready and go get some breakfast. I have plans for today."

Once they realized I was taking them somewhere, off they ran to the bathroom. It was interesting to see that they did not mind going to the bathroom at the same time. I would have had a fit. Coming from their culture, I thought that was odd. This was another example for me to learn to accept people the way they were. I also realized my filters were not of great value when dealing with cultures that were so different from my own. Frank used to say, 'Acceptance, Julienne, is a quality.' I was beginning to understand.

Their hair was still wet, but it was summer, and they did not mind. Each wearing new jeans and blouses from my closet, they were looking like the girls they were meant to be. Their dress code had changed a great deal. They no longer felt compelled to cover their heads in public. They now looked people in the eyes. As best they could, they expressed their feelings, and though they did not know it, they were learning the meaning of freedom.

More and more like Suzannah, I wore skirts. This day was not an exception.

It was time to begin the exploration of Boston. We had achieved what I never thought we ever would. At breakfast, I gave them choices: shop for a dress for the opening at the art gallery or go to the museum or the cathedral across the street.

"Where is museum, far?"

"Better ask the waiter. He will know."

"I want to see cathedral, is like mosque, yes! We not go in?"

"Leila, we can go to the cathedral, and we do not have to take our shoes off. We can walk all the way to the altar. Let's go to the cathedral, and we will continue to the museum. Ask the waiter about the museum and the stores, too. We will do everything. I must run to the toilet."

"Who ask waiter?"

"Both of you! Ask him to write the directions, it is all right. It is time you practiced talking to others. Do it!"

CHAPTER 16

A Cathedral

From the breakfast table, we walked down Washington Street. It was the perfect time to tell my girls about George Washington. They were fascinated that I knew the history of the country. They did not know the history of theirs. I even knew some things about this cathedral. Once I told them about books I had, their thirst to read became voracious. The more they read the more their language skills improved, it was a daily occurrence.

It was a short walk—one block, one turn, and there she appeared in her grandeur: the Cathedral of the Holy Cross. Saadia stopped. She was taking in what neither Leila nor I could see: the architecture. She made a quick sketch and continued to walk toward the entrance.

"Good, beautiful sketch, many workers I know. We go inside, yes?"

"Yes, Saadia, we are going inside. You will be able to see closely the details of its architecture. This style is called Gothic. As you study art, you will probably also study many things about architecture."

"Julienne, I want to go school now. Make drawings of house, cathedral, and hospital, too."

"Nothing will stop you, Saadia. Come, let's go in."

Leila, taking Saadia's hand, began to walk up the granite steps. I followed, something I did often, just for the sake of observing them together. At the door, they both turned to look at me only a few feet behind them. They seemed unsure, wanting me to be with them.

I took their hands and we went in. To our right was a marble basin filled with water. An old woman kneeled, dipped her hand in the water, and made the sign of the cross. Both girls looked at me.

"You do not have to do that, but it is not a sin if you do. The water is called 'holy water,' I believe because it is blessed. People who are Catholics use the water to create with their hand the symbol of a cross on their chest."

"Why water, why cross? What is cross?"

"I do not know the reason for the water, but Catholic people make the sign of the cross, possibly to remind them of Jesus on the cross. In Christian societies, he is a very important figure, like Mohammed is to you. If I find a priest, I will ask him. You are Muslim, and you have rituals. This is a ritual of the Catholics."

Saadia looked inside the church, seeing everything at once. "Julienne, in Afghanistan and Pakistan, too, village women and girls not go to mosque. Only behind the—what you call the separate wood?"

"I believe you are talking about a screen."

"Look the sky. Many glass like mosque."

"Yes, the windows are stained glass, and they represent scenes from the bible. See the center of the church's ceiling? Beautiful!"

"Big painting. Beautiful. Hard work. Where to stand?"

"This sort of painting is done on a scaffold. When we travel to Italy, I will take you to Rome. A most important little chapel has one of the most magnificent works of art from Michelangelo. I will show you a picture when we get back home. I can also rent a special movie about an Italian painter called Michelangelo. The most important person of the Catholic church lives in Rome. He lives in a place called the Vatican, and he is called the pope."

"Like the *ayatollah*, or *imam*, or prophet?"

"You know, Leila, I do not think the pope is like the *ayatollah*. The pope is the head of the Catholic church. Judaism, the religion of the Jewish people, came first, and after that Christianity, and after that Islam. The rituals of the Catholics are older than the ones from the Muslims, but I think some Muslims say that Islam was always around. I am not a student of religion, so I cannot argue that."

"Pope good person?"

"Yes."

"Look, a man with a long dress, like a *burka*. He is talking to the old lady."

"He is a priest. Maybe we can go and talk to him. We cannot stay too long, as he has work to do, and we have other places to go."

We approached close to where the priest was, and immediately he realized we had some questions or concerns. He walked toward us and blessed each of us.

"They are Muslims."

"We are all children of one God."

He had his hands over their heads, a gesture I did not anticipate, yet evidently one that was not menacing to the girls. Somehow they did not feel threatened.

"I have never been to a mosque. I am very happy you came to Holy Cross. It is an old cathedral. I am Father Perry. I want to welcome you. What are your names?"

His soft voice suddenly was drowned. The organ and a choir we had not noticed before began with a series of high notes.

"The Bach choir is getting ready for practice. Girls, you may enjoy the music. My best wishes to the three of you, but I must go now."

Obviously late, the priest left us in a rush. The girls had never heard a choir. They listened attentively, and soon enough Saadia pointed to Father Perry, who had a conductor's baton.

"No music in mosque, no music in streets, no music in home. I like this. Listen, they sing good. Listen, Saadia, this is good music. Julienne, you know."

"They are very good. Maybe we can stay for one complete song. The music is by Johann Sebastian Bach."

"Remarkable, Julienne, how you know music, painting, so many things you know? You know these?" Leila pointed to various spots around the cathedral. "See on the side, the walls up, see, here, here, here? Different, but same. Twelve. Who is this, Julienne?"

"His name is Jesus, and those are the stations of the cross. The old lady is saying prayers and remembering the incident that happened over 2,000 years ago. I do not know much about all that—just enough to give you the wrong information.

"Why he carry the wood?"

"Leila, it is a long story. When you read and understand English well, I believe the story can be found in the Bible. Jesus was a Jew, killed because of his beliefs. He was crucified on the cross he is carrying. It is more than a bundle of wood. Look at the picture closely. Look at the shape in each of the pictures, the shape makes it a cross. When you see this shape now, you know its name. It is a cross."

"*Jihad!*"

"No, I do not think crucifixion and *jihad* are the same."

"Yes, dead. It same."

Saadia, silent up to now, had to let us what her thinking was, and there was something righteous about it.

"Do people in church kill many people? The man with long dress nice to us. Maybe he not knowing Leila and me Muslim."

"He knew. I told him."

"And no kill us! No hurt, too! Remarkable."

"Most Christians respect the religions of others. They do not kill people of different religions. "

"Good people, I like. No stoning?"

"I think most of them are good people, but like any people and religions, some are good and some are not. As for the stoning, I believe in many ancient cultures stoning was the punishment for many crimes. I believe only women were stoned."

"Julienne, why you say ancient? Stoning *now*, not ancient. Now, Julienne!"

"You are correct, since you are a perfect example of what happens in some parts of the world today. I am glad you are here now, with Leila and me, and we are all safe." The choral piece came to an end. "How about we go to the museum now? The music is over. We can eat some lunch at the museum—they have a cafeteria. Then the big event of the day is to go find your clothes."

We left the church. I think they were both impressed with the artwork, the lady, and the holy water. They liked the priest because he was not threatening. Most of all, the organ and the Bach choir impressed them.

It was time for our next adventure. The Museum of Fine Art was waiting for us. It took a while to explain to them it would be a very quick tour only to familiarize them with a museum.

"Julienne, you know music, you know church, and how you say 'Jo Ann Bak'?"

"Leila, repeat after me: Jo-HHHHan—you see your nose does the 'hhhhh.' Jo-hhhhhan."

"I know Johann Sebastian Bach."

"Good for you, Saadia! Work with Leila so she can pronounce the words well. Do you want to see anything else before we go to the museum?

They were satisfied with the cathedral and ready for the museum.

CHAPTER 17

Art Make Happy

The Museum of Fine Art was not difficult to find. Neither girl had ever been to a museum. For Saadia, this was a treat she almost could not fathom. Leila was not an artist but appreciated things of beauty. If I understood correctly, she had a grandmother who was educated in Turkey and, for a very short time, this woman had exposed Leila to some art. At the front desk, she collected every brochure possible. Saadia was mesmerized and interested in the masters I had told her about.

"Julienne, thank you for take me to museum." Saadia had tears in her eyes. "Darkness in my head going away fast, like a horse. My body is happy! Inside I happy! No one make present like this for me."

I gave her a hug and told her this was only the beginning of her art education. Otherwise, we did not talk very much. Leila and I followed Saadia, who was in a world neither of us had visited. As we walked, Leila and I had to stop again and again. We became expert at finding benches. Saadia examined each piece of art, each brush stroke. The frames fascinated Leila, yet the Renaissance was not the period of her liking, something neither Saadia nor I understood.

Witnessing and being part of their world was very gratifying for me. Thus far, my life after Frank had not had room in it to care for or about any one else. I had become rather reclusive, and it was evident these girls were changing not only the people they had been but also the person I had become.

At times Saadia called us so we could be at touching distance of a painting. She wanted us to see how the artist must have held the brush to create this or that curve, or how this and that pigment became what we were seeing. Never before had I witnessed such jubilation. She was in a trance.

To think that, not so long ago, this girl was to be stoned to death necessitated that I pause to think about the people who were willing to kill her. Her parents were responsible for her brilliance, yet they were unable to see it. Though I did not have children, I knew I could never kill my own child.

Judging by Leila's sudden openness to converse about what had been unspoken for such a long time was indication enough that retaining, hiding, or stuffing trauma inside in any way would not serve Saadia in the long run. One day she, too, would have to tell her secret. First, I had to learn why stoning was still a form of punishment is some countries. For now, she was appreciating the best this museum had to offer.

We moved from one hall to the next very slowly. It became evident that we must return to this museum. Now that Saadia had made such a discovery, I knew museums would be a regular stop wherever we went.

"Julienne, in Teheran we have big museums. Ancient art. Look—they have art from Persia. We must see—I never see museum in Teheran."

"We will see as much as we can. We do not have to go anywhere else today. I think the museum closes at 6:00 P.M."

"So much see, Julienne, I like museum. I want to be a good painter and architture, too."

"Saadia, you want to become a good painter and an architect, too. Architects make architectural drawings. I know your work will surpass many architectural designs I have seen before. One day, I will read about you in a magazine."

"First school, Julienne. We learn English well, yes. See I know 'well,' not 'good.'"

"Yes. When we get back home, I will get you the right person to teach you all that you need to know to go to school with other kids."

Leila chimed in. "I like that, Julienne. I want to study laws of different countries. I want help other women and kids like me. Many need help. I rescue women and children, too. In law court, like you show me in book."

"Wonderful. I will have an international lawyer and an architect. I am very proud of both of you. Your progress is remarkable."

They both laughed, because I was using their newfound word. Still following Saadia, we veered to a long and wide hall with glass cases. Behind them were costumes from many countries. Not one *burka* was part of the exhibit. They both liked the Spanish flamenco dancer's costume; they remarked that I could dance for them with the red dress Leila was not allowed to wear at the reception. It was fun to watch them. Far from the many tears they shed, they were now in a wonderful, jovial mood.

The next room took us to a French impressionist art section. Saadia nearly fainted when she saw a Monet. She told me she had seen a picture book with that painting. She kept repeating that the paintings were free. I did not understand what she meant, with arms in motion, and as she imitated brush strokes, she explained the free-flowing movement of what she was looking at. I had never thought of impressionist art as free, but, yes, they were all free thinkers creating free forms of art. This young girl was able to tap into something most people knew nothing about.

"Julienne, painters here all husbands?"

"I do not think most were married. I know most were men. I am not sure I understand what you mean."

"You answer good. Why men not allow women to paint? Not good, Julienne."

"You know, many societies are patriarchal, and not only in the Middle East, Asia, or Persia. You are looking at paintings from the 19th century. Women of Europe were liberated, but although they were educated, they had a hard time distinguishing themselves as artists. I can think of very few who achieved fame. Berthe Morisot, Eva Gonzales, and Mary Cassat—I know there were more, but I do not remember their names. In most countries, éven today, women have a hard time validating who and what they are. This world is constantly changing, and the place of women in it changes every day. This is why people from Judeo-Christian societies do not understand why Muslims want to keep their women in darkness.

"As you get older, and you enter the work force, you will probably encounter some difficulties, but men also have a hard time. The idea is to be very good at what you do, no matter what it is, and then, when this happens, you can shine like a bright star.

"In Western Societies, the more education a woman has, the more assertive she becomes. She is sure of herself and who she is. This is something women everywhere need to learn. Maybe when Leila is a lawyer and a defender of human rights, we will know more about many forms of abuse, especially in the Muslim world."

Saadia looked pensive. "Julienne, they stone women painters?"

"I have never heard of that. In Europe, it was not the customary mode of punishing a woman."

"No one punish you. You like Frank, marry Frank and no punish, no shame."

"You are correct, Saadia, I liked Frank. I also loved him. I married him, and no one could punish me. Different cultures have different rules. In some places, the rules are ancient and have not changed. I think ignorance has a lot to do with all that and also something called brainwashing."

"What is brainwashing?"

"This is going to be a little difficult. Let's say I want you to believe something, even if it not true, and

I repeat it thousands of times, for many years, for many centuries. After a while, you will believe it, and you will teach it to your children. Brainwashing works like that."

"Dangerous Julienne, but one thousand years, I dead."

"Yes, it is dangerous, yet armies do it, religious leaders do it, and even parents do this. What is left behind are people who do not know the truth about many things—people who continuously teach the lies to their children because they do not know enough to question what they have been made to believe. Centuries later, you have people who advanced and people who stayed in the dark."

As we talked, Saadia led us to various halls of the museum, but she paid attention to what we were saying. She was appreciating art for art's sake. She was asking questions because, in her world, there had not been any art or freedom of expression.

"In dark, makes ignorant people, like my father and his stones."

"I believe you are correct, Saadia."

At precisely ten minutes before six, a loudspeaker announced that the museum was about to close. With a sad face, Saadia looked at me as if I could change the rules.

"Tomorrow again, please?"

I looked at Leila, who was showing some wear and tear, but to my surprise Leila said, "Only in the morning, Saadia. I want to see stores in Boston."

"Fair enough," I said. "We will come back in the morning, and in the afternoon we will go to mall."

125

"What is mall?" Leila asked.

"It is a place usually with more than one floor and many stores. You get to choose where you want to go and what you want to buy."

We headed to the same restaurant where we had breakfast. The same waiter served us, and by this time he was the girls' best friend. He decided what they should try, then looked at me and made a suggestion. Our delicious dinner arrived moments later. We were all tired, and after paying and tipping Patrick, we left and went straight to our room.

CHAPTER 18

A Stone to Kill

Saadia was elated, she spent time admiring Renoir, and some Cézannes that were on loan from another museum. The idea of more than one museum was, as she said, 'extraordinary' More than once she told me of her amazement when she saw the nudes. She mentioned the nudes; the images did not feel dirty to her. A couple of time she mentioned how lucky and free some people were. They understood that the body was a carrier of something divine. We turned a corner and a full exhibit of work by women greeted us. She was overtly overjoyed. Turning to me she began to talk about women and their art.

"Women painter very good Julienne, look writing on wall say 'Women in Art,' Saadia is lucky too. My painting in gallery, not yet museum. I like museum. Thank you bringing me here. I like artists to be not men only. No Taliban in France, yes! Old painting maybe Taliban not yet."

"Saadia, I know the Taliban had not made its appearance anywhere in the world when these painting were done. We could find out more if you wish by going to the library, you need to learn to look things up. When we get home we will go to our library and do some research, write their names down. I will teach you how."

"Julienne, if no Taliban, everybody happy. French artist woman are lucky, no stoning, can make beautiful art. Lucky people. I lucky too I can see, I can feel no can touch, yes?"

"Saadia, in most countries today, stoning another human being is not acceptable or legal. Women artists in France are lucky for sure; they can create whatever art they want. That is true of female artists in most countries. Some women like you are very talented and make beautiful art. France happens to be a country where many people understand the idea of what it means to be free and they express that in their art. There are many ways to be free."

"Julienne, too many words. English very hard, you know."

"That will only be true for a little while. Soon you will speak English the way you paint."

She smiled in approval and decided to talk about more personal events.

"Julienne, you know why men soldiers help me? Took me fast when I in hole drive fast, surprise my father and other men going to throw stone to my head. Far far far fast and after that in … now I know, helicopter. Julienne, they not hurt me. Good people they are. I scared, I not know what they do to me. But not hurt me."

"I am sure they were decent men who decided to do something about a tragedy that was soon to happen and they knew they could do something about it. You were a lucky person. Maybe when we go elsewhere we can talk more about that. The museum is not the right place for this conversation."

"Woman, too, soldiers, nice woman. One gave me many clothe to put on my body, soap too, nice soap smell like flower—I don't know. She take me to bathroom, not like yours. She give me special napkin for blood, like you. Nice women. One day I want to write and say thank you very much. Beautiful woman, like art. I paint her face one day. I see her in head. I remember, I paint later, I talk later.

"Saadia, do you know if they were American soldiers? If we knew that, we could do some research and find out the names for you. I think this could be done with American soldiers. I do not know anything about military protocol, but I can find out, I am sure. Do you know the date you were rescued?"

"Yes, same flag, American soldier gave me hamburger, I no like. Leila, do you like hamburger?

"I like hamburger. The soldiers helped me, took me to mess hall. They give me hamburger and French fries, different foods, very greasy. I hungry, not food for many days."

"Leila, was that in Iran?"

"Yes, with soldiers from other place, maybe two. They say nobody know. One speak Pashto, another one speak Farsi, a girl soldier. She not look like a man."

"I have no idea what that could have been. Are you talking about American soldiers? I do not know what the

129

military does. We never know what governments do—
espionage, maybe. As far as I know, American soldiers
were not in Iran. Whoever they were or whatever they
were doing, I am glad they rescued you."

"I am glad no stone for you, Leila. Me very scared,
me shake my body."

"It is very sad that, in countries like Iran, Pakistan,
and others, they still stone women. Leila, maybe you
will be one of the international lawyers who will help
change that. Some people have not advanced with time,
and they kept ancient modes of punishment to instill fear
in order to control people. As cultures and people evolve,
practices change. In most parts of the Middle East, as
well as parts of Asia and Africa, people have not yet
made the changes that are needed."

Saadia said, "Julienne, you know when stoning
comes. The men, they make a hole. They put bag on
me head covered. They did that to me, Julienne. I see
them making the deep on the ground. I scared but no
cry. I angry because my grandfather and many friends
had stone to throw. My father say I shame him. My
grandfather say I shame him. Many woman I know look,
they too had stones. No good reason for stone me. Leila,
when you do law, can you help other girls? Not fair, not
right. I am happy I can do art now. I never go back to
Afghanistan, Pakistan, too. Never! You know they make
deep hole, they tie my feet and my hands no can run,
they put bag on head last. I see all preparations."

Her voice showed no anger. The tone of her voice
remained even, and I could not detect pain or hate, and that
surprised me. Although she was talking about herself, it

felt as if she was speaking about someone else. She was somehow detached, and I became concerned about her lack of emotion. Without experience or knowledge, I had no barometer to judge what emotions she should have had. No studies about people like Saadia that had been so deeply victimized by her own family had been done, as far as I knew. I imagined this was because victims of stoning did not survive.

No one could enlighten me, but I kept thinking about the long-term costs to this brilliant girl. She had known nothing at all about matters of birthing. I wondered what postpartum feelings she might have had. Would she ever be able to trust anyone, including me? I knew this was an issue that needed professional help. By this time, half asleep, I decided to ask Ursula if she knew anyone who might provide advice.

"How do you feel about all this? You are a very lucky young lady."

"Yes, lucky for you, I know. I am happy now."

I must have been quiet for longer than I thought.

"Julienne, what you thinking, no can talk?"

"Saadia, I am thinking about the pain you must have suffered and about the baby you had that did not survive. I was thinking about your family who betrayed you. I am concerned because you do not cry about it, and you do not seem upset."

"Julienne, my baby better dead. I too young to take care of baby, I not know how. I not know how to be mother and teach if baby stay alive. If baby stay alive I not come to America. I do not know you, I do not go to museum, I do not do art, I do not know about art. I stay

131

with husband, get beat up and maybe, if the Merciful wants, more baby, more hitting me, more sad. And all baby boy be like husband one day because I not know how to make better men. I not educated in Afghanistan. I not know to be mother like in America. Girl baby get big, maybe nine, many before I not know, like me, suffer like my mother suffer like me to have husband. Not good Julienne. I pain sometimes. I lucky now, I like Leila, I like you, I like Ursula. I have family now. You my friend, you my sister, no more pain. Poof, pain stay in Afghanistan and Pakistan and Iran too."

"Sweetheart, I want you to grow up to be a strong woman. What happened to you may hurt you for a long time. Do you think you can trust anybody? Can you love anyone? I want you to grow up a balanced human being."

"I strong, Julienne. I trust you, Leila, Ursula, too. I not know other people. I say hello to people, but I not know them. One day, I can trust them like I trust you. I like peace you teach me. I like changing me. No need blaming, father, grandfather not know, people standing afraid and not know how to have peace. Feel happy to be with you and Leila, too. No fear, Julienne. Much love in house we live. My heart happy, full too. Julienne, we different, but we the same."

"That is true, Saadia. You are a wise young person. I love you very much."

"No, you are wise person, Julienne. Suzannah teach you well. Maybe Frank, too. Now you teach me good, you teach Leila well. I very lucky, like Leila. I like that. You are lucky you know a good man that did not hurt you. That is important, no?"

"Yes, I am lucky. I knew it was important to choose a man with care. I did not always do that. Choosing Frank was a decision that did not take a long time, but I knew it would work because we both talked about doing all that it took to make our relation work. To have a good marriage, you have to like the person and you must love him—yet sometimes people have long-lasting relationships that have respect, even when the people are not in love. Relationships and marriages are complicated. I think the two people must be willing to have the needs of their partner in their mind. As we become more independent, many people believe this is not necessary. I think they are wrong."

Leila yawned. "Saadia and Julienne, lets not talk too much. I want to go to sleep—and Saadia, if you talk too much, you will not wake up early, and we will not go the museum."

"I be no more talking, I go to museum tomorrow. I see much, I learn much."

I smiled at my girls and said, "Good night."

CHAPTER 19

Let's Talk About Love

"Julienne, tell us about you and Frank getting married."

"Leila, in western society, marriages are different than what you were subjected to. First people choose their mates. One can be married in a church, a temple, a mosque, by the courts and by anyone approved to handle the legal aspect of a marriage. By the way, there are many types of Christians and Jews and they all get along. They worship with different rituals but, as you say, God is God. I do not know much about Islam—only that some sects are less tolerant of others and some are not tolerant at all of non-Muslims. With the idea of one god, I do not understand when people do not go out of their way to get along, but I suppose it is something we must do for ourselves. What do you think?"

"In Iran, we are told not to accept the faith of infidels. Saadia, is that same in Afghanistan? But you know some people think it is crazy. People are people,

God is God, all the same people."

"In Afghanistan same thing," Saadia said. "People afraid to think. If warlord, mullah, father say not trust infidel, people not trust. In Afghanistan, soldiers by other country, many country, are devils. If warlord, mullah say infidel are nice because they do business, people say infidel are nice. Julienne, when people do not know to think, they follow what they must, you know like sheeps, yes?"

"In Iran only Mosque, one church in Teheran, I don't know it. Saadia, you see church in your village?"

"No."

"There are many varieties of religions, like Hindus, Buddhists, and other religions of the east that have temples. They also worship differently. In each religion, the rituals are different. One can also choose to be married in the court, as I said—it is called a civil ceremony, which means there are no religions involved. That is what Frank and I did. My mother was there, along with most of Frank's students.

"After the wedding, we all went to Frank's tiny apartment, which became my home. The plan was to find somewhere else to live, but that never happened. His students brought us a lot of various foods that they liked, and my mother brought champagne. We celebrated in his apartment in Paris, France. It was a simple celebration with a lot of love. There's not much to tell about it—only that we felt the magic of our love." I paused. "Saadia, what was your marriage like?"

"Scared, very scared. I do not talk now, another time make me cry like Leila. I no want to tell, I no want to cry. Museum more important."

"I am glad to know you can choose to talk about what you want. That is called exercising freedom of speech. See—you are learning to make up your own mind about what you want to do. Congratulations. At the same time, if you think about it a lot, if you give it a lot of your time or energy, let me know, and Leila and I will try to help you. If we cannot help, we will find others who can."

"We know you help us. Me and Saadia, too, we know. I know what to tell now—I tell you about weddings of Persia. You already know how terrible it was my wedding night. But maybe not all wedding night are like that. Your night was good, Julienne, I am glad. Sorry you not have children. I am glad we are now your children. Now I tell you what is beautiful in the ceremony in Iran. I went to a wedding, my cousin, she was 17, old you know! She was very old."

"Yes, do tell me about the Persian wedding of your cousin," I said. "Is it like *Nowruz?*"

"Julienne, you are smart. It is almost like *Nowruz*, but different meaning. Like you have many words to say the same things."

Leila looked at Saadia, who shrugged. "Me, I not go to cousin wedding in Afghanistan, only my wedding. Not nice, not happy. Only husband happy because new bride to own, to beat like a drum with hard fist and kick too. Husband like to hurt, make him feel good. Many husband like beast, and monster too. Not nice."

Something wonderful was happening. The girls were talking about their cultural heritages. They did not seem to know much about Islam—only that they had to do what they were told without ever questioning anything. It was all a matter of blind obedience, and that was fairly easy because they were not educated. Within this same context, I realized they knew very little about Islam as a religion. Leila remembered the rituals attached to a Persian wedding but did not know the reasons why they performed the various rituals. Talking about weddings, any wedding, probably had healing properties for them. Though they were both young, remembering their ancestry was important—it was culturally necessary for their self-esteem. Although they were no longer part of the world they had left, I felt they still should retain their roots.

"All right, Leila, tell us about it. I wish I had some tea; remind me the next time we travel, and I will bring some. Then, when we talk in our room, we can drink tea."

"I will tell you about marriage in Persia with no tea. You already know that parents make arrangements, so I do not tell. I think all marriage in Iran and other Muslim countries do same, but I not know. In Persia, there are many parts to a wedding. First there is *aghd*."

"What is that, Leila? I never heard the word. Saadia, do you know what she means?"

"Shh, I telling you," Leila said. "*Aghd* is when the contract is signed. After that, there is a celebration. It is *jashn-e aroosi*."

I repeated the word.

"Julienne, you will never speak Farsi. Your tongue does not work well. *Jashn-e aroosi* is a wedding party. It can last a whole week. When you have a wedding, you decorate the room to look pretty, yes?"

"Yes. I think almost every body does. Frank and I, we did not have any decorations. His entire apartment was smaller than our living room. He brought me a wonderful bouquet of white roses and in the bouquet there was also lavender and two birds of paradise that represented us. I liked it very much, and I still have the dried rose petals and the lavender."

"Okay, I tell you about tradition. You have no tradition. The *sofreh-ye aghd* is on the floor, and everything look at sun. East is important, you know. It is so the husband and the wife can see light, I think, I not sure. This ceremony at the wife home of her parents. After many persons come, the new husband arrive. He take seat to the right. Like east, right is important, too. In Iran, the first culture, Zoroastrian culture believed the place to the right, the place for respect. After a while, the bride come in the room, she go to his left." Leila paused. "Julienne, is it 'go' or it is 'goes'? So confusing most times!"

"I go, you go, they go, but he or she always *goes,* and 'does' works like that, too. Those are verbs, and I will teach you how they are conjugated when we get back. Once you know this, your language will improve a great deal. It is confusing now, but after a while, there will be no confusion. Okay. What happens next?"

"On the floor or on a table, there is a beautiful cloth, sometimes from Cashmere, Tibet, or the Himalaya, those have special goat's hair. Sometimes the fabric is satin or silk, too. There are women, special women, they know how to embroider well. I do not know how. On that cloth is a beautiful mirror, the frame of the one for my reception was made from brass, it beautiful. Two candles, how you say this thing for candles? They holding candle for husband and candle for wife. The mirror mean light and fire. Everything has many meaning. You use words, we use things. I forget to tell you, when the bride comes to room, she has veil on. When she sits next to husband, she take veil away. First time he see her face, only in the mirror.

"There is tray with many things, seven things. The first are seeds of poppy, they make wishes go. There is wild rice, something we call *sabzi khoshk,* but I do not know what you call it. There is salt, some seeds you do not have in the kitchen, I do not know what they call. Many words I not know. Good black tea, and *kondor* that burns the evil spirit. I look in the dictionary, it call itself frankincense. We get some, Julienne, smells good.

"There are more things—flatbread that is decorated, almonds, eggs, walnuts, and hazelnuts. Things we eat a lot.

"There is basket with apple and also pomegranates you brought the other day, I happy, I know they very expensive, thank you, Julienne. You know they are fruits from heaven. There is also a cup with rose water, we use rose water a lot. There is a bowl with the sugar cube you buy for us. There is another thing that hold burning coal. There is a needle with seven different color threads.

"During the ceremony they put a cloth over our head, and they sprinkle sugar so life can be sweet. That big was a lie, no sweet in my marriage. A cup with honey so life can be sweet, that too is lie, you know.

We not have a Qur'an, only Haviz poetry. The only book in the house not destroyed, that book between

139

husband and the wife. We have lots of cookies and other sweet things every people had with tea. It was beautiful ceremony for ugly marriage to very ugly bad man. No one know I am so happy he dead. That was the way Allah punish him for being very bad to me. He burn when he want to kill me, no burn me. My little daughter in paradise now, she okay, no man will hurt her. I am glad."

"Leila, the marriage ceremony of Persia is complicated. You described many beautiful and symbolic things. I am sure not all marriages are as bad as yours was."

"Not to worry, Julienne. You not have to make marriage ceremony in your home. I never marry again. I know choice now. When I am lawyer and after that, I will not have time for husband. What about you, Saadia? Will you become married again?"

"No, never."

"Well, ladies, I am not getting married either. No man will ever be as remarkable as Frank was."

They laughed heartily, and inside I cried a little. Often, while talking about the miseries of their own lives they brought back to me the memories of Frank. I knew decency, tenderness, love and affection, partnership and more in our marriage. This night, we were having heartfelt conversations, and I was glad they had lost their fearfulness. Watching them grow more each day, I witnessed them venturing through new doorways without hesitation. They had gained a sense of emotional freedom.

But we were all getting tired. Saadia looked at both of us, covered herself as only she could do, letting only her nose show. From her cocoon she said, "We talk too much. I tired. Good night."

"You are right, we talk too much. I am going to sleep, too. Good night, Leila. Good night, Saadia."

In unison they answered. I was fast asleep before they turned the light off.

CHAPTER 20

New Habits

In a couple of days, we established a ritual: after we were dressed, we went to the same restaurant. It was the closest one, and we enjoyed the walk. The girls liked the waiters and waitresses, though Patrick had become their personal servant.

After entering, we waited a while until Patrick, our waiter, came to get us and told us our table was ready. I knew he was breaking a rule, but we wanted to eat and get our day started.

At each of our breakfasts, he had the address of another place we needed to visit.

Just before entering the restaurant, we had heard the cathedral's bells, and both girls asked me why they were "making a loud song." I asked the next person I saw, and he told me it was Sunday and it was high mass. I asked the girls if they wanted to go and see a ritual at the church.

We arrived as a series of fully garmented priests and other high-ranking officials were making their entrance. They had white long robes complete with lace, and one had a purple sash on. I could not explain any of it to the girls, but we were impressed.

Toward the center right of the church, I saw three seats on the side. We walked where the procession had walked moments before and sat, and I made it clear to the girls they should do whatever the rest of people in the church did. We stopped talking, and Leila touched my arm.

"Why we standing up and after down?"

"I do not know, but everyone else is, so we must."

A while later, all was quiet, and the choir we had heard the day before began to sing. Somehow their voices and the organ seemed amplified.

Saadia said, "I like that, Julienne. Any music in museum?"

"No."

From behind us, came a rather loud SHH! We looked at each other and knew we should save questions for later on. At one point, half the church went for communion. The girls wanted to go and experience whatever was going on. As quietly as I could, I explained what I knew about communion, including the idea and representation of the piece of bread and the wine.

"I not go. Leila, you go?"

No one from our row went for communion.

When the service was over, six priests dressed in full regalia and some alter boys walked toward the front of the church. In orderly fashion, the people attending this high mass began to leave. Being in the middle of the church gave us more time to listen to the choir's angelic voices. At the door, the priest we had seen before and also another one were greeting people. When he saw us, he again put his hands on Leila's and Saadia's heads. He was the one wearing the purple sash and none other than the priest we had talked to a day before. Both girls lowered their heads, and he blessed them. He wished us a good day and carried on with the rest of the people.

"Julienne, what did he do? He is nice man. Gentle he is."

"Leila, he blessed both of you. That is one of the rituals of the Catholic church."

"Lot of peaceful in this place, and girls can go in. What did they get when many people went near the alter you showed us yesterday? Now you explain more."

"Saadia, that is called receiving communion. It is a symbolic act. Christians believe that Jesus, who was the son of Mary and Joseph, was also the son of God. When people receive communion, the small piece of bread represents the body of Jesus Christ. The wine represents his blood. Do you remember the paintings with the man and the cross? It is a long story, but that man was Jesus, and he was killed. He is the most important figure in any Christian church."

"Really complicated, Julienne, but peace too. I like that church. Why do you call it cathedral?"

"Girls, I am not a Catholic, and I do not have all the answers for you. I think cathedrals are bigger, and they are the churches where the high priests have their place. I am not sure. We will ask Mr. Rand. He is a Catholic."

They both laughed, and Leila made a smart remark that she was under the impression that I knew everything.

Since we had not had breakfast, we doubled back and went to the restaurant. Everyone seemed to have the same idea, and the restaurant was packed.

"Julienne, it was nice to hear the music and see the costumes in the cathedral. All the people looked nice. Maybe we should not wear jeans. Next time, Saadia, we wear dresses, yes!"

"No afraid, mans, womans and childrens too, all together. Remarkable!"

"Husband touched children and wife, too, not hit them, smile many time. I like this church. Julienne, do we have church near home? I want to go one day, I want to know more. I want to paint a church. Can I do that?"

"Yes. There is joy and peace in churches. I think anyone can go to a church. There is one not too far from us. I will get some information for you. Maybe you can incorporate that church in your next canvas. It is not like this cathedral, but it is beautiful, I am sure. By the way, girls—when there is one man, you say 'man.' If there are many, you say 'men.' The same goes for 'woman' and 'women.' Leila, will you have an interest in going to the church if Saadia goes?"

"No. I enjoy this, but no need to go again." She smiled, making sure no one could see her missing tooth, which reminded me that I needed to find a dentist. I decided to ask Patrick. He was from Boston and hopefully he knew of a good one not too far away.

The time we spent in church took away from our museum time, but Saadia appeared satisfied. The service afforded us a beautiful new experience we each enjoyed.

"Julienne, can we bring Saadia to the museum again and we go to the mall? She can look at the art, we can look for dresses?"

"No, we cannot do that. How would you like it if I left you someplace and went off somewhere else?"

"Leila, I know art not mean much to you, we go fast to two rooms we not see yesterday. Okay! I rush very fast."

They were easy people, flexible enough, and ready to accommodate the wants and needs of each other. They made my life easy, gave it focus, and great pleasure. As time went on, I felt our relationships were not of responsibility but of companionship. Whatever loneliness there was in my life had been replaced by two most astonishing people.

That afternoon, we went to the mall, and I got to watch two kids in a candy store.

CHAPTER 21

Me Sit Under Burka, Me Learn

After shopping for hours to find the right dresses, we were tired and hungry. We found a wonderful Italian restaurant a block away from where I had parked. The girls were getting adventurous. Their palates were accepting flavors and spices they had not experienced before.

We were in a celebratory mode, as this was our last evening in Boston, and they had experienced a great deal more than I had planned. There was no point staying longer—the dentist was booked, and I made an appointment for the next month, for which they were both delighted because it meant we were coming back. The conversations were light, and I marveled at how well and quickly they were learning the language.

When the waiter came to take our order, Saadia and Leila chose what they wanted on their own. The real treat for me was noticing that the two scared girls who moved into my home less than a year ago had discovered a sense of freedom. Covered with a blanket of pride and great satisfaction, silence became my partner.

When I asked if they wanted to go anywhere else, they made it clear they wanted to get back to the hotel. We were all tired.

During the short ride, I told them about the tutor I would hire to help them make more progress in speaking, writing, and bringing themselves to grade level. They were pleased but apprehensive about the school idea.

Once in the room, and ready for bed, I was curious where Leila learned to read. "Leila, when you were very young in Iran, did you go to school?"

"When I four, went to a school. It large school with many windows to see outside. One day when we get up, my mother dressed me to go to school. During the night, people we knew changed. Something happened. They used to work in the field. Now they had guns. Soon after they started growing beards.

Those neighbors we know, one day they stop my mother from take me to school. They very nasty and showed their big guns to the face of my mother and me too. We go back home. My mother said they were people without understanding or education, but now they had guns, they had powerful. She said ignorant people with guns very dangerous. They could be made to do anything. Like puppets. I did not know what that was. My father was afraid of them and after soon they told him he must go to mosque. They scare him more, he got a beard, soon he became one like them. My mother and him had many fight. He hit her a lot and told her she was not to disobey husband. He never did that before. Very soon she wearing a black *burka*. I five year or maybe six. All the women in the village must wear *burkas*, some blue, many some black. Other girl like me *hijab*.

"My mother knew how to read and write. She go to school outside of the village where she was born. She had books, she put them far away, my father did not find them. She started teaching me when my father was away. I don't know what he did, but he was not home a lot.

"When my father go away, my mother took a book and teaching me many things she knew. When there was too much excitement in the streets, I sit under her *burka* and she told me many stories about Persia. She not like what happen to our village, she did not talk very much to the people. She did not go out alone. Only when my father with her, she was to go out. She told me in Iran no more freedom for woman they lost. She said she was not allowed to talk, must not tell me about freedom. My father said she was stupid. He started hitting her very often."

When Leila was on a roll no one could stop her. Saadia looked at me as if to say, "She is at it again!"

"Now is funny to say, I learn reading under the *burka*. I also learn about numbers, with my mother, some stars too. She said the men of the village, all ignorant, very dangerous, she said that. She said me often to remember to read, to learn a lot. She said the only thing that will save me another day. She said every woman in Iran in danger and I must learn a lot to read.

"Difficult for my mother, but she give me understanding in me the advantage of education. I loved my mother very much. She was very kind. After a time, she hated my father. He was hitting her every day, for no reason, Julienne. He became a very mean man. He was not always like that. We did not laugh anymore. The radio we had disappeared one day. My father took it away. The windows had cover. Could not see out anymore.

"Sometimes I could see her arms and her face, with bruising. At the beginning, she say she fell, but I was always there, and I knew she did not fall. My father hit her sometimes, pushed her hard, too."

"Leila, what happened to your mother? You did not talk about her when you talked about your wedding."

"Julienne, it is not nice a story, what happened to my mother. One day, my mother and me, we were on a rug on the floor, everything was clean. She had a book with images of the world and many stars, too. I saw rivers, oceans, and places not like Iran. We read the words under each picture. Germany, France, Great Britain, I think you call it England. We laughing because the houses and the people are different. My mother said she used to dress like that a long time ago.

"We did not expecting my father. He opened the door, and when he saw the book, he grabbed me by the arm, he throw me on the other side of the room. I fall like my toy baby. I hurt my side. A lot. He start to hitting my mother, with his arms, with his legs, with his fist. He would not stop. I screamed at him but he not hear me. He hitting her in the face a lot. Kick her stomach a lot. She fall, he kick head now. She hide under the *burka*, he break the *burka*, he say teach lesson to her. Blood from her nose, from her mouth, and even her ears had blood coming out of them.

"After a long time with kicking, she not move anymore. He kick her again she not move. He take her on his shoulders like an old rug, Julienne. He told me to stay and clean mess. She was a disrespectful woman he said. That is happening when woman is not respect.

"He left, blood fell from her head. I took a rag and water. I cry, I clean my mother blood. I cry again when I think of that day. My mother was not disrespectful, she was wanting about education for me. Before he started going to the mosque, it was fine for her to teach me all she know. Other women in the village that know to read, teach their children. They not go away like my mother. No disappear like my mother.

"Julienne, some bad things happen. My father very bad man. The day my mother go away, a piece of me go with her. I do not know where. I feel, you know when you cut a string and you have two pieces, I am one piece I do not know where the other piece is. My father threw it away.

"Thank you for taking me in your home, thank you for treating me respect. I love you very much, Julienne. You are like my mother. You want me learn. I understand about going to school. I scared, but I know it is good. I love you, Julienne."

She paused a while, looking down at her hands. When she raised her head again, the moisture in her eyes told us what words did not. I opened my arms and embraced her. I did not know I would be speaking while sobbing.

"I love you too, Leila. Our different roots, different cultures will not stop us from growing in the same garden. You two will bloom in the garden I call the world."

Saadia smiled and said, "Julienne, you tell poetry like Rumi, maybe different. You must learn with me art and architecture too. We build home and church many many. We teach children beautiful things. What is bloom?"

"Saadia, when you are in a garden, and there is a bud from a plant, you know it will become a flower. That is blooming. The bud blooms and becomes a flower."

"Leila, we bud, we blooming!"

"Yes, you are two beautiful flowers. I love the way you are learning English, and I love your sense of humor."

Saadia and I looked at each other, knowing Leila was not finished with her story.

"My father return late that night. I never see my mother again. I do not know what he did to her. When I ask where is my mother, he hit me hard. I not allowed to ask. From that day not allowed to go outside. He burned the book we were reading. He did not know about the other books, and when he away, I take them from under my sleeping mat. I read more.

"I made his dinner at night. My mother show me how to make some things. In the daytime when he was gone I read, same books, I know them, first page until the last page came. I prayed so my father would not find me read. I want to know every word, every meaning. I read the poetry of Hafiz. I saw your book on the shelf— one day I read Hafiz in English. Must learn English well number one.

152

"I missed my mother, but allow never to ask where she is. I think my father killed her. She was a happy person, Julienne. She loved books, music, and she liked to dance too. Saadia, she love art, too."

Leila looked at me again and started to cry. She was discreet. Many years of silent tears had trained her to be quiet. Tears laced with pain rolled down, and her cheeks got red. I walked to her bed and held her in my arms. We did not need words to express the feelings we had. It became clear and amazing to me that pain of any kind had a bonding effect.

"Leila, maybe you go to sleep now. It is late now."

"Saadia, you go to sleep. I want to tell Julienne about the books. You know Hafiz but not know about Sheikh Bahali. He an architect and many other things. My mother had a book with his name. He know a long time ago about stars, where they travel when we are sleeping. He know about Islam but not what my father is. He know about numbers a lot—I do not understand numbers, do you? Saadia, do you like numbers? Julienne, do you? He know Sufi, and he could turn and turn and turn more."

"I know very little about the whirling dervish—that's what that turning again and again is called. I like their white costume and the head dress, too, but I do not know anything about them."

"My mother have another books, only six book we have. When my father take her away, three book at a neighbor, but I not go out, I not ask to have them. It be disrespectful. I do not know what happened to them. The other book, the man was Muhammad Iqbal. He was very important man, the king of Great Britain called him 'sir.' He had poems. Lots of poems." Leila's speech was interrupted by a yawn. "I am tired now, too. We go to sleep, yes?"

Saadia nodded. "Yes. No more talk, Leila. Dream about many books. I dream about drawing church."

"Sleep well ladies. I will not dream tonight—I am too tired."

CHAPTER 22

My First American Friend

Bright and early, they woke up. We had gotten home late and slept well in our own beds. Refreshed, they were up and ready to take on the world.

First, they needed to parade around and show me the new dresses one more time. After making me a cup of tea, they advised me to wait for the show in the living room. Around me, something delicious was erupting. They expressed their gratitude with broad smiles, and they were no longer afraid to hug me—I got plenty of those. My favorite chair was ready for me, it was time to be patient and wait for the show.

I heard Saadia's foot steps down the hallway, and once she saw her image in the mirror, she told me she would be using one of my shawls. She came moments later. Her cream chiffon dress had sleeves she felt were too short. The silk shawl from my closet was light and translucent with swirls of violet, blue, and a green that was neither sage nor jade. It was airy and light. She wore it European style, covering part of her back with the sides folded around her arms. She walked in and immediately turned from side to side, creating with the flowing skirt a whipped cream effect. Though the shawl was long enough, she did not cover her head. Her choice of colors embraced the hazel and green of her eyes. Wearing her hair loose, Saadia appeared as a beauty to be reckoned with.

"I know how to make choice now."

"And you made a wonderful choice. Saadia, you look beautiful."

Leila, now 5′7″ tall, came into the living room wearing her new black patent-leather pumps and her midi-length, powder-blue linen dress with long, tapered sleeves. She was the more classic of the two. Capturing an air of dignity, she wore her jet-black hair in a high bun. Her neck was exposed to receive the new pearl necklace I had given her.

"What do you think, Julienne?"

"I like it very much. Beautiful color, and the linen makes your dress perfect for you and the occasion. You remind me of the wife of one of our presidents."

"You know empress Farah Diba Pahlavi? Beautiful lady, I not look like her, maybe hair color."

"I was not thinking about her, but you have that same demeanor. I was thinking of Jacqueline Kennedy."

"Who is Jacqueline Kennedy?"

"She was married to one of the presidents of the United States."

"Okay, we talk about her another day. I know

whom you mean. What will you wear? Do you want us to go to the closet and tell you?"

Saadia shook her head. "No, Leila. Julienne wear red dress. You try it, Julienne."

"I know I will not wear the red dress. I am sure I have something else that will work just fine."

"We go to closet, we tell you. Yes?"

"Fine, Saadia, but that does not mean I must accept your choice."

"What you say, no accept? How? Leila look like president or wife? I look beautiful. We tell you."

I burst into laughter. They both must have thought I was nuts. I told them as much as I could about Jackie Kennedy, except her hair was not in a bun.

"Sweetheart, just because somebody chooses something for you does not mean you must accept their choice. You can always make up your own mind. You can say no."

"Leila, what the word you find in dictionary?"

"Remarkable?"

"Yes, remarkable. Julienne is remarkable. I not know that."

"Well, now you know. In most places, people can choose for themselves what they want. It is not exactly remarkable. Most of us take this for granted."

"What is granted?"

"Time for you to start using the dictionary again. Look for 'G-R-A-N-T-E-D.' You will know what the word means. It means many things, but mostly we take for granted the things we do not even think about. I think things and people we do not even appreciate."

"Okay, look for dictionary another time. We go to your closet."

"I tell you what—you find a few dresses in my closet, and I will choose one. While you are amusing yourself, I will do the laundry."

"This is great machine. Washing is easy. When the American man took me, when he took me to Saudi Arabia, the barrack had many washing machines for the people that were there. Lots of soldiers from many countries, many lady soldiers, and one spoke Farsi. I was not allowed to go out. I was not a soldier, but I wore soldier clothes. There was a small girl, she was a soldier, and she let me use her uniform. I did not have a gun."

"Leila, I did not know you were in Saudi Arabia. When and how did you get there?"

"It is a very long story, Julienne. Do you want me to tell you?"

"Yes, if you do not mind. What do you think, Saadia? The laundry can wait."

"I make tea, lots of tea, long story. Need Kleenex, too, yes?"

"Good idea, Saadia. I do not cry anymore, maybe you do, Julienne, too. I put my jeans on first. No more dressing up."

Off she went to her bedroom to change, and so did Saadia. The show was over, and I had no idea what story I was about to hear. It wasn't long before she returned and began her story.

"You know my husband try to burn me, yes? He was very mean to me. After I scream at him because he try to kill my baby girl, he wanted me to have a boy, but Allah said a girl was fine. He was a disgusting man, I am very glad he is dead. He got the gasoline and was throwing it on me, but the wind change and gas went to him. Lots of gasoline fell on him, and next to him was the fire for cooking. He was cooked. My baby girl screamed, she was burn bad. I run to her, took her and run, she did not stay alive long. Had a lot of pain Julienne. The house burned. I had no doctor to save her.

"She lived three days, but after the second day she did not cry anymore. I cried for my baby, she was red and black with burn she had no more skin, no hair. But I know it is better for her, a man like my husband or my father will never abuse her. I pray often for her because I love her. I not always know who to pray but that is fine. God is God.

"She was very small. I made a hole with a garden tool, it did not burn. I put her there, she had nothing to cover her little body, Everything was burned, my mother give me a bracelet, I give it to her, I put it next to her heart. She looked very bad all black and red, I remember that always, it is hard. No skin left for her body, not good smelling, too. In her time, she suffer enough. After I made the hole next to the flowers in the garden, next to the roses did not burn, I planted her. I know the flowers and the trees will shade her always. The roses will make perfume for her."

Though she said she no longer cried about it, there were lots of tears. Talking about the event was a release of emotions she had not anticipated. Saadia got very close to her and caressed her hair. Despite being the younger of the two, Saadia was wise and caring. My tears also fell freely. I am glad she was able to talk about it, yet the sadness of it all left me speechless. There was a hole in my heart. No one should feel the pain Leila had to endure. No one! She was not finished with her story. She drank some tea, wiped my face, and kissed my forehead.

"I did not see any neighbors. Did you know, when things not right, people stay away, they are afraid, even if they have guns? Most people are coward. The guns do not help touch the hearts. I decided to go away, but I had no idea what direction to take. It did not matter, because I was very sad, but more I wanted to die, so I started walking away from the burned house. I walked—I remembered when I got married, this awful man took on a road, it was night, so I do not know if it was where the sun rising. He said it was not far from the Persian Gulf, I remembered the direction from the map on the book.

"I walked south. I did not really know if it was south. I walked and I walked. I walked some more and after a long time, I could not walk anymore. I was thirsty. There is no water. I remember my mother telling me the people of Australia, aborigine she called them, put a pebble in their mouth and that made water in their mouth, saliva you know. I did that. It helped a little.

"I was tired, I lay on the ground not too long, then I was crawling, my belly was flat from the no water and no food. My elbows lost the skin. That did not matter. I had to go far away to die. I moved all four arms and legs, like this, front left, back right front right back left, again and again like an animal I had never seen.

"In some parts, there was brush, and it was brittle.

160

I ached all over, but I knew if it grew, there must have been water, so I chewed the desert grass. My long, black hair was red with lights of tan looked like fire. I was dirty, very dirty. I was bleeding, too. That did not matter. I was not crying anymore, I was crawling. Not even thinking anymore. Night came, and soon all was dark around me. I was lost, I was thirsty, but I crawled away. I prayed that I was going south. I prayed I would wake up dead. I knew I would find my way. All four, left, right one after the other, my limbs did not give up.

"It would have been nice to go home. There was water at home, but also it was where the abuse started. My father was not a nice man. He killed my mother and would to kill me, too. I could not go home. I had not home. I wanted to die, but not from my father. I walked a lot, not sure where. I found a small tree, it made me feel good. Under the tree, like under the *burka* my mother wore, I rested. I was dreaming, perhaps it will rain, miracles happen, but all I saw now were stars. The moon I could not find, I did not know where to look.

"I must have fall asleep. When I opened my eyes, it was not yet sunny. I see a man looking at me. A tall man, not menacing, he walked closer, on his feet were sure big shoes, now I know boots. Something told me he was kind, not the feeling when I met my husband. I could not see the color of his eyes, it was still dark for that, I knew they were calm and kind. Maybe a man that never raised his voice or hit his wife. I could feel that about him. He wore clothes of a foreigner, maybe from another place far away. I never met anyone from far way. I know some of them had blue eyes like the ones I saw in he picture books. I had seen pictures of soldiers, but he did not have armor.

"A breeze made it cooler. The air was almost salty, I was less thirsty, and maybe I was only afraid. The man walked closer to me, very close.

"I sat up, straight this time. I did not care if he killed me. I looked at the man, and I did not want him to know I was afraid.

"When he got close to me, he took a bottle of water from his side and gave me water to drink. He did not hurt me. He had a box, he talked to it, a language I did not know. He stayed with me, never said a word. After a while, there were three cars, no there were not cars, they were big, big wheels, they looked like large animals, bigger than three elephants or four or five. They stopped and many other people jumped down from the side and ran toward me. I was shaking, I was so afraid.

"They talk to me, but I not understand. One woman, also dressed like the men, came next to me. She spoke Farsi, she told me they were American soldiers. She asked me what I was doing there. I told her the story I just told you. One wrote what she said, and she asked me more questions.

"They put me on a thing like a bed but it was not. Four men carried me to a car, but it was not a car. When I woke up, I had something in my arm with a balloon with liquid hanging from a piece of metal with legs on the floor. I was so afraid, but a few minutes later; the girl who spoke Farsi came in the room. She told me I was in a hospital because I was—I do not remember the word, not enough water."

"She said you were dehydrated."

"Yes, that is the word. I must remember now, dehydrated. I stayed in the hospital many days. The lady soldier told me her name was Nicole, that is the one that spoke Farsi. She said there was an organization that agreed to take me to the U.S. I asked her where U.S. was She said United States of America. I knew that. I was excited because I would be somewhere else, but I was very afraid. I did not understand any person. They all dressed the same way, with the same uniform. They all looked the same also. The men had no beards, Julienne, and that felt good to me, short hair.

"Nicole came to my room one day—it was not a room, it had a curtain, and next to me there was a man, he was in bad shape, Nicole said. He was a man, he cried a lot. Crying I understood, but I do not know why. Nicole told me the NGO was taking me to Boston because they had a family there that would adopt me. Now I know what adopt is, but at the time I did not know. I am glad they did not adopt me. The husband was sick, and before I got there, he died. When I arrived, the lady did not want me anymore. More afraid. Nicole was still with me, and she was very good about explaining everything to me. She told me they would find me another family.

"No one wanted me. I was in another, bigger hospital. One day Nicole came to visit, and she told me a lady in Maine who spoke Farsi said she would take care of me until they found a home for me.

"I am lucky. Gale found you, and now I am here. I like that a lot. You do not hurt me, and you are teaching

163

me about making choice, about me. I am receiving education from you, and soon from the teacher and the school. I am lucky, Julienne. Thank you!"

"Both of you are blessings in my life. I thank you."

CHAPTER 23

What Do You Miss?

"Julienne, I am glad I am here with Saadia, you understand books and education, you know what we need. My mother liked books and education, too. You know, the more I read my three books, the more I understand and I want to know my mind. I not have big mind when I was small, but I understand many things.

"The *mullah* did not want a girl or a woman to have a mind. Every day, when I read a page, I feel more alive. The words had a message for me every day. I know when I understand words I understand the world more better. I was learning about me. Maybe if I lived in Teheran, that would have been different, and I would have been able to go to school. I not know. I had no friends when I lived with my father, and I did not know anybody when I was married, so I never talked very much to anybody. Sometimes, I hope I had friends here, but I do know for sure. When I go to school, I will meet people, and maybe

I will have friends. I am glad I am here because now I know me. I know my value.

"When I home alone, I read one page. After that I sit, it was time to think. The only disturbances are always outside. The neighbors with the guns sometimes shot in the air to scare people. Sometimes they hurt people for no reason. People that be friends before be enemies. I am glad I never go out. Maybe I would be like them, afraid all the time. I do not like guns. In my books, the writers talk about love and peace, never guns. I miss nothing. I miss no one. I am happy here, Julienne."

"Leila, it is so wonderful to hear you speak. You now know English well enough to express your deeper thoughts. All the reading and learning you did became tools you use now to learn more. Your mother gave you a great gift. This is what your favorite word means: remarkable! But I have a question: I wonder what you think of the young people in your village who became terrorists? Not too long ago, you did not have the words to explain that to me. Can you tell me what you think their reasoning is?"

"I know why. They grew up without education. Many did not have books, they never saw books. Mothers did not know how to read. My mother tell me ignorance is very dangerous. She was right, I did not have to go far to know that. Julienne, it is like playing with dominos, because the young people have no education, they are ignorant, they believe anything anybody tell them. They are frustrated, they do not know about thinking. When they received guns, they feel superior. They could scare people, and they could kill them. That gave them power!

Growing their beard did that, too. I am not sure why that is, but they scared the parents in the villages, and they do not want mothers and girls in the streets. They are scared of them. People they came to trust told them stories, and they believe many things that are not true. I not with them, so I do not know what is said, but soon, if they saw a woman or a girl leg, that is dangerous to them. Every girl and woman had to cover head and legs and feet, too. If they saw a woman they decided was not properly dressed, they beat her up. They rape and kill some, too. The many woman not fight back because afraid, husband afraid, they ignorant people grow. Crazy stupid, no?

"I believe when people are dissatisfied with life they have, when they have a gun, it gives false satisfaction and the illusion of power. To keep the power, they must scare more people everywhere. After a while, they believe what they do is the will of God. I am glad I am here."

"Leila, how come you said God instead of Allah?"

"Julienne, there is one God, and it is God. You can call him almost anything, I think. Saying Allah is fine, but I think it should not be in fear that one uses the word, but if they don't they will be killed? God maybe other words too, I don't know. I do not want religion in my life. Because of religion, I was very unhappy, almost dead. I liked the Cathedral, but I do not need to go there. Maybe one day I can explain better. I must think about it."

"I understand. I am glad you know your mind."

All this time, Saadia was busy sketching, and she had been silent. She looked up at both of us.

"You know, like Leila, I have no friends, I too much work to do. If I did not do the cleaning, I was hit by

167

father mine. He said he loved me, but when he is angry, that was most times, he hit me, he pull my hair. I do not miss anything. I like the cathedral, it shows peace to my heart. It told me that many people care a lot to design and build it. When I go inside all the way to the—what you call it, Julienne?"

"The altar. I think it is also called the sanctuary. I am not sure if they are the same. When you are in school, if you really want to be an architect, you will know the difference. You will also know the words used to describe different parts of buildings."

"Yes, I will learn the right words. I want to learn to speak good. I know I do not talk right like Leila. I am glad she knows to read well. Yes? I am learning that. I must learn to read and talk good—better, yes! Faster, too, yes! Because when I do school, I no want the kids to laugh all the time at me. You help me a lot, I know. You think the person teacher will be a good teacher? I want a good teacher, so I speak very good. Julienne, why sometimes you say talk and next time you say speak. They are the same! Also, why good and after well? That is confusing to me."

"Saadia, you will have a good teacher, and you will learn to speak well. There are many words that mean the same thing, and as you learn more of the language, you will also know when to use the words you need. Do not need to worry about kids laughing about you. Some will help you, and, yes, some may not be so helpful. Yet, once they know you were born all the way in Afghanistan, they will find you very interesting to talk to. Everything will be fine."

"Leila is right, because too many people ignorant, the Taliban can get more dangerous, more bigger, too. They are ignorant, and they getting orders from men that are dangerous. Not all ignorant, but all wanting more power. They like to kill and hurt other people, girls and women, too, so they make the other men do the same thing. It makes them feel big."

"Are you saying ignorant men can be manipulated?"

"What is manipulated?"

"Let me think how to explain this. An ignorant person can be manipulated with greater ease. Saadia, to manipulate means to control. You can control people with fear, you can be very clever, and you can make people believe what you want. That is to manipulate. The more ignorant people are, the easier it is to manipulate them."

"Julienne, if the people receive education, can they stop to be manipulate?"

"Yes, they can, but it can be difficult, because when people are used to doing something, it is not easy for them to stop and also become responsible."

Saadia looked pensive. "Did I say thank you for teaching me to read and write and talk, too? I know much more than before. I am glad. I want to know more. I think when Taliban come to Afghanistan and make everybody afraid, they manipulated, yes! Men, too, they grow beards, and they be mean. When they close schools for girls, that is because they are afraid of girls. When they bombed schools and library and even museum I never went to, they killed the people. No art, no music, no education. There is no spirit, there is no hope for anything, Julienne, everything is dead, people are walking even talking, but they are dead. That is very bad. Only terror and fear left. That not good. Not good for Afghanistan.

"Now I understand why my husband was the way he was. I understand my father also manipulated, ignorant, scared, they believe what the men told him he must believe and he must do. My father, my husband do not know how to think for themselves. You know, Julienne, I am sorry for my father. He is a ignorant man. Many ignorant men and many people die because men are ignorant. Very sad.

"I think, if every person learn to feel more, and not feel for itself only, maybe the world will be different. Because if you thinking about a person, you are not only thinking about you only. Like when there is a fire in forest, the animal mothers pick up baby, they are thinking not about themselves only, they are thinking about another life to protect. Not like the Taliban thinks. Remarkable no?"

"Saadia, this is profound. You are right. When we think beyond ourselves, we become better human beings."

Leila nodded. "Of course, Saadia, we would not be in here, if she did not. Julienne is a good human being, a good woman. We are lucky to be in her house."

"Thank you, ladies. Let me give you my understanding of a house and also a home. A house is a building. It is a place where people can live. To me, a home is a little more. Here we have a home. We have hearts, compassion, love, and we can talk about important things, like we are now. We can laugh, and we can cry, and there is understanding everywhere. I think, in a house, there is not much of that."

"I like this home. What do you think, Saadia?"

"I like my home, too."

"I will never be able to tell you how much I love having you here."

"Why not able, Julienne?"

The bell saved me. On the phone, Mr. Rand needed to speak with me. He had found a tutor and wanted to bring him by to meet the girls and me.

I looked at the girls. "Mr. Rand is coming with a tutor. He should be here in a little while. When this man comes, let's take a good look at him to decide if we want him or someone else."

"Julienne, you decide for us. Saadia and me not know how to choose tutors."

"That may be true, but you have to like the person. You are the students, and I think you will learn better if you like your teacher."

"You think we learn well English because we like you?"

"I don't know if it's because you like me, but you are learning to speak English well."

"Still so confusing, Julienne."

CHAPTER 24

A Turn of Events

.

As the girls learned to communicate with greater ease, their conversations surprised me. They may have been young, but certainly their thinking processes surpassed mine at the same age. They spent a great deal of their time reading and learning about their individual countries and the one that had adopted them.

We were surprised when Mr. Rand arrived with the new tutor. Our needs had been met—she was young enough to understand the girls and, being a woman, she was the right person for them. Elizabeth managed to engage and push the girls beyond anything I ever imagined. She was great! As a reward to their progress, she offered each of them driving lessons.

At the small public library, a wonderful librarian made it a point to have a supply of history books for my girls. She was amazed that their interests were so broad. Leila told her about Hafiz, and before we knew it, Mrs.

Jones called me to say she had two translations of his work. My *Essential Hafiz* took a back seat, as Leila felt the translations now available to her were better than the volume I had. Mrs. Jones was also good about letting books stay in their possession for longer than the two weeks the library allowed. Both girls were surprised that we had books in our country telling us about theirs. As a trio, we were learning about each other's cultures.

While this was going on, I was teaching them as much as I knew about the history of the United States. Remarkable, extraordinary, amazing, outstanding, and more became words I heard every day.

The autumn weather made its appearance faster than I had hoped. It was good timing to call the dentist in Boston and make an appointment for the three of us. The real excuse for the visit was the purchase of better and warmer clothes.

One day, after our morning walk, the dog we called Jake followed us home. He had no collar, no tags. He was skinny, and the girls had been feeding him every day. Jake must have had sensed we were going away. He knew where his few morsels came from, and was not going to let those go. The girls promised they would take turns caring for all of his needs. This smart dog knew what would be best for him, and he stood between them, looking at me, as if saying, "Look, they want me. I like them. I like you, too. I will be a good guard dog."

Caught in a conundrum, I reminded the girls about our upcoming visit to Boston. They felt he would not survive winter by the ocean—he was, after all, very young. They both felt he could not have been more than six months old. Under protest, I agreed and told them we would get some dog food and have a dish on the patio. He would stay there, if he wanted. They both protested. In an instant, Jake had become their dog and a member of the family. The patio was a place to be visited but not to remain indefinitely. Once home, I called the local vet, who agreed to take care of Jake while we were gone. It was the best thing to do. During our absence, he would have all his vaccinations, get tags, etc. When we returned, our Dalmatian would be groomed and ready to begin his new life.

It took a while, but we had crossed most cultural barriers. Saadia no longer felt a need to cover her head. They both liked their clothes to be discreet—something I appreciated. They had not lost their individual personalities. They had strong personal values, something I had not accomplished until much later in my life. Remembering the wild person I was at their approximate ages, I was glad their lives and their circumstances had made them who they were.

The original group formed to take care of the foreign people visited us less often. Ursula, Gale, and Mr. Rand continued to be the surrogate parents we all needed. It pleased me a great deal to see their astonished faces at every visit. My girls joined in conversations, and the others could see the progression of language skills I had become accustomed to. As weather permitted, we were often on the seventy-five foot patio with our dog, making sure all was fine.

From a local antique store, I had located a trestle table seventy-two inches long. I was told it had been made in South Carolina. The wood looked like pine, but it was a hardwood with a well-established patina. A local craftsman, recommended by the store, made eight chairs to go around my table. He was from Germany, and when I showed him some Frank Lloyd Wright designs that I liked, he was able to capture my idea. He created the most comfortable and beautiful chairs with hardwoods from the region. The potted plants became Leila's green thumb domain. One of the two rocking chairs became mine, while the other belonged to Jake.

Mr. Rand was the advocate, handling matters of school and tests to verify grade level. Both girls were surprisingly and naturally adept at mathematics. He had another person in mind to bring to the table what Elizabeth could not.

Gale was working with the state department to change their legal status, so they could eventually become American citizens. The process was long. It seemed to me that the bureaucrats of Washington were merely there to collect paychecks and file away documents they received from me, never to be seen again. Ursula, always cheering and optimistic about everything, kept telling me all was in order. Everything had to go through channels. A thousand times, she reminded me to be patient.

One early morning, Gale called me. She sounded exited and wanted to meet the group at my home that very day. Calling everyone took a while, and Leila and Saadia prepared lunch. Every one agreed on one o'clock.

With the air a little cool, Leila decided a soup would be good. I had some potatoes, onions, and celery, so the soup selection was made. She sent me to the store to get some bread, butter, and a few more things. Saadia had acquired a taste for German breads, so she took it upon herself to call Ursula and ask her to bring some. We had plenty of butter, so I knew she would be happy. A salad was in order, so we got the makings for this, too, and returned home. The soup was almost ready. As always, Ursula would bring sweets for all.

There was something wonderful to note in the new sense of initiative my girls had developed.

Leila had made the most magnificent table setting. Linen tablecloths and napkins, ironed to perfection, were graced by an abundance of the last wildflowers from the garden as an attractive centerpiece. The girls had found some blue dishes at a garage sale, borrowing money from me in order to buy me a present. For special occasions, such as today, my most valuable dishes were on the table. Water was served from my mother's silver pitcher, polished enough to reflect our faces.

The girls were good at entertaining. This impromptu lunch brought out the creative, positive side of my girls. They took over every detail, and showed each one of us where to sit. I joined the rank of guest. I liked that!

"The girls bring you a lot of joy, Julienne, I see it in your face. You love them as much as my sister loved you. I can see it."

"Ursula, I know I love them a great deal, but no one could possibly love as Suzannah loved me. I only wish to give to them what she gave to me."

"My dear, love is not something one dreams about. My sister showed it to you, and you show it to the girls. Love requires action, and you do that, just as she did.

I know I am right." À la Ursula, she was done.

Gale spoke loudly enough to get our attention. "Julienne, Ursula, Mr. Rand, Leila, and Saadia—I came up with an idea while dealing with the State Department. The hired help in Washington does not understand a thing about the girls' situation because they did not arrive here via the right protocol. They are, therefore, hopelessly lost in an antiquated system. We have nothing but idiots there."

"What are you saying? I am not sending them back to Iran or Afghanistan. I will take them to France, before I do that. We may have to start all over again, but I know there are solutions. They have gone too far, made too much progress, for some idiot in Washington to decide their fate. Too many sacrifices and hard work have gone on. We must find a solution that benefits the girls—not some congressman looking for reelection."

"Calm down, Julienne. They are not going anywhere. I have a solution."

"Do you mind being clearer? I have no idea what you are talking about."

"I am—I am—" She paused, as if unsure how to say what she was thinking. "I am talking about adoption."

Ursula spoke before I could even digest the idea. "Gale, you are a genius. Is this a real solution, or something you dreamed of? I do not want my niece strapped with hope and have the world crashing down on her."

Both Leila and Saadia had their eyes on me. They understood. They were stunned, hopeful, and scared all at once. Their eyes were wet. They sensed both my excitement and anger with a system they knew nothing about.

"Are you saying I need to adopt them?"

"Yes. That will solve some of the problems. I spoke to a lawyer in Washington. He works with matters of immigration and is willing to take the case to the Supreme Court, if he has to."

"You are telling me that, no matter how romantic the idea is, there are no assurances. Does this lawyer care or understand that I am not interested in advancing his career? I want my girls to be safe, and I want them to say right here."

Leila got up and gave me a kiss and a hug like I had never received before. Saadia did the same and told me she would like to be my daughter. She already was, she said.

"I talked to the lawyer, Julienne—he understands. He is even willing to come here and meet you and the girls on your own turf."

Ursula broke in again. "What does he want? Most lawyers are not trustworthy. I never met an honest one, although I am sure there are exceptions. How can you choose the right one? When I came to the United States from Germany after the war, the one I chose took every penny I had and did nothing. It was a neighbor who helped me."

"Ursula, you said the magic words. Your neighbor had an interest in helping you. That is what this lawyer is all about. He adopted two boys from Afghanistan two years ago. He is a man with a particular interest!"

"Gale, how did you find this person?"

Mr. Rand sat forward and said, "I introduced Gale to Mr. Roberts. He is a good man and he helped people

178

I know who had similar challenges. It seems to me, your life and the lives of Leila and Saadia are surrounded with pure magic. If you want these girls to be part of your life, I suggest you give this adoption thing some serious thought."

I had no idea Mr. Rand's words would touch me so deeply.

"They are already my girls, and have given thought about adopting them. I have their best interests in mind, and they are now an integral part of my life. I just do not want deportation to enter the picture. That is my only concern. Can your lawyer address this issue?"

"I have his number. We can call him. He is expecting our call."

I never saw Leila get up but she did. The phone in the kitchen had a long cord, and she brought it to Gale. As she did that, she looked at me and smiled. Ursula gave me a hug and called me "Mom." She actually had a sense of humor.

Gale dialed from Maine to Washington. The connection was sketchy, but she got through. She talked to a secretary, I believe.

"Mr. Roberts, this is Gale Wilson from Maine. I am at Mrs. Fairchild's home with the two girls I talked to you about. Mrs. Fairchild has some concerns and would like to talk to you."

She handed me the phone. I was not prepared and shaky from the events.

"Good afternoon, Mr. Roberts. Gale told me about you. I am indeed ready to adopt both Leila and Saadia. My immediate concerns are both with the State Department and the Immigration Services. These agencies do not always talk to each other, and I do not want the possibility of opening a can of worms and having my girls deported in the process."

He sounded like an older gentleman. He assured me that, once the girls were adopted, no one would be deported anywhere. He offered to start the procedure. He had my address from Gale and would send me some documents. He told me the rest would be easy—that he did this with his sons. He was brief, clear, and sure of himself.

After this conversation, I felt a little better, but my nerves were frayed. Ursula proposed that we eat lunch. She could tell I was shaken with anticipation and fear. Both girls went to the kitchen and returned with bowls of soup, bread, and butter. Leila asked me to come and prepare the salad dressing, the one she liked.

We ate with few words, as we had more than food to absorb.

CHAPTER 25

Julienne, Mom?

"Julienne, we like calling you Julienne. Do we call you Mom, now?"

"Leila, you can call me whatever your heart tells you. What is in our heart does not require a change in what you call me."

"I like that. What about you, Saadia? Do you want to call Julienne Mom or Mother?"

"No, she Julienne. I do not know Mom or Mother, I know Julienne. Maybe sometimes Mom, sometimes Julienne, how is that?"

"Okay, that is settled. I will remain Julienne and Mom when you feel like it. I like that, too, because if you called me 'Mom' now, I would not know who you are talking to."

They both laughed, because, like me, they felt the relation we had did not require a change of name. Yet there was still the matter of their last names.

"Ladies, you will have to think about your last names. You can have mine, you can even have mine before I was married to Frank, or you can keep your own. You do not need to answer now. Take your time, because this is a big change in your lives."

"I would like to be Leila Fairchild. With that name, when I become an international lawyer, I will not be associated with Leila Shainahah. I like your Fairchild name, and Shainahah has not served me well. Fair and Child, exactly the right name for me, for what I want to do. Is that okay with you, Julienne?"

"Leila, it will be an honor to share my name with you. Frank would have loved that, also. He, too, never had children. I like how you broke the name in two very meaningful words. Smart woman, you are!"

Leila looked at her soon-to-be sister. "Saadia, are you going to keep your name Bazareik?"

"No. I am Fairchild, too. Julienne is best person for me. I was too young when my mother was dead. I have one Julienne. I like Fairchild. Good name for me. Good name of architect. I make my hair the color like you, Julienne, what you think? Leila, your hair too black, too, but get some red and brown, like Julienne."

They both laughed. It felt good to see the two perfectly safe in their home, even making fun of my auburn hair.

"We cannot make these changes right away. The lawyer will have a lot of work to do. I will call him on Monday. He said he would have some documents in the mail. We may even have to go to Washington, where he practices."

"Julienne, can I visit the White House? Lots of places for sketching in Washington. I go, okay?"

"Yes. If necessary, we will all go."

"I want to see his office, Mr. Robert. Maybe I will ask him for a job when I am a lawyer. This town is too small for the International Human Rights lawyer, Leila Fairchild. What do you think? One day, I will have to move to New York or Washington. I will miss this town, because it where my heart is, but I want to help those in need. I must be where I need to be."

"I think you are right about that. I am not even sure that there is a lawyer in Owl's Head. When you are a lawyer, if you still want to practice international law, you certainly will have to be in a place like New York or Washington, or maybe Boston, and perhaps California.

"Here too small, Leila. You go to Washington, I stay here with Julienne. I take care of Julienne. I paint and make design. Maybe Boston, Yes! We go to Boston."

"Ladies, I have a friend who says often that all things will be accessible, if we are willing to do what we must do. There seems to be some truth to that idea. Before we can achieve what we want, we must do certain things—in your cases, studying and practicing with passion what you studied. You must be true to yourself. A great man named Joseph Campbell said, "Follow your bliss." To me, that is great advice. I hope you each will always be true to yourself while you follow your bliss. I can assure you, if you do this, you will accomplish all that you wish.

"I believe we came to each other's lives for good reasons. As you grow to adulthood, I will be able to assist you to be all that you wish to be. You have survived difficulties most people cannot even imagine. This gives you the advantage of courage and fortitude most people know nothing about."

Almost in unison, I heard, "I am ready!" and I trusted they were. My two brave girls proved to me that, with intention and effort, many things were possible. The more we talked, the more I learned. They were two people whose emerging potential was about to explode.

Nothing had changed around me, but my life's purpose had been drastically transformed. I was going to be responsible for the successes of two human beings. We were all in transition, looking forward to a continued good life.

I had to go for a walk. Jake and the girls came along. Like me, they had gotten into the habit of coming back with seashells.

"Julienne, will you be married again?"

"No, I do not think so. I like my life the way it is. I get to do what I want without having to share mistakes or joy. Maybe one day, I will have a boyfriend, but I have not met a man I would consider. Leila, why do you ask?"

"If you get married, your husband not like us. I not like that."

"Have no fear—you girls will come first. No man, boyfriend, or otherwise will ever have any say in how I conduct my life with you. You are my children. Maybe you will get married one day, and your husband may not like me."

"Julienne, whom would I marry? Never a man from Iran, because I married one already and would not take chances and marry another one. Not an American, because I do not think he would understand me—the Leila inside of me. It is difficult to say, but no, I do not want to be married ever, too much pain."

"Sweetheart, things change. Maybe you will meet the right person for you. I understand what you are saying. People of different cultures can encounter difficulties in a marriage, because the way they see and understand life is different, and many people are not accepting of others. I was very lucky that Frank had lived in France for many years before he met me. He understood the soul of a French person."

"Leila, I think you are right. Finding right men difficult. We do not know people from our place, and, if we do, maybe I would not want anything to do with them. I do not want a man to control my life. You showed me how to become independent. My education will make that happen for me."

"Sometimes I wish my little girl did not burn to death. If she were here, she would have had a chance to be happy. But maybe if I had a baby that day when I was fleeing and crawling, I would not have been rescued. You know, Julienne, we never know anything that will or may happen. I am glad that I was rescued and I am here with my new family."

"Good thinking, Leila. Maybe, when I am older, I will do like Julienne—I will adopt two children. Too early to tell, you are right. I do not know what the future will be. I can tell you, if I am given an opportunity,

I will adopt two children—I do not think one is enough. Children need each other to grow strong, like you and me. I know I will honor the children I am responsible for. Julienne is a good teacher."

CHAPTER 26

Metamorphosis

While I continued to be engaged in the lives of my girls, time passed. The transition happened much faster than I had anticipated or noticed. No one told me that, in my hands, I had a lot more than I bargained for. Something happened. It was subtle; they were no longer who they used to be. The two girls who walked into my kitchen four years ago were now young women.

Leila had graduated from high school *summa cum laude*. Even before her top honors, it was clear that her life would take her to places I would have preferred to be different. Saadia, two years behind, followed her older sibling's academic footsteps. They were both people who were conscious of mankind and both cognizant of the inhumanity of mankind, no matter what the country or circumstances.

We talked a great deal about these things. The world was their community. Often, I wondered if this was because of who I was and my own life circumstances, or if it was innate to their individual character. I recognized early on that they were both amazing human beings.

They had mastered their new language and studied a couple more. Every summer, we traveled abroad, and often I wondered if this might have been reason enough for their world views. Wishing they be exposed to their own cultures was important. They had found no friends from the areas of their birth, but our library at home became filled with books by authors from the region. In all areas of their lives, I wanted them to become people who were able to make intelligent choices based on what they knew. Passion for what they could accomplish turned hopes and wishes for their own futures into palpable successes in school. Self-knowledge and assertiveness became their guides, elements of character I knew would not have been afforded to them had they remained in the milieu in which they were born.

They were admirable people. Through various programs in school, they became involved with many community affairs and volunteer work. Saadia visited the small local hospital, sketch pad in hand; she made quick seascapes for the patients. For the children, she made their likeness into clowns. One doctor had her do a portrait of his wife and daughter. Leila became active at a shelter for abused women, where she helped with the children of the abused. The director felt she was too young to deal with the abused women. Little did he know!

One day, while we were having a delicious dinner, compliments of Saadia, she asked me if she should tell the director about her own life, so he would understand that she knew about abuse and misery. We talked long hours about this. Saadia felt she needed to be exposed to the children, so she would learn about patience—a quality Saadia and I both realized she sometimes lacked. I, on the other hand, felt that, although she had experienced abuse, the context and differences of communities, faith, and circumstances required she should give the matter a great deal of thought. Though she could be an example of what one could become, I felt she had not traveled far enough into maturity to counsel women she encountered at the center.

She remained silent a while. "Do you think, because I am not old enough, I couldn't help or guide an abused woman in distress?"

"Leila, at many levels you could, but I am not sure you have lived enough of your life to have experienced the subtle differences to understand why a western woman might stay with an abusive mate. We are not talking about child brides here.

"There are many reasons women choose to stay within an abusive household. Education, background, exposure, and a multitude of other reasons are partially responsible. Often, the women are fearful of what will happen to them. Then there is fear of the unknown— something that is very real for most human beings. Lack of self-confidence and self-esteem must have a great deal to do with it all as well. I cannot be certain, because I know almost nothing about abusive relationships, but cultural and emotional baggage also play a part in what people do. Much like your husband, who came with his baggage and exposure and could only act as he had seen around him, so are the husbands of other women. The women themselves also have the baggage that weighs them down to immobility.

"The differences often are the laws from one country to the next. To guide a person effectively, you need more than sympathy. An understanding of the psychology of the lives and backgrounds of the parties involved, coupled with knowledge of the law, may be the elements needed. Leila, you must live a little longer to offer these things to the women you are talking about. Your boss most probably has a valid point. Knowing you are a busy high school student, the process beyond what you are presently doing at the shelter would interfere with your studies. Sweetheart, I support your altruistic desires—they are valid—but let us also remember that it is important to be sensible."

As always, Saadia was a great listener. She added to a conversation only the punctuation that gave it strength. "Leila, if you were still in Iran, and your husband did to you what the husband of this woman at the shelter did, would you be able to change yourself or your husband? Lucky for the person you are talking about, she is here, she can find help, she can change her life and her circumstances only if she wants to. She is at the shelter, and that is the place that will give her the time to think and go forward or backward or even continue to live with what she has gotten accustomed to.

"Remember, the person you were when you were abused is not the person you are now. You decided to change. It was your decision, and the wishes of Julienne could not have helped, if you were not intimately engaged in your own transformation. I think it takes a lot of study and understanding to help people. Taking care of the children is exactly what you need. I also know the children will gain a great deal just by being around you.

"I do not think you can go around attempting to change every one in the world. You need to know about yourself more, and once you do this, you can change yourself every day of the week. I do not think it is easy to change people. You can promise them many things; you can even promise them that their lives will be better, but you can't make anything happen for them. From what you told us, most of the women in the shelter go back to their husbands or boyfriends. That tells me that most are looking for miracles, but they are not willing to work at it. Leila, this is not unique to the shelters in the U.S.A."

"Saadia, I hear what you are saying, but in my heart, I want to help some of these women. If was able to change my perspective of myself, they can, too."

"Maybe you can, but think about it. If you had your baby, would you be able to change the things you wish were different? Could you take a chance on yourself and on your baby? I remember, when we came here, how scared we were. We could not trust any of the people willing to help us, because we did not trust ourselves. We were two very fragile girls. I am not sure we are still not very fragile."

These exchanges were delicious to watch. Both girls were people who had become sure of themselves. They had passion for what was possible. From being victims of their societies, they had transformed themselves to the essence of assertiveness. Often, I found myself smiling, and sometimes my eyes filled with tears. After reflection, my only explanation was that I did not want them to grow up. Yet, without my help, they had.

The two-car garage I once believed to have been too large needed an addition. We had grown into the American family, and we all drove our own cars. Though we traveled together as often as possible, as the girls grew, they became more independent. These changes were happening all along. I saw the signs but could not assimilate them. Most times, I failed to see that the two young and scared girls had left the premises.

Our dog had suddenly gotten old and very sick. For the first time in my life, I had to decide on a matter of quality of life. The veterinarian was kind. He came to our home, and our dog took his last breath surrounded by the three of us. His head was on my lap. He looked at me, and I knew he understood. The tears we shed were not only for Jake. With the help of our neighbor and the incredible vet, we buried him under a blue spruce. When it was done, Leila offered the men a cup of tea. They both declined the offer, knowing we needed time by ourselves.

That day, we talked about the finality of life, the finality of love. One moment there was life and a lot of love, and a moment later it was gone, leaving us with only memories. We cried for our dog, and we cried for the things and the people no longer in our lives. That night, in the privacy of my room, I could not hold the love I had lost. I was empty. My tears came from my solar plexus—they tore my gut apart. I cried for the love, short as it was, that was no longer in my life. I could only hang on to memories and a faint smell my nostrils could not dispense with.

The next morning, we were able to talk about our feelings. We acknowledged we were strong people and with time we would get over Jake's death. We each had lost parts of ourselves when our dog died. We had been reminded at one point or another, during the course of our lives, we each had given our love, to a human being and now a dog, each time after the loss the memories endured. We would keep the memories of Jake alive in our hearts. We decided we would fill the empty vessels inside of us with love and passion for the things that were important to us.

Life had to continue, as dictated by forces we did not understand. We knew it was a condition that we, as humans, had to fulfill.

The school year was almost over. My girls received numerous awards in school. They developed a few new but strong friendships. Because of their personalities and also their age difference, they each had their own friends.

A few weeks before her graduation, Leila received the official letter from Stanford. We were proud. The tremendous work she did for four years earned her a full scholarship. The distance overshadowed my pride. No matter how great the school, it was far away.

Perceptive as she was, Leila reminded me with the clarity of a seasoned lawyer that Stanford was not an education one could easily dismiss. She had checked out the faculty and knew everything she needed to know. She was certain to be the international human rights lawyer she had worked toward and dreamed of her entire high school life. Stanford was the place.

Letter on hand, she gave me a hug and a kiss on my forehead to thank me for being in her life. She did her best to assure me she was ready, and all would be fine. I never doubted that—it was I who was not ready.

Leila was more than a survivor of horrific circumstances; she was able to make choices based on logic, knowledge of a projected future, and an unburdened assuredness. She was a young woman to be admired. During her high school years, she kept in touch with Mr. Robert, the attorney in Washington. She also informed him of the next phase of her education. She reminded him with a formal letter that one day she would ask him for a job.

I had to learn to let go of this brilliant star and watch her shine over the Pacific Ocean.

CHAPTER 27

Changes Are in the Air

Leila's graduation was the event of the year. To have a party for all the students in her small class became the plan of the season. Most of the students were college bound, and all had worked hard. They deserved this party.

The temperature permitted this affair to be on the long porch. Renting tables and chairs from two towns over, tablecloths, dishes, and more were delivered three days before the dinner and I was able to accommodate the eighteen students and their parents. There were no catering services in Owl's Head, and again I had to find help outside of town.

The arrangements and coordination demanded a great deal of energy and patience. Both girls helped by going in and out of town for all the things we needed. Ursula's bakery provided us with rolls and cookies, while she made two enormous cakes representing caps and gowns. All went well. The party was a success, and two days later, our homes were back to their usual decor.

Stanford had not moved. I had to prepare my daughter and make sure she had all that she needed. I also had to prepare myself for the distance that would separate us. In the long run, I was afraid that her choice of becoming an International Human Rights Lawyer would make her life difficult and dangerous. Leila reminded me more than once that I had been the one who had nurtured her to let the feathers grow on her wings. It was normal that she develop the need to fly. Her sense of duty toward the women of the world came from her own experience, and I had nothing to do with that.

"I am not going to blast the world, I am not going to behead or use stones. I am going to use the laws of the world and do my best to assist some women in their struggles against oppression. I have no illusions. It will be difficult, and I do not know where my ideals will take me. We both know that, and Mom, just think: I accept where I have been and the very circumstances I faced. I am now comfortable with me as I am. I have you to thank for that."

As planned, the three of us traveled to California. I needed to know where my child would be. We needed to know everything about this place, and, in no time, the three of us became familiar with the diverse cultures we found in that state. We called it a fact-finding mission that would put me at ease about being separated by distance. The other reason for this trip was that, as we did every summer, we went on a vacation. This time, we stayed right here on U.S. soil, exploring one state.

The girls both became protective of me, and that,

too, happened without a moment's notice. I made sure they learned to live their lives fully. Faced with the results of my fostering independence, I found myself challenged by feelings I had not anticipated. There were waves of happiness, because of their accomplishments, and also extreme sadness, because they were soon to fly away from the nest we had so carefully built.

Before Stanford, the exploration of California had become the object of our conversations. We prepared well for this! We rented a car from the Los Angeles airport and went first to San Diego. This was a voyage "full of Zs," as Saadia said. Going from one place to the next, we wanted to see as much as we could. Saadia, our tour director, felt we needed to see San Diego. Her motive demanded plenty of sketching material.

All prior trips offered Saadia a chance to view what Leila and I missed most times. Always with a sketch pad and plenty of pencils, sometimes with inks on hand, she found a variety of subjects to sketch. Contrary to Leila and her Louis Vuitton satchel, at the last *Nowruz*, I had given Saadia a backpack—a nice one, but a backpack just the same! Her concern was not one of esthetics, but one of comfort. My two girls were sisters at heart, but they were completely different. Looking at her tourist guidebook, Saadia found what she was looking for. It was nearly noon, and she invited us to visit an old mission basilica. The bribe was easy, as she found the key by assuring us that she also found two multiple-star restaurants around the corner from the basilica.

San Diego de Alcala was our destination. Saadia was a good researcher and could find old churches and other ancient buildings where no one seemed to know of their existence or that they mattered. She often told me the new world was not so bad—nothing was too ancient, but there were lots of interesting places. Her love of architecture took us many places we otherwise would not have visited. When she saw the basilica, she said it reminded her of some buildings she had seen in the only book she ever read in Afghanistan. The whitewash of the walls and the bricks on the floor captured her heart, while they reminded me of both Spain and Morocco.

The girls were both surprised that numerous churches and many restaurants in the San Diego area clearly displayed their Islamic influence. The girls knew that the Moors had occupied Spain for 700 years, and they were Muslims. They had no idea, however, that the inspiration in design, textiles, tiles, styles, and colors all around them were also due to an occupation close to a thousand years past. What most believed to have been an obscure culture had crossed an ocean to arrive in South America, Mexico, and southwestern parts of the United States.

"You know, if a person knows a little history or has the right background, it is evident that cultures travel. It is good, and it is scary, because when people travel and bring their culture, they bring it all—the good and the bad."

"Saadia, I never thought of it that way, but you are correct. What bad thing would you be talking about?

"One thing for sure—Islamic rules and laws would not work well in the United States. While I hope this never happens, I know that, if you get enough Islamism here, you will approach many of the sharia laws. Mom, we are not a country where we have laws that do not bend to accommodate some groups and not upset others. We do these things at the cost of our own selves."

"I hope this never happens too, but one never knows where history will take people. Loyalties to any given country and certainly religions make for some strange associates."

We had an entire summer to be vagabonds from southern to northern California. We did just that, but the cloud above my head continued to grow.

I was about to lose a daughter to a very good school. I found myself walking with pride and sorrow. No one ever told me these things when I agreed to take in two refugees.

Saadia was right. After the basilica visit, we continued on to a small bakery. This one was French, and the *pâtisseries* were different from the ones Ursula made. While we enjoyed some coffee with heavy cream, I remembered Suzannah, who would have loved both Leila and Saadia. So many years had gone by that Ursula had gotten older and no longer manned the bakery.

My girls were no longer children, and I was getting older, too. I missed Suzannah. I wished I could have told her about my girls. As I watched them grow, I understood what she must have felt. I understood the abuse they suffered. I cried with them, and I swelled with pride because of them. My children had not only survived violation acceptable by a culture. They had grown past it all.

A Note from the Author to the Reader

A note to readers in the middle of a book is not a customary literary occurrence, yet I feel compelled to do this. I trust you will be tolerant and accept my departure from the norm.

It was before and also during the penning of this book that I began to meet many extraordinary people of conscience who, much like me, were neither pacifist nor activist, religious nor agnostic. However, they embodied love of country, love of culture, love of the people of the lands of their birth. They were people of integrity and scruples. Not from the rural parts of the world I was attempting to understand, they were people who had been elegantly educated. They understood what I did not. My pen has no words to describe their courage, fortitude, and trust. People I did not know lent me their own pens to bring understanding to you. They wanted their stories understood. They wanted to be heard. They wanted you and me to feel the gurgling blood in the veins of the females.

It took many breaths and many risings of the sun to muster the courage to contact one particular author who was, at the time, residing in Jordan. He had touched a cord in my soul. He wrote of my sisters, and he wrote for my sisters and to my brothers.

Graciously, and without knowing me, he accepted my request and gave his permission to include his poem in this book. Khaled Hishma retains all rights to his poem. Take a breath and read with me, as I single out Khaled Hishma for the power of his words.

Killing in the Name of Honor

I am...
    The victim of your ignorance
    The sufferer of your disrespect
    The bearer of your crimes
    The inflicted with your sins
    The scared by your despotism
    The imprisoned in your hostility.
    I am the Female...
Without me...
    Existence cannot exist
    Life would not persist
    Dignity does not manifest
    Humanity could not depict.
I and my pair...
Were created...
    From the same single sole
    At the same exact moment
    With the same given rights
    By the same Gracious Maker
    On the same parity grounds.

My Murderer...
Is Always...
    A man who is not a man
    A male who is not a human
    Masculinity loaded with stupidity
    Virility plunged with ignominy
    A mentality polluted with partiality
    A religiosity distorted with deficiency.
There is no...
    Honor in your act
    For you know no honor
    No logic in your doing
    For you have only enormity
    No virtue in your behavior
    For you are molded with evil.
It is ...
    The culture that brought you
    Is born out of heresy
    The tradition that formed you
    Is promoted by savagery
    The custom that shaped you
    Is made through loquacity
    The idea that possess you
    Is fashioned from idolatry.
I Am...
The Mother who...
    Carried you in her womb

The Sister who...
   Walked beside you at home
The Daughter who...
   Held your hand for love
The Wife who...
   Provided your life with tranquility.
I am the Woman...
   My passion is unmatched
   My affection is incomparable
   My tenderness is exceptional
   My allure is undeniable
   My charm is unforgettable
   My delight is irresistible
   My elegance is graceful
   My brightness is nonparallel
   My mind is sophisticated
   My intellect is electrifying.
I Am...
   The splendor of living
   The infatuation of realm
   The dazzle of being
   The eminence of prestige
   The fluency of serenity
   The charisma of glamour.
I Will...
   Outlive your indignation
   Survive your discontent

Eveline Horelle Dailey

Ridicule your malice
Scorn your absurdity
Surpass your idiocy.
For I Am The Female...
The preamble which start life
The script which inscribe inception
The substance which create pride
The warmth that deluge ardent love
The glory that envelop regret
The devotion that acquire nobility
The proof to dispel falsity
The narration to diffuse falsification
The authenticity to expose deception.
I Am The Female...
I cannot be concealed
I will not be repealed.
I shall not be veiled I am vibrant and breathe.

Khaled Hishma

If a word is necessary here, it is to ask you to stop
and ponder.

CHAPTER 28

Apprehension Before Higher Education

"Julienne, if Saadia went to school in California, would you move here? You seem to feel at ease in this area. Wouldn't be great for all of us to be here, at least until I graduate?

"Leila, you are being very selfish. Mom and I will be just fine in Maine. She lived there a long time, before you came into her life. Why do you think she should move, just because it could be convenient for you? You are something else!"

Leila burst into an avalanche of tears. They were both on edge and, for that matter, so was I. We did not know how to cope with the emotions rising within us.

"I am so afraid to be alone here. I know it is the school I want for my studies, but at the same time, I am

207

very scared. I know I am being selfish. It's just that I will be alone without you; the two of you are my support. Since I came to the USA and even before that, I can't think of any family that have given me more and meant more to me. You are all that I have, and it scares me to be without you. Saadia, I did not mean to upset you."

"Leila sweetheart, stop crying, you will be fine; we will all be fine. At first, it will be hard for all of us, but we are strong people, remember that! You chose the career you wanted to have years ago. You have looked into many schools. You and I both know this is where you belong. During every vacation, you will be able to come back home.

"I am also sure you will meet new friends, and some will have similar interests. I believe California is a state that attracts those taking chances and doing things differently from the status quo. I have a feeling there will be people in your classes with comparable ideas. You will be an advocate for the rights of the female children and women here and in the Middle East. Give yourself a pat on the back for the courage of your conviction. Sweetheart, we will worry about you, but we know you will be fine."

"Leila, she is right. We will miss you. We will talk to you maybe every night, how is that? I love you very much. You are my sister, and I will even miss you teasing me about my cat eyes."

One street over, we continued to a destination only Saadia knew.

"Look! There is a shelter for animals here. Can we go in and see? I want to sketch a dog. Maybe we can rescue one or two. You rescued us, and you rescued Jake. What about going to check this out?"

Saadia defused the difficult moment. I was not too sure about her method—for certain, going to an animal shelter was not going to happen. I suggested that, since we had to visit so much of California, we would not have time for a shelter visit. There were other things to explore right where we were.

The possibility of an animal or two in my life at this time was not going to happen. I did not want to experience any more pain. The departure for school was enough for me.

We arrived at a mutual agreement: after Stanford, we would visit a shelter. For now, breakfast awaited us, and so were a couple of museums. After that, if we still had energy, we would walk to the beach.

The rest of our California vacation took us to Los Angeles, with stops on Rodeo Drive, as well as a long stop at Madame Tussaud's, where some of the likenesses of famous people were impressive. The Getty Villa and other museums kept us hopping from one direction to the next. The girls were not terribly impressed with Hollywood. Leila felt the opulence of the area contrasted too much with places like Chinatown and other ethnic neighborhoods. With the apparent differences in their socioeconomic factors, she saw the potential for civil unrest. Her activist mind questioned the American system of evaluating the worth of a human being. As always, my passionate daughter had some good arguments supporting her opinions.

The more I observed my children, the more it

became clear to me that Leila would touch people with her thoughts, her words, and her deeds. Based on her inclination to pay close attention to the movements within the entire Middle East, I prayed it would not be the blood that she spilled to would make a mark on the ethos of a society she was part of.

Saadia, the pacifist, had shifted her interest about architecture. She now wanted to specialize in the design of schools, hospitals, and other healthcare facilities. Museums and the cathedrals she had often sketched now took a backseat, but some of them still made their appearance in her landscapes. She was young, and I was sure she would change her mind many times.

"Leila, as I read the news and now also spend time on the Internet, I become more conscious that the women of any country where there is oppression and abuse have to gain their own freedom. They must be willing to lift a finger. I don't know how, but it seems evident to me that freedom is something that is earned, not given."

"Saadia, for a pacifist, you sure are one good thinker. I agree with you. The women must do something. They must do their part. They must act, and only after that will there be support for their causes. We are perfect examples of this. When I walked away from the burning house, though I wanted to die, I had taken some action. One must find a way to accomplish the movement that takes life from point A to point B. Only at that point can meaningful help be given—otherwise, apathy sets in, and we know what that looks like for millions of women.

CHAPTER 29

It Takes Passion

Our journey around California took us to all sorts of places. We were not the typical tourists; we saw the real state, from the slums to where the movie stars took residence. Our conversations about the entire place were sometimes intense.

"Maybe because of my interest in law, I find myself observing what surrounds people. I wonder if every state displays such differences between the haves and the have nots? You do realize this is how the fundamentalists recruit armies of people? They are in the neighborhoods where education is at a minimum, where drugs are rampant, and no one has a sense of value. They are there—lurking, waiting for the prey to fall. They are there, ready to pluck the fallen and give them what they want to hear, or a sense of importance—a place in the world and, therefore, fulfilling the need they have to be recognized. Maybe there are no jihadists here, not yet

211

anyway, but I can assure you it is not difficult to change the behavior of uneducated, frustrated people. It takes very little to manipulate these masses, and one gun in the wrong hands, and *voilà:* you have riots and much more. I am afraid this may happen in California. I will go to school here, but I would not spend my life here."

"Leila, we know your interest is all about human rights, but you have to know these conditions exist everywhere in the world. People make attempts at distinguishing themselves. I know they are not always successful, probably because they do not have any idea of the directions available to them.

"I realize what you are talking about. You make a great deal of sense. At the same time, I hope you are very wrong. Who knows? Maybe this is why I want to build schools so kids can be educated and hospitals so they can be made healthy and well. People have a need for such establishments. Through my own eyes, I know this is what is needed. Maybe, after you graduate, you may realize that enforceable laws covering disparities, abuses, or rights of people are needed everywhere. But when most of the world operates from patriarchal societies, I do not see how being an international lawyer will help anyone. You cannot save the world, Leila. What do you think?"

"I think this conversation is fascinating. I am so proud of both of you. When I was your age, all that concerned me was where the next party was. Your minds approach issues that I did not know existed. I am so proud! I know I say it often, but today, I feel like a peacock! My feathers are fanned to show the world how proud I am of you. I know you each will both be true to yourselves, no matter what you choose to do. I am sure of it! You are two people with a great deal of determination and courage—I do not think you know what people see when they meet you. You bring me a great deal of joy, and you bring others a sense of wellbeing. You both exude something magical, but overall, you bring a sense of human fairness. I will support you in whatever direction your lives take you. I admire who you are becoming."

I got up and kissed them. I thought back to the time, soon after their arrival in my home, when they had to get used to my joyful outbursts and my hugs and kisses. At first, they were stiff and scared. It took a while, but they, too, started giving me hugs and kisses. Saadia often told me, the winds of happiness ruffled her senses, and I had wings to make winds. My artist was almost a poet. During these usually non-verbal moments, Leila looked at her sister and, with a smile of approval, told me that Saadia was being ruffled. We had our private language. No one knew what it felt like inside of us—only we did. In our own ways, we were survivors of great pain and great love—the stuff that made better humans, Leila recounted regularly.

"We are proud of you, too. I do not know any young and beautiful widowed woman, with or without money, who would have burdened herself with children from different cultures, children who did not speak her language, and abused ones, at that! Julienne, remember when I was learning English and you got us the dictionary? I found the one word I now know describes you to me. 'Remarkable.' This is what you are! You took us in, educated us, and gave us a kind of mental freedom

213

most kids our age could not understand, no matter where they come from. We are lucky, very lucky. You took who you perceived us to be, gave us the tools to explore who we were, and showed us how to become people who have pride and purpose. Yes! You are remarkable."

"Leila, now I am going to cry."

"No need to cry. I think watching you, listening to the stories you told us about Suzannah and your life, empowered us to grow into our own individuality. You taught us values, because you learned them from Suzannah and others, too. I give all those around you credit because, ultimately, they arranged patterns in your life that permitted you to become who you are. You did and are doing the same for us! I am glad for all this, because we both benefited. This also showed me why women are so important to young people they are raising. You took us from ignorance to the burning desire to know and know more. You have a freedom about you that you imparted to us without even trying.

"When I am a lawyer, I will be dealing with issues of female abuse. I hope to convey to women the lessons I learned from you. The gift you gave was much more than a roof over our heads. When we came to your home, as two very scared girls with not a soul in the world to turn to, you opened your heart to us. You showed us how to get to the content of our own hearts and minds, and you gave us wings. We learned to trust who we were, and that is something few people experience. You showed us how to become women of power.

"I already know, from history and experience, many men are not comfortable with women of power. I feel, in general, men have a hard time dealing with powerful women. I see it more than I ever thought possible. It is subtle, but I see it often. Regardless of where they come from, men and women will ultimately have to educate each other. We need to engage each other and become partners, not enemies.

"I may never be able to trust a man fully. I do not know. Wow—I am admitting I may have to grow a lot more! In the meantime, I think most men like to treat women like cattle. When they have a sense of ownership, they feel like men. I am under the impression that many men are somewhat brittle when it comes to their manhood. This is perhaps why, in more places than I care to acknowledge, women and certainly girls are not allowed to express a personal thought. They are only vessels for the pleasure of their captor/husband and the production of children. This is the way the men of these societies want them to be."

"Wow, girl, you need to let go of anger!"

"Maybe I do, but Saadia, sometimes when we are watching television, I sense such behavior in the programing of people. It is subtle, but it is there. I see it in school with some of the boys. I suppose, in some American societies, this is the way it is. Not that all the men brutalize their mates as we were, but the need for shelters for battered women tells me a story I will look into as I get on with my studies.

"I may also have to take on a psychology minor. There are reasons why people behave as they do, and I need to understand the behavioral psychology of humans. My concern will not be the women here—they have enforceable laws to protect them. The women of too many other countries, particularly the Middle East, are the ones in need of help. The problem with these countries is no implementation or enforcement of the law. That's where I feel I will come in."

"Leila, you are on that soap box again. I am trying to draw a calm sea here!"

"Saadia, put ear plugs on! Why do you travel with pen and ink anyway? Can't you wait till you get back home?"

"Art is not something you put on hold. Lawyers can put things on hold, but an artist must answer the muse, or creativity itself goes away. You are not going home!"

Like most sisters, sometimes they verbally attacked each other. It took me a while to accept that as part of a normal process, since I had no sisters.

"What angers me is the fact that women have accepted being victimized. They raise their children to be victims. When one falls out of the fold, she is stoned to death, decapitated, or eliminated by any possible means, and the women around her just stand there. They are either paralyzed with fear, or they have been so conditioned for centuries that they do not know they are people with a mind or a voice. They have no hope, nor do they know what hope looks like.

"I remember, when I read Victor Frankl, it became clear to me that, when people have no hope, they die. They have no will or reason to demand life instead of death. Victor Frankl was talking about Jews in concentration camps, and I am talking about my Muslim sisters. They, too, have no hope. They are like sheep, going with the flock without aim or direction, without knowledge of who or what they are. They are born out of rape, from servitude, to create more of the same. Julienne, I get so angry sometimes."

"Leila, you are a passionate being, and you believe with all your heart that you will have the solution. I do not think anything is wrong with that. You probably will encounter some hardship, but I realize you must follow the dictates of your heart."

"If I can join a group of international lawyers, at least I will be in a position to help the women who are courageous enough to flee their world. I will assist them and show them the possible changes available to them. If I can help younger girls, like you did for us, that will be great. If I can help, assist people, I will do what is necessary to continue to strive for the freedom each woman deserves to have. If I can impart to one or more that they must do their part, they will become free, and I will have lived my life purpose."

"Leila, you are an admirable, remarkable young woman."

"I will have to start thinking about building communities, yet I am not sure a community of battered people is what is needed. Leila, I want to be part of your world. I want to assist you with the goals you have so deeply set for your life, but I am not sure that I know how. Maybe we are not all supposed to change the world. I must be satisfied with the little that I will be able to do."

Something extraordinary happened after Saadia made this statement. Leila got on her knees, took both of Saadia's hands. She looked at Saadia with pure love and admiration.

217

"Saadia, without you and Mom I could not be the person I have become. You both are the instruments and the compass I use. Saadia, when you paint a sky or a seascape, you show me what freedom really is. When Mom traces the terrain for us, she shows me what a person of freedom is. She is the teacher who takes us outside of the limitations we sometimes set on ourselves. Saadia, never abandon me, because without you I would have only a dim light and no rod to navigate my life."

Often my girls brought me tears, the only expression of gratitude available to me.

CHAPTER 30

Careful, My Daughter

"Leila, I appreciate the commitment to your truth, but I have some concerns because, ultimately, you will be endangering yourself. I am sure, regardless of where you are, on U.S. soil or anywhere overseas, people of fundamentalist tendencies will have a hard time swallowing the pill you are going to give to them."

"Mom, here is the thing, and I know I am repeating myself. Yes, ignorant men, Islamic or otherwise, are bent on humiliating women. They feel they are elevating themselves by doing just that. I may be very young, but I have observed one thing: the more a man feels badly about himself, the more he needs to belittle others, mainly women. These men seem to need to make a woman feel as badly as they feel about themselves. They are frustrated with their lives and possibly who they are, and they do not know how to handle it. They blame the woman. They want to hurt her, because ultimately she is part of who they are—she made them who they are. To this type of mental state, add some misguided religious teachings, and you have the formula that allows for stoning, beheading, rapes, and so on.

"Those are crucial issues that must be addressed from various perspectives. This is why I must study both law and psychology and possibly something else along the way. The circle is vicious. Their station in life doesn't permit them to free themselves, and wishing for girls or women to be educated is not part of their mindset. That scares them senseless, because an educated woman can show them the fallacies of their lives. Their mothers were accomplices, even if they did not know it. They, too, were encoded from birth."

"Leila, this is a mouthful that will demand a great deal from you and many others. You have a theory I feel holds a great deal of truth. My girl may have found a needed key."

"I have a thousand and one theories, but I don't know if any of them are right. I think women gave their power away because, possibly thousands of years ago, they figured it was easier to stay home, whatever home may have been at that time, take care of the crying babies, and create more of the same in order to control the man they had. He had to go hunting and planting, when he learned how. In other words, he had to bring the bacon home. That elevated him, and removed the sense of equality between the two. I do not know how long it took, but I believe, from that place, men began to feel themselves to be more important.

"Soon, their hunting and gathering was not enough.

They had lust. All those baby girls were tempting to their loins. The men had to create an environment for this to be acceptable. Multiple marriages became a reality. The women who had given their power away were overcome and subdued by the younger women who replaced them. I have a feeling this was not such an easy transition for mankind. To keep women in their place, rules became important to the men who were still not too sure of themselves.

"I have not yet found the answer to my theory. I suppose I need an archeologist and at least another person able to tell me about the neurology and biology of the brain in the context of my interest. If I am ever to understand anything at all, I need a whole team of people around me. I already know the positioning of left and right brain and what could also be called the female and male brain. Can you imagine telling this to one of those ignoramuses? I do not know when women gave up and accepted that they did not need to be educated. When they did, they further augmented the power the men had over them.

"Move a few thousand years ahead, and you have all sorts of male-initiated religions devised solely to serve men and subjugate women. You know, in most religions and philosophies, there is a female figure. She started the ball rolling. I have not read the entire Qur'an you got us, but as I recall, there is no Eve, no Shiva, or any other female deity. She has been eliminated, much like they do to their women today."

"Leila, in school you will align your self to many students and professors, too. You will have the answers you seek."

"I hope so, Mom, because no matter where I turn, I see a sort of accepted isolation of the female. The last vivid case in mind is the last pope. I remember the garments, the pageantry, the processions. They called themselves the College of Cardinals. You did not see any women in that group, nor did you see any when they went in private to vote. Women cannot be pope. In that religion, with its big cathedrals, women are not elevated enough to serve their god equally. There is a lot of similarity between Christianity and Islam. They are both patriarchal institutions. In both cases, the woman is not equal. I have a feeling, in both cases, those in power would argue my observation false.

"In the Islamic world, ayatollahs are all men. So are mullahs. You do not see a woman Taliban. I know, at one time in history, many armies were headed by women. That, too, I know nothing about. This part of history seems to have been redacted. In today's world, women must regain their power. The only way they will do this, I think, is through education. One day, one woman will have to stand up and say, 'It is time to count me!'

"As liberated as women think they are in the U.S., I do not think this will happen here, or at least not soon enough. Some country in Europe or South America will probably be the first one to elect a woman president. I am not an historian, but my point is that we women have given our men the power to control us, and we are the ones who must change that. Julienne, you got me on that soap box again!"

The young waiter took that moment to break in. "Ladies, would you like more tea or perhaps coffee now?

We make a good cup of java in this establishment."

We looked at each other, realizing we had been talking in the small café for hours. We decided to switch to coffee; we had been taking room in the restaurant for three hours and did nothing but talk. It did not appear to matter much, because the place was nearly empty. With the view of the ocean, it was the perfect place for us. Saadia ordered a slice of apricot pie to go with her coffee. She remarked that the apricots most probably came from Turkey but not Afghanistan.

I believe, at times, she missed the land of her birth. Leila did not like sweets; she ordered an English muffin and a two slices of American cheese. Waiters were not accustomed to such a request—at home she ate muffins with any kind with cheese. She got this from me, because I did it. The cheeses we ate were different, however. Saadia, on the other hand, put pounds of jam on anything made of wheat. I joined Saadia and asked for a slice of strawberry pie. The young waiter had never heard of a place called Turkey. He only knew that the strawberries were from California.

Moments later, he returned with enormous slices of pies and a double toasted muffin. On a different small dish were two slices of American yellow cheese. He again asked if she wanted any jam or jelly, and she politely reminded him she wanted nothing else. The coffees met with our approval, and we continued to talk about many things, but Leila got off her soapbox. She was passionate about women's affairs and the issues around them. I could not call her a feminist, but she was pretty close. She wanted all women to be liberated from the chains of oppression. Her wish that women had the ability and freedom to make up their own minds about who they were and what they would do with their lives was in the forefront of a quest I did not always understand. Leila had discovered her own potential and calling and felt this was possible for others, no matter where in their world they found themselves. The idea that too many girls were never given the opportunity to learn how to read and write was intolerable to her. She reminded me how difficult and gray it was for both of them when they were unable to read.

Leila had long discussions with Saadia about literacy. Saadia, who left Afghanistan totally illiterate, often attempted to explain what it meant to her to be illiterate, saying it felt like being in a dark tunnel. She had seen a book in the small village where she grew up. She remembered when the Taliban destroyed it and killed the owner of the store. She was young, but after that incident, she never heard anyone talk about books, and she no longer even knew the word in Pashto. She also did not know the name of the village where she was born. She knew her parents moved from one place to the next to follow the work given to her father. She did not know what he did.

For many of us coming from other cultures, these things were unfathomable. From the descriptions she gave, Saadia's life was more like one ordeal after another, Her father was physically cruel to her mother. Until she moved to the United States, she had not heard anyone talk about education, schools, or books. In her world, these things or the conversations they would bring about did not exist. Once language permitted conversation, and all the taboos and ice were melted, she told us she believed this was the reason it was so easy to manipulate both men and women in the villages in Afghanistan where illiteracy was rampant. She told us she learned what was on the other side of the deep darkness of ignorance only after she met us. She did not question how anyone could interpret the world for her and those around her—there was no other way.

With complete ignorance it was easy to believe what was said. Self-proclaimed men of knowledge made this easy. The rules they made became the laws. Entire villages had to abide. The fact that no one knew or ever questioned where these rules came from was perhaps a result of extreme fear for their lives. People were familiar only with the tasks they were born to do.

Saadia did not speak as much as Leila, but she was a deep thinker. She observed at a young age that the way of life in her village made complete and fervent believers of every man, woman, and child. At the mention of the prophet's name, every one stooped. She could be married off when she was only nine because someone made a rule and no one questioned it. Many things were done to people in order to make certain all would obey completely. Now she understood how it worked. You behead one person, and it takes no time at all, and no one raises a head. You cut off one hand, and the person prays to Allah and is thankful for the hand that was spared. People who behaved like flocks of sheep populated entire villages. The abject ignorance around was the cause of many of the problems, and she knew well that something had to be done. Being young, she was passionate and impatient.

These were troubling moments to experience with my girls. I still remember the first time we walked on the beach. At first, Saadia was petrified—she had never put her feet in a body of water. She did not know that water from oceans was salty, nor did she know that this infinite body of moving water was not out to kill her. Saadia had never seen a seashell. She did not know she could enjoy picking up a shell and examining the mother of pearl. Because she had the soul of an artist, she saw the beauty immediately, and she soon began to augment my seashell collection. She also learned to swim, and often I referred to her as my fish.

She told me how petrified she felt in the plane that transported her to the USA. "You have no idea what ignorance does to people. The darkness I speak of is deeper than an ocean. You have nothing to draw from, and I know no words to explain this to you. It is like being blind. People of Judeo-Christian societies, most people of Asian societies, such as the Japanese, and others too, are born with a wealth of experiences and exposures. They have books and art all around them. People in those societies are able to speak freely. They are able to express their creativity. The list goes on. The simplest things we enjoy without a thought are unknown mysteries to millions of people.

"Mom, I think this is why I am able to feel no hatred toward my father. To believe that I had to be stoned to death is deplorable. Yet, I know I could not hold him responsible. His mind was under the deep darkness I once experienced. This is very sad! Men like my father are under some sort of a hypnotic state. I don't know if that is brought by faith or fear. It does not matter. What matters is my father was far from being an oddity. The men around him were all just like him, and so were the women. I am certain that today, in the same village, nothing has changed. This is the way it is, where people have not advanced toward new centuries."

CHAPTER 31

Many Things to Weigh and Consider

Reminiscing about the past with my girls, I came to know it was not culture or praise I was seeking when I agreed to have them living in my home. The fact is, at the time of the agreements, I did not give it any thought. In retrospect, thinking about it would have scared me, and I would have declined. It was my lack of fear of the unknown that persuaded me to accept the challenge. Permanence was not on my mind and, to be honest, I believe I treated this as one more experience to have in my life. Many years later, I have come to the conclusion that my children were the best teachers of culture I could ever have had. The exchanges between the three of us educated all of us.

The level of satisfaction I feel today continues to

be tremendous. My own sentiments toward freedom and adventure were passed on to my daughters. From them I learned about acceptance and, despite the circumstances and their age, they came to me with a great deal of wisdom. The independence to explore and experience, along with the tutoring and schooling they received, helped them become the extraordinary people I saw before me. When I think of what they left behind, I appreciate the broader tête-à-têtes and logic they express around me. Because of Leila and Saadia, I reached a level of understanding and acceptance I would otherwise never have known.

"I think, as time goes on, my intention is to have a non-government organization of my own, or be part of one at a high level. Being part of a NGO, the focus would be to help girls and women in the Middle East. My idea would be to educate them from where they are, and from that point, they would help themselves."

"Leila, that is a wonderful and altruistic plan, but think about what you are saying. You know that most countries in the Middle East keep their women in bondage. They are prisoners in cages without visible bars. I can imagine such countries would have no need or reason to release a woman or girl to any western NGO. You need to do one thing after the other. Take baby steps my dear. Your education first! You are talking about an organization with boots on the ground. I do not see how this would work, but I know you can think outside the box. To do such a thing, military forces would probably have to be part of it, and, to my knowledge, the commitment of military personal is usually of a different nature."

"Leila, when the military is in hostile countries, they are not there to help young girls. We both were lucky; I am sure our cases were oddities in military maneuvers.

"I doubt that there are many more girls like us. I do not think soldiers have any manuals that tell them to find people and rescue girls. If such a manual existed, I bet you the order would be to bring them to their homeland. In matters of war, occupation of country, hostility, etc., what happened with us could be considered a set of freakish accidents. Both of us met with people who had a frame of mind permitting them to go outside of their training. I do not know how to explain the reasons they may have had—perhaps they may not even know why they came to our rescue. They just did! For sure, more people could learn from them. I know our presence with their individual units must have been a problem. The only fact I know is that they were all people with great character. I wish I knew their names, because it would be an honor to thank them now. I think they would appreciate what they did with greater satisfaction based on who we are today. It is not every day that two different groups of soldiers do the same thing in different places and change lives to the extent that ours have been. The humane factor or their other reasons put two people on their way to becoming productive citizens.

"Leila, you also know that occupation of a country or war with any country comes with plenty of destruction. It seems, in matters where military forces are involved, destruction is a by-product, and people die. What may have been in order must change to impress the citizens not yet ready to join their fold. Armies do that well. My understanding, from what I have read, when there is war, it is necessary to destroy and rebuild so the next generation has no concept of the old ways of being. The people who are old die off. Of course, I could be wrong, but I think it is the way of religions as well. The feeling deep in my heart is for those who rescued us, and for certain they were unusual people. That is good enough for me!"

"What you are saying makes sense, Saadia. You know, centuries ago, Muslim women were free. Some were heads of states. They were educated—think of the queen of Sheeba. Now, in various Muslim countries, girls and women are stripped of their human rights. They cannot go to school. They can't even go outside without being accompanied by a male. What is absurd is that, in some countries, I read that a woman can go out with her five-year-old son. Does that make any sense? Is a boy of five a man? Is this the rationale that allows adult men to marry girls who are six or nine, rape them as they please and be protected by some ruling? In places like Saudi Arabia, it is the same thing. To think a woman can't go out on her own, and when she does go out, she must be covered from head to toe.

"Do you know, in places like Azerbaijan and I am sure in many other places, gender selection infanticide is routine. I do not remember the ratio of male vs. female, but they let the boys live and kill the girls. That is not exactly my ideal society. This is not about abortion— it is about the selection of the female child that is born and killed immediately after she takes her first breath.

She has no human value. That is one of the things that concerns me about the world I came from.

"To have any questions answered, to have changes in societies, women need to be educated because they cannot weigh the issues of their lives without understanding what it is to be a human being. Right now, we both know that not enough women in villages in the Middle East have a sense of self."

There was a long pause between the three of us. A lot had been said.

"You know what I find beyond ridiculous?"

"What is so ridiculous to you, Leila?"

"Mom, when a western woman travels to a Muslim country, she must cover her head and be dressed modestly. In other words, she must do as custom demands. Yet, when a Muslim woman travels to non-Muslim countries, it is not politically or religiously correct, or so it seems, to ask the woman to dress as per the dress code of that country. Sometimes, I am ready to scream. I am outraged and offended that western countries bend their own ways to accommodate the beliefs of others. This makes no sense to me."

"Leila, let me tell you about the drawing and construction of buildings. I know I am not yet an architect or a contractor, but one thing is certain: nothing can be built before creating a foundation. This is probably true of building what you seem to want to correct in a world larger than we know. At the foundation is where you need to be."

The more I listened to them, the more amazed I was. They were sensible young women concerned about the workings of a world they were born to and found unjust. They had a sense of honor.

"I am pretty sure you must have a plan, and you must know what areas of women rights you want to engage yourself in. You can't be all over the place. If you are, you will accomplish nothing."

"Mom, how did you make Saadia so logical? I hate that!"

"I believe you are each very logical, methodological people. You are different, but observing you, I find that each of you uses your mind the way most people wish they could. What Saadia is saying is true, and I am sure you will come to that conclusion as you go on with your endeavors. You will examine what your heart tells you to do, and your mind will provide the guidelines and boundaries. I know you must be true to who you are and what you believe you must do. I do not think you are one who could settle for a life without meaning. In a sense, you two rescued me. You gave purpose to my life. As you go on with your studies, you will be exposed to more than you know now, and I am sure your passion will continue to solidify itself."

"Would you prefer it if, right after high school, I found an immature boy, got married, and had a bunch of screaming kids? Grandma, I do not think you would be too pleased with that scenario."

We all laughed. Suddenly it became clear to me that my children had no intention of ever procreating. They had seen too much, at too young an age.

"I think I speak for both Saadia and me—having survived all odds, we can't stand by knowing what goes on in our countries. I can hope to be of service to womankind by helping the women of my country; that will remain part of my priorities. Saadia, with her idea to design and build shelters and schools no matter where they are, will also be following a calling from within. We may have come to you with our own baggage, but Mom, you took the broken people we were and gave us the tools to find our own dignity. Ultimately that is what I want for my sisters, and not some man using them as if they were drums to beat and strike with a stick."

"Have you girls given any thought about ever going back to your homeland?"

They both looked at me with a puzzled expression. I must have touched on something they had not verbalized deliberately.

"After both our escapes, I believe we are both *persona non grata* where we come from. Being a Fairchild may fool them for a moment, but our activities will not."

"Mom, Leila is right, but in order to grow to be strong human beings, I feel we must give up the people and the baggage that wounded us. Both family and the laws of our countries failed us. I believe Leila's calling to become a lawyer will serve her justly. What has taken thousands of years to become a way of life will not be dismantled overnight, we know that."

"Saadia, you are so wise. While I am at Stanford, I know I will learn and grow a lot during those four years. I also know it is going to be very hard, because not only I will miss your love, I will not have the balance you give to me."

"I love you girls! You do realize we have spent the last three days in Malibu. The idea of this trip prior to going to school was to visit all of California. If we want to do this, no more talk. We must continue to travel toward the university. We will have to meet with your counselor and buy the things you will need in your dorm. There will be a multitude of things we will need to take care of. Tomorrow we need to get back on the road. We have appointments to keep."

"Can we decide tomorrow? I am really not ready. I am so afraid!"

"I understand, but when we wake up tomorrow, we have no choice. We will be on the road."

"Mom, sometimes you have no mercy."

CHAPTER 32

A Change of Title

"Good morning. You know, I spent half the night thinking about your question. This hotel's internet is terrible. I could not do the research I wanted to do. Maybe this café's internet service is better than our rooms. Do you mind if I use the computer while we eat? It will take just a few minutes."

"Leila, darling, I have no idea what research you are talking about, and if I questioned something that demanded internet and research, put it in the same file as you do my thousand and one other questions. I have no idea what you are talking about. I'd much rather eat without looking at a computer."

"You asked if we would go back to our homeland. I wanted to back up my answer with some data. Anyway, after some soul searching, I can speak only for myself, and the answer is no. As a lawyer with an international bent, I feel the women's issues of my interest will be best served right here in the U.S.A. I will do more good with the international courts from this country, or possibly the U.N., traveling only when necessary. As it stands today, the local courts of Iran would not produce favorable results. Who knows? By the time I graduate, Iran may change many things. I think the question you asked can't be answered. Only time will tell."

"U.N. is not bad. I would much rather have you somewhere in the U.S.—yet I also know that you will do what you judge best, and you will follow your dreams."

"I love you, Mom, and I am glad I have your support. That's what you get for giving me all the Joseph Campbell books. I am only following my bliss."

An avalanche of tears came running down my cheeks. I was overwhelmed with pride and joy. When I adopted the girls some six years ago, they decided to call me Julienne, and only sometimes Mom. Lately, Mom was the dominant name, and I liked it. Now, being called Mom gave me something I had not anticipated. A pride or something even greater enveloped me. I am sure only a mother could feel this, and I felt it.

Leila came close and hugged me.

"No one would have known that, in only a few years, you two would master a new language and excel in school, when you were not even at grade level when you got there. And now Stanford!"

"Yes, but the kids graduated at eighteen, and I am twenty-one or maybe even more."

"My dear, you have advantages that no other student in your class will have. You have a great deal of maturity. Your life's journey has been a hard one. Because of it, you see the past and the present with clarity, and you have great anticipation and hope for the future. You seem also clear about what you want to do with your life. By the way, if you ever feel that you wish to change your major, by all means, make it happen. Life is sufficiently complicated without ending up with a career that does not suit you."

"I know what you are saying is true—but Mom, I do not feel ready for such a great institution. You are the only mother I have had for a long time. When I call you Mom, I have a feeling that my real mother would be proud of me and would approve of you, because you guide and encourage me. We may not have biology, but we have everything else. I love you, Mom!"

Saadia smiled and said, "I am so glad Leila took the lead. I had been thinking about this a while. When we talked about my father the last time, I became aware that you could never have been his wife. The thought was almost funny. At first, I felt as if I was missing something important in my life. It didn't take long for me to realize I was not missing a mother, because you had become my mother. What I missed was calling you mother. Mom! Leila and I are on the same page. So, Mom, you already call us your daughters—what was missing was your daughters calling you Mom!"

"I love you so much. You are my daughters, even if there is no biology; we have a bond no one I know has with their mother. Of course, you know the new title obligates you to listen to me when I say no to something!"

They both laughed, looking at each other as if to say, "What have we gotten ourselves into?" Saadia got up and came back with her enormous map. It was time to move on.

We had already decided we must stay one night in Paso Robles. Weeks before, Saadia found a place for us to stay. It was a villa, and when she saw the pictures on the Internet, she said they reminded her of one of the inns in Tuscany. With my credit card, she handled the booking. During this adventurous western trip, they had each taken turns making reservations. They also had decided what we would visit.

So far, all was comparable to that unforgettable Tuscany vacation, when we celebrated the entire summer with Italian foods, something they both discovered they liked a great deal. Symbolically, we also celebrated their birthdays: Leila on the 4th of July and Saadia on the 14th. This time, the culinary experiences took us to Mexican restaurants, and to this we added food from Vietnam that I liked and they did not.

Feeling much like a group of gypsies, we packed our bags and stuffed them into the rented car, as the trunk got smaller at every stop. Paso Robles was going to be a good destination. Leila asked if she would be allowed to taste some wine. Up to now, my children never had alcohol. Because of their Islamic background, I felt I needed to respect this custom. Until she asked me, I had no idea if it was custom or religion that suggested no alcohol. We discussed that a bit, and I still had no clarity.

Our inn had an enormous vineyard, and since I grew up drinking moderate amounts of wine, I felt wine tasting at the chateau would be fine with me. I had to remind Leila that the owner of the inn would have to decide. When

239

we went to the great restaurant she found, I promised we would have wine with our dinners. Saadia, no longer wearing any type of head scarf, asked me if she could also have some wine. I mentally reviewed the laws of the land about drinking age. She was not yet eighteen. I came up with an alternative and suggested that she taste from my glass. Satisfied with my answer, she went about sketching the sky as it changed to the colors of sunset as I drove.

The inn was within gated walls, and we all felt a sense of warmth. Our room was elegant and spacious. It was a good choice. Leila was solemn. One more day of freedom, and she would be a new student at a large and prestigious university. I believe she was feeling the transition in her life. I reminded her that she would be fine, and if all went well, I would fly her home for Thanksgiving.

"What about Christmas? You know the pine tree I planted five years ago is tall enough for lights. Oh my God, can you imagine how beautiful it will be? We will enjoy it from home, and people walking the harbor will enjoy it too. Maybe we should have a big party when I get back. Saadia, don't you think that would be great?"

"Leila, we don't need a big party."

"Mom, do you think we could have another dog?"

"Wow! From party to a dog—I will have to think about these things. It costs plenty of money to fly back and forth. Which holiday will give you more days—how is that?

"What about my dog?"

"Girls, has anybody ever told you how spoiled you are?"

"Yes. Ursula always says that we are spoiled. She is getting old, and she says things without thinking. You do not spoil us, but you are very good to us. Right, Saadia?"

"Right!"

"Saadia, when we get back home, since we will come to Logan airport, we will look for a dog rescue place in Boston. If I approve of your choice, we will get you a dog. One dog!"

"Mom, I love you. Thank you!"

"So I won't have anything to say about this dog?"

"Leila, you will be in school. I will be home alone with Mom, and I need a dog. Besides, Mom needs a dog, too."

"If I am being replaced with a dog, make it a beautiful one!"

We laughed. No matter how old they were, they were children. My children.

"When on vacation, it seems that the time goes too fast. It is already time to have super, our last supper. Leila, I believe it is your turn to decide where we will eat."

"Mom, during this entire trip, you never chose what you wanted. How about you chose a restaurant for Saadia and me?"

CHAPTER 33

Almost at the Gates of Stanford University

Dinner at a small continental restaurant was the ideal place to end our vacation. We talked of new phases in our lives. The food was good—a blend of American, Italian, and Spanish foods. I skipped the wine, and after dinner we went for a walk. We were on a hunt for an ice cream parlor. Two doors down was not exactly an evening walk, but we found what we were looking for. This evening needed to remain with us a long time, and enjoying ice cream together would possibly do the trick.

"Miracle!" said Saadia, when she saw the ice cream parlor proposed by our concierge come into view. My girls, Americanized to some degree had special preferences about eating their ice cream. They each had two scoop, one of vanilla topped with a mountain of chocolate and nuts, and another scoop topped with a jam that looked like apricots was also topped with more nuts. They would mix it all together making lumpy syrup. The small paper bowl looked dangerously fragile, we sat at the nearest table.

The server, a young man probably Leila's age, was too generous with his portions, and he had to give them additional empty bowls. My scoop was a rum and vanilla combination. I tasted the vanilla but the rum must have been left out. From our position, we noticed a park for far ahead. It was not a ball game going, as there were not enough lights, yet half the town appeared to have gathered. We did not finish our ice cream and decided to go and check what the excitement was all about.

Soon our gait followed the rhythm of the music. I could detect violins, ouds, and other stringed instruments I was not sure I knew. Lots of drums dictated our pace. The air was one of festivity. Some people were singing, some were dancing. The audience was young, peppered with some respectably old men and women. As we approached, Leila told me they were singing in Farsi a song her mother used to sing to her while she danced. She often told me her mother was a good dancer. Saadia, who always looked as if she were miles way, again did not miss a beat and told Leila it was a good omen. The spirit of her mother was with her and would guide her in the new school. We had to work hard at keeping our eyes dry.

I knew Leila's mother would probably never have had the opportunity to see her daughter off to Stanford University. One after the other I hugged both. A kind gentleman, who must have been watching us and sensed something important was going on, gave me his seat as I approached. I thanked him and told him there were three of us, so we would keep on looking for a spot. Before I took another step, in a baritone voice, he told the two young men next to him they had to move. He took time to tell them about what gentlemen were to do when ladies were in their presence. Without a word, they got up, their attention shifting from his voice to smiles from ears to ears toward Leila and Saadia. My girls were visibly taken by their display. Since the three seats were at the end of a row, the gentlemen and the young men stood next to us.

The next song was a festive one, something that demanded dancing. Before I could think, almost everyone was up and dancing. Without prodding, Leila got up also, and her hips began to follow the tempo of the drums. Her hands were like wings of a bird riding a thermal. Barely moving, I sensed her arms were free of the chains of tradition she left behind. From the curves of her hands and fingers, I saw the power and grace she did not know she had. Imperceptible movements were felt rather than seen. She was holding the waves of the ouds. She may have been going to the college of law, but she was born to dance!

Many eyes fell upon her, including the young man next to me. Since he had given up his seat, he was now in front of her. To my knowledge, no words were spoken, but he began to dance with her. The older gentlemen, smiling, turned to me and said the two young men were second year students. The dancer was at the college of law and the other was a brain for all sciences. They were both from Iran and lived with him. They had been in the U.S. for the last four years. How curious, I thought—the dancer was the law student.

"I am sorry. I should have introduced myself. I am John Sheppard. I am in the law department."

"I am Julienne Fairchild. This is my daughter, Saadia, and the dancer is Leila. I believe Leila will be in your department. This will be her first year—pre-law, planning to major in international law. She will have a great deal to do before she actually enters the program, but she is determined."

"Amazing how destiny works. Does she speak Farsi? She seems completely Americanized and very young. If I may ask—Fairchild does not seem to be an Iranian name."

"Sir, we were adopted by Mrs. Fairchild about ten years ago. I am Saadia. I am glad to make your acquaintance. I did not mean to intrude and, if I did, please accept my apologies."

"You did not intrude. I am professor Sheppard."

For the first time, I realized my daughter to be very protective of me. I had not encountered this before with either of them.

The music stopped, and Leila looked at us with the broadest smile I had ever seen.

"Mom, Ali is from Iran, can you imagine? He is a law student, too. While we were dancing, he told me he will introduce me to many students and professors, too."

"Well, Leila, I am one of those, and I will spare Ali. I am Professor John Sheppard, Dean of the law college."

"Sir, I don't know what to say."

"Say nothing at all. You met Ali, and this is Kazim. In about two more years, he will be one of the best biomedical engineers in the world. He lives with me, but he is not one of my students, of course. Kazim is already working on a vaccine for a disease so far contained in Africa. You may be standing next to a future Nobel Prize winner. Ladies, since the music in the park is over, and it is only 9:00 p.m., would you come with us to our favorite teahouse? It is part of our ritual: first the music and, after that, hours of tea and conversation. Leila, you will meet many of last year's students and, who knows? You may find one or two to become friends with. What do you say?"

"Mom, what do you say?"

"Fine. We will go for a short while—you know we have a lot of last-minute things to do. We have to go get the car across the street."

"You car will be safe. The teahouse is half a block away."

We followed the leader. The young men and my girls talked in English. I learned that, while they were in America, they had to speak the language of the country. As I walked, I thought about how someone in that school had a brilliant idea about how foreign students could more easily learn the language.

Two cups of tea later, it was time to head back to the hotel. Many telephone numbers were exchanged. Leila met both female and male students, not all of whom were of Islamic background, but all looked quite studious.

"Mom, thank you, this was the best evening ever!

I am glad I met all those people. I have lots of names and phone numbers, but I am not sure I will be able to remember the names, faces, and numbers according to their owners. One of the girls, a sophomore, told me she will call me tomorrow morning early and meet us by the entrance alley toward the dorms. She is a volunteer who helps new students. She said she can show us where to park."

"Leila, you did well," Saadia said. "I still want to go to Columbia University, but after this, I am beginning to question my choice."

"Saadia, you have two more years before the final decision. By the way, changing your mind during the next years is something that is quite acceptable. However, let's concentrate on one student's adventure at a time."

CHAPTER 34

Scared No More

.

Knowing we needed to wake up early did not stop us from our long, continuous conversations. Leila, who was apprehensive of the new unknowns, found solace with the students she met at the café. They were a stimulating group from around the globe. The encounters with the dean, the students at the park, and those at the café opened a gate for Leila to walk through. The experience was also good for Saadia, who was still timid among strangers.

"I did not have many friends in high school. Too many of the kids were nerds, and the rest were just plain stupid. The kids we met last night were all bright. I recognized that any and all of the interaction we were having would not have been possible in any Islamic country. Males and females, students all together, talking and enjoying each other. What a blast!

"I saw no one violating a perfect balance between humans; it was amazing! I have a clearer understanding of freedom. There is a lot of self-expression and restraint to that simple word. It is something that does not exist in countries where fundamentalism exists. I feel, unless a person is a female from the Middle East, I do not think she would understand my thoughts. Maybe Ali, the one who was dancing with me — not because he was from Iran, but because I believe he has acquired a balance within himself. The men I met from home where not like him. There was the other guy — what was his name, Saadia? The guy who kept gawking at you?"

Saadia had something to say, and, as usual, she took a breath or two. Observing my two girls and their exchanges was pure delight. I also knew a void less than twelve hours in the making was outside our door. I was going to miss my daughter.

"Are you talking about Kazim, the biomedical engineer? He was not gawking. He is from Jordan, seems brilliant. You will get to know him in no time. He is dating one of the law students, the one who sat next to him at the coffee shop. She seemed bored or something. I did not talk to him much, but he told me his interests were varied, from chemical, to medical, to research only. I guess he will go where he finds the most advantage to his career. He appears to have a plan, whatever it is. There was too much noise for my taste. I did not speak to the girlfriend at all — she was aloof."

She was smiling as she spoke, but she became serious with a turn of the head. "Leila, freedom is something we must all achieve inwardly first. I think we are lucky because Mom was able to show us how to be free because she is a person who is free. It is the examples of parents that teach us most, not the words they speak. In our case, the moral police in an Islamic country would have all three of us stoned for sure. If not that, we would be given at least ninety lashes with a horse whip for talking to people of the opposite sex."

"You are right. The more I read, and the more I meet people such as those from last night, the more I realize there is an entire segment of the world population that is enslaved because they are ignorant of their own potential or are afraid to express it.

"Mom, maybe you can help me. Inside the Middle East and parts of Asia and Africa, people are told by their religious leaders what they can and can't do. The element of choice you worked so hard at teaching us does not exist, because the people of those regions do not know there is such a thing. A choice is not an option for a female. We are prime examples.

"Do you remember when we moved in with you, and Gale explained we had to choose the room we wanted? You said that the choice of room would have to come from us. Neither Saadia nor I had ever had such an experience. To choose. We came from a system that had not grown beyond centuries past. The room thing was huge for both of us. I am no longer certain that we made the choice based on any thinking mechanism. Saadia saw your canvas and it made a choice for her. Regardless, it was the beginning of a new opening into a part of us that had remained dormant our entire lives. The sad part is that we did not know. That is what ignorance does to people. That day, you gave us a key to our own soul and intelligence to be discovered.

"Male members of the societies we came from become the Taliban we read about or see on TV. Other similar groups will develop from that because it is the way of human kind. They do not know themselves as human beings with free will. They do not know their personal potential because it does not exist in their mind. These people do not know how to thrive or desire anything. They are led in whatever direction the leader tells them. They are similar to a herd of sheep, and ignorance permits them to be molded according to the dictates of any self-proclaimed person who presents himself as an authority. It is a lot about who has power over whom. I think it is the way the world works. Those in charge get to do as they please with the lives of those who have nothing. This kind of power is not removed with ease, because, at the core, those being manipulated do not have any sharpness of mind to view the picture.

"I am under the impression this type of a world brings with it frustrations—the same kind of frustration I saw in some eyes when we drove in parts of Los Angeles. Many of the men had void in their eyes, the same I saw when I was growing up. Those are the ones anyone can manipulate with a few simple and empty promises for a better life. Those are the ones who can be talked into any behavior. I do not think the society has much to do with it. I have a feeling it is a human behavioral trait. You know, Mom, the more I observe people, the more I know how lucky Saadia and I are."

"Kids, it is 3:30 in the morning. We must get a few hours of sleep. Leila, you are to be in school by 9:00 A.M. Lights out, and no more talking."

Like two- or three-year-olds, they came to bed with me, kissed me, and went to their own beds.

My eyes had not been closed more than a minute when I heard Leila's telephone. It was 7:00 A.M. and time to get going.

CHAPTER 35

The Gate of Stanford

The new girlfriend, Farah, kept her word. She confirmed the appointment with a phone call to Leila at 7:00 A.M. We were to meet her at 8:30. Leila looked at the map she had drawn, and all was set! We got ready, talked about calling her back and inviting her to breakfast. It was a passing thought—we needed a little more time together. The continental breakfast was great, and the owner of the inn, Agostina from Italy, gave Leila a small bouquet of flowers—a mix of California poppies from her garden and store-bought dried lavenders. The bunch was gracefully arranged and a white ribbon that was part of a small bag, tying the whole thing together. Agostina gave Leila instructions to save the lavender in the bag and hang it in her closet.

When we left home to begin our California vacation, I was very excited. By the time we made it to the San Diego area, the realization that my daughter was going to be dropped off far away from me, to a school I knew was prestigious, left me empty and morose. Nothing I did could stop the feeling. The more miles we put on that rented car, the sooner the life we had known and enjoyed was reaching an end. Not emotionally prepared for the separation, we each became very quiet, sorting through what we had not experienced before.

Finally, Saadia spoke. "Leila, you are not the only one who feels like it's the end of the world. I already feel a great loss, yet I know this is what you want and need to do. I am just going to miss you a lot. You are my sister, and I like having you around. You are fun, even if you drive me crazy sometimes. I love you, Sis."

I could only smile knowing we each had the same feelings. I also knew we were going to experience the separation differently, but we would be fine. "The three of us were brought together in what, at the time, was my home only, for reasons I may still not understand. The point is, we were brought together, and I did the best that I could without a parenting guide. By opening my heart for love to come in, I was showered with degrees of love I did not know existed. Somehow, I managed to sow the seeds to help both of you become successful people. I am very proud of this. We all will adapt and make contact with each other as often as possible."

"My God, Mom, she has a brand new computer. What could possibly stop her from emailing us every day?"

"School!"

It was understood: school had to be a priority. We got in the car packed with Leila's stuff.

"Oh, look!" Saadia said. "Have you ever seen so many palm trees? How can they grow here? I love the red tiles of the roof. They look handmade. I like this place."

"Well, in two more years, you could come here instead of Columbia, and Mom could move here."

"Mom, do you know which way to go? This is a very large campus. Very large! I don't know what I was expecting, but it was not something this big. The brochures they mailed us with the application only showed the building coming up. This is huge! Do you know where you are going?"

"Kids, you better pay attention to the signs, because right now I have no idea where to turn. I do not want to make it difficult for the cars behind me, and I do not want your friend waiting more than she has to. Watch the signs and tell me when you see the name of the hall. Leila, where did Farah say she would meet you?"

"Oh, no! She said to take the second right, but I was busy looking around and did not pay attention. Maybe we didn't pass the turn, because she said she would be at the corner so she could hop in our car and get us where we need to go."

"Mom, slow down. There she is, dressed in red, on the right. Do you see her?"

It was a breeze. I veered to the right. She recognized Leila and, before I knew it, she was in the car, had introduced herself to me, and began to talk to Leila. Though she respected the rules of social etiquette, she talked nonstop. She had no idea that, once in a while, she needed to come up for air. Leila told her to stop a couple of times. Saadia and I looked at each other and smiled.

A couple turns right and a few left, and we were in front of the door.

She produced a placard to hang on the rearview mirror, and I parked six feet from the door. I was happy because we had a multitude of things to take to the second floor.

I never realized Leila had packed so much. Saadia complained that it was all junk and no one needed that many books. She also felt Leila bought too much for her dorm. Regardless, up the steep stairs we went. It took the four of us about five trips. When it was all done, I think the rented SUV took a deep breath. Farah mentioned she did not know a microwave was so heavy. We laughed, and I was grateful we had done our part because, in the dorm, one student was asked to bring a microwave, and Leila had volunteered.

There was an awkward moment. We did not want to leave . . . so I invited them to lunch. Farah suggested a café right on campus, in walking distance from where we were. It was a great idea. I did not feel like driving all over town.

Down the stairs we went, with Leila walking behind me, holding my shoulder with her hand. When we got to the street, she took my hand.

"Mom, I do not know if I am scared or apprehensive, happy or exited. I know everything will be fine, but I am . . . Oh, Mom, I do not know how to be brave."

She started to cry. Luckily for us, there was a bench a few steps away, and we sat to compose ourselves. Farah assured her that all would be fine, and she told us she too had such feelings on her first day two years ago. The difficult moment was defused, and we started walking toward the café. Farah informed us she had to go back on duty; another student was to arrive in about twenty minutes.

It was obvious we did not want to let go. The pace slowed, yet the café's door suddenly opened. Another mother came out with her son. They walked past us, looking distressed, and Saadia remarked how 'cool' it was to see a young man as upset as Leila was. It was not funny, but we understood.

We found an empty table and, before we sat, a young woman was in front of us ready to take our orders. The menu was on a blackboard in front, but I hadn't seen it. She obliged us with some ideas. We each ordered a bowl of soup and a cup of tea. The food appeared almost instantaneously. We did not speak.

"Saadia, now you see why I have a microwave, and Mom, although I'm sorry I took some tea from home, I am real glad. I don't know where this tea comes from or what kind of tea it is. It tastes like colored hot water!

"As time goes by, let me know what you need, and I will send you care packages."

It was time to get up and leave this establishment. Again the walk was slow. When we got to Leila's door, she embraced each of us and told me, holding back her tears, that she would be fine. She had her phone and her computer, and she would communicate with us everyday.

Another phase had started for Leila. I left her, knowing she would regain her balance. While I understood this transition was part of her growth, it tore me at the gut.

CHAPTER 36

Saadia Talks

A few small stores and a couple of cafés helped our aimless state of mind the next morning. Saadia and I felt ill at ease. We were happy for Leila, but we already missed her. The next day, we would visit Sacramento and see the capital of the state. From there, a series of flights would take us to Salt Lake City, then one layover in New York, and back to Boston and Bar Harbor. Going back home minus one made both of us at odds with our own skin.

Today, we would tour San Francisco. Saadia's interests were the Crocker Museum and a couple of churches. In Salt Lake, she wanted to see the Mormon Temple. To maneuver these visits and accommodate what she wanted to see, the layovers were going to be long, but she deserved a treat.

It was Saadia's time, and my attention had not yet shifted to her only. I had never had the opportunity to be alone with only one of my children. Something agreeable was happening, yet something wearing was also going on. Neither of us talked about how we felt. I knew we each had to process feelings foreign to us. Going to a museum would ease these unfamiliar emotions.

Saadia and I shared a love for art and architecture, and this gave us something to focus on other than ourselves and the disconnect we felt. The cellular telephone kept in my purse for emergencies took on a different type of importance. It had become the best means of communication with Leila. One more time I had to hear her voice, just to make sure she was okay. Once I was sure all was fine, we could be on our way.

It was a wonderful drive, and soon enough we were at the Crocker Museum. Saadia knew all there was to know about the place and architect Seth Paris Babson, who designed it.

It was wonderful to see the world through the Afghani eyes Saadia inherited. She saw and described every detail in art and architecture; she knew their reasons for being. With every movement of her eyes, she saw the wonders of life itself. She was a gifted personality, who had not yet discovered her own strength. Once I parked the car, she began to tell me about the architect's body of work. She was one who needed to know the "who" and "why" of everything around her. She had taken the time to learn as much as she could about Babson, including the fact that he designed Victorian houses—something directly opposed to the façade in front of us.

"Mom, thank you for spending this special time with me. I know we could have gone home without exploring anything else. I appreciate the wonders of western life. It saddens me that the girls and women of Afghanistan are not afforded such experiences, not even in books. They do not know of a world beyond where they are. They know misery, abuse, and no one has a sense of who they are. Certainly, they do not know who they could become. I know that because, before my rescue, I, too, did not know these things about myself.

"I could never know enough words to tell you what you gave to Leila and me. Simple things, like playing outside like the boys and girls we saw this morning, were not possible. After about six, girls were kept inside and went out only with their father. I know this is not the way humanity needs to be, because it serves no purpose. No one gains from such closed societies. The young girls who become women do not have the acumen to pass on to their children the art of being a decent human being. They never met one. The girls see their fathers abusing their mothers, so they think it is the norm, and, of course, the boys learn from their fathers. After centuries of that—there you go, you have me! But I am no longer in Afghanistan. Mom, I would not have known what to do to change my life. It seems that there must be a spark from outside. In my case, I was rescued and not killed. I was granted a reprieve."

"Saadia, I feel we are each born with a map, and no matter what, we get to walk the route highlighted on that map. Not much different from the road map you created for this trip. Out of the bigger map, you saw the smaller places and the stops you wanted to make. Life is kind of like that, and when we deviate from the highlighted area of our map, we get lost. Perhaps it is the same for the whole of humanity. Many left the road, and those following them did not even realize the route was no longer the same. It is not easy to find the correct and best way for society.

"If I understand correctly, this is a circle that has gone on for many centuries. I do not know what the answers are, but I believe it is from each woman, girl, boy, and man that change will happen in the world. We are all part of the world. We must all partake in making it a better place, and I do not think any of it can be accomplished by raising levels of fear. We must all do our part, no matter how small. Blaming one another is not the answer either."

"Mom, I must admit, as we traveled the length of California, I was amazed by the diversity of people. At home, Leila and I are the only two who had a different look. That made us special, although sometimes we were not exactly accepted. We had to learn to deal with that, and I think, because of you, we got tougher. We became emotionally resilient in a way that most people may not experience. It was nice of you to be strong for us sometimes.

"Traveling coastal California, and for sure Los Angeles, I saw a lot of anger in more faces than I would have cared to see. It also showed in postures. Most young people I saw dressed in a way that only showed anger. I could not help but think the moral police from the Islamic world would have a field day here. I know I am wicked! At times, I could not believe how some of the girls were dressed, and their mothers, too. I think there is a direct relation with what people think of themselves and how they behave and dress. I am not saying that girls and women need covers, as in Islamic places—not at all—but I feel a woman does not need to express her femininity as a bag of flesh.

"I do not believe the Islamic world has it right at all, but I also believe that too many women here see themselves as sex objects and only that. They seem not to aspire toward much better. I felt disturbed by the apparent measure by which a woman judges herself. This is the impression I got from looking at them and the way men looked at them. How strange is that? Some of us are given as sexual slaves to our husbands in exchange for a goat or two. My observation and impression here is that too many women want nothing more than being sex slaves. I never gave this whole thing any thought before or maybe I guess I never noticed that before. I do now and the sad thing, I think, is that the people I am talking about may not even be conscious of it. You know, Mom, this is a difficult world to digest."

"Saadia, you are observant. I believe you are right about many things, there are segments of societies evolving without establishment of boundaries. At the core we all need guidance, from parents, from state from religion, in other words we need to know what is acceptable within the society we belong to. At the same time, this idea finds conflicts, because what is acceptable to a Christian may not be acceptable to a Jew or a Muslim and the opposite is equally true. This is why people of Judeo-Christian background and also some Muslims find it appalling that some men within a segment of the population, where you were born, see nothing wrong with the violation of a young girl they call a wife. In such cases, I do not know how we can apply non-judgment, no sanction or a degree of acceptance. The reason to find the behavior despicable is one of biology."

"Mom, you know it is because of your thinking and of course our history that Leila chose to study law."

" I doubt that I influenced Leila, I think Mr. Roberts, the lawyer, had some effect on her. The grooming of a human being is something that starts in the cradle. This is one of the many reasons why it is so important for women to be educated. I may have pushed for both your education. What a Muslim girl will not do, because of fear imposed by religion, a western one will do, because she is free of fear. Humans are so complex. I do not know that there are any simple answers. I feel fundamentalism has no place in societies that are evolving. It does not offer an avenue for people to grow, evolve, or accept others. What is done to women in the Middle East, parts of Asia and Africa, and some other countries, should be sanctioned by international laws. Leila is right about that. Perhaps this is where she and those sharing her opinions will make a difference in the world."

"Mom, I am going to miss her, I already do. She was my scale to measure reality with."

"Sweetheart, I understand Leila's passion to make changes for the benefit of girls and women. Your talent will take you to a place where your work will enhance life in another way. The world needs more like you, too."

"Do you think, as the species goes, we can evolve past some god-forsaken oppression of women? Mom, when I came here, I did not have the tools to think with. It now I feel that I had no mind—a complete void between the ears. Now I find it unconceivable to think about growing old in a society like the one I left. I suppose I wish for a type of utopia only found in books and within my ideal."

"Until all the answers are in place, the only thing that is required of you as a human being is to make all attempts at reaching your personal potential—to allow whatever guides you to show you where you need to go and what you need to do. By the way, none of us can do this, no matter how much planning goes on, other than one moment at a time. We must be flexible. In life, there are many boulders to go around. It is good to have ideals and general directions; coupled with education, you become the best human you can ever be. Sweetheart, life has a way of presenting us with opportunities we did not look for. You will find all that you must find as you grow older and wiser."

"Like having two girls come and live with you and become your daughters?"

"Exactly! I could have had all sorts of excuses. I never had children, I did not speak Farsi or Pashto. Logic said 'no' and my heart said 'yes.' I followed my heart. I always do, you know!"

"Do you have any regrets?"

"No, not one."

CHAPTER 37

Hard to Let Go

We spent more time in San Francisco than we expected. Inwardly, I believe we were waiting for a call from Leila, asking us to come and get her, but the call did not come. Onward to Salt Lake we went. Before leaving San Francisco, we went to the local postal service store, packed a few things, and asked the gentleman to mail them to our address. Transaction done, we returned the much lighter rented car at the airport, and we flew to Salt Lake City, Utah.

We had become expert at renting cars. Saadia wanted me to get a Corvette. Out of luck, I rented a brand new Toyota. We did not have any preconceived idea of what we would find. When we asked for directions, the gentleman told us to follow the route downtown. He told us it would not be difficult to identify the temple. He pointed to the picture of the structure that was on the wall. Once in the beige Toyota Camry, my copilot proceeded to guide me. She had the map; I had the visual.

We were set!

When we arrived at our destination, Saadia suggested we eat before going to the temple. The hotel did not have anything we wanted, so we looked for food elsewhere.

A small café along the way seemed perfect. Light and bright in appearance, we went in. A bubbly young woman dressed in plain clothes, very opposite to what we had seen in California, took us to a table facing a large window. She must have sensed we were new to town. We asked for two cups of tea and a minute with the menu. She arrived with a tray bearing a variety of teas to choose from, and I noticed they were all decaffeinated.

We decided on an apricot tea with cinnamon. As they had many times before, Saadia's eyes changed color to suit her mood. She did not like her tea.

"This is not what I expected. What kind of a public place does not serve coffee? Do you remember, when we were in Rome, for some reason I was expecting the same type of feeling and pastries too, with espresso. You know, Mom—prior to this trip, I did not give much consideration to religions. Now, having been in many churches, I feel some disenchantment with religions. I had no particular expectations, but this does not feel like a place I would want to spend time in. Last night, I read about the Mormons. Did you know they had a prophet, too, and he had a bunch of wives, and some were pretty young? Now, I know prophets like young flesh."

"Saadia, it is now against the law for men to have more than one wife. Be open minded. Things changed within that church, and we have not been here long enough to judge."

"I can almost hear what Leila would be saying."

We both laughed, still looking at the menu. We each switched to lemonade and had a pastry.

"You know this is not any kind of a breakfast."

In no time, we were done with our meal and continued on to visit the temple. Temple Drive took us there, and once the car was parked, we continued on foot. Very much like the picture from the car rental place, we walked on. A young man dressed in black pants and a white shirt approached us and welcomed us to the Church of Jesus Christ of Latter Day Saints. Saadia wore her crooked smile but greeted the young man politely.

We wanted to visit every room of this place, but he took us instead to a wonderful garden and explained that a Mormon temple was a place special to Mormons, a place where they make contact with higher spheres. We were not Mormons. At the end of his polite chat, he asked if we had any questions and offered us two Books of Mormon. Saadia took one and told the young man we did not need two. It was time to continue elsewhere.

"Mom, even if I had no expectations, I feel totally let down. When are we going home?"

"Saadia, did you not enjoy at least the apparent architecture of the place? If I understand correctly, this is the most important temple for the Mormons."

"Very bizarre is all I can say. We couldn't go in, just as I could not go inside a Mosque."

"You could have asked the young man. Maybe they make exceptions?"

"No, I only I wanted to get out of there."

"Okay, we are out now. What do you want to do?"

"You think we could drive someplace and find coffee and some decent food? I am hungry."

"Let's go back to the hotel. They will tell us where we could go."

The front desk gal was not a Mormon, and she gave us the name of an Italian restaurant complete with instructions for getting there.

"Mom, don't forget to change the reservation for tonight only."

This took me by surprise. Saadia was not impressed and wanted to go home. She took no paper or pencil to sketch anything. Definitely odd!

I wanted to talk to her before changing the reservation, so we went to our room for a moment.

"What is going on? This is not like you."

"Maybe I am tired, but I can tell you I do not like this place. I want to go home."

"Sweetheart, are you coming down with something. You are not being you."

"Mom, there is a feeling here that takes me back to Afghanistan. I feel a sort of oppression, and I do not like that."

"Okay, I get it. I will let them know that we are departing in the morning. Let me call the airline first."

All was worked out, and off we went for some Italian food. Saadia asked them for two coffees to go. The waiter, lusting after my daughter, made them complimentary.

It was an early flight out with layovers, but we were on our way home, en route to our own beds. I think we were both ready.

CHAPTER 38

A Letter from Leila

The way back home was nearly as long as a transcontinental journey. We had two stops. We were tired but pretended for the benefit of the other that we were not missing anything or anyone. The car was parked, our luggage out, and I was glad the bulk of our belongings had been mailed rather than taken onboard. The roundabout driveway never looked better, and it was a relief to see the mailed boxes left by the garage door. I made a mental note to compensate the mailman handsomely. Saadia's multiple sketch pads and newfound treasures made their way to her room.

Tired as she was, instead of waiting one more day, she did what I used to do: she went to get the mail. This daily routine took on a different meaning on that brisk and sunny afternoon. It was fall here in Maine, and the leaves we left had taken hues to remind us that it was not Photoshop that had transformed the scenery. Saadia ran back to the kitchen, where I was making us a cup of tea. Now that we were the only two inhabitants of this home, I realized that, with Saadia being generally a quiet person, this home would feel too quiet. I called the vet to get our dog back.

"Mom, Leila wrote you a letter. Here, open it." The rest of the mail stayed in a pile on the table. Saadia gave me the envelope and sat on the floor by my feet. She never gave up the comfort she found cross-legged on the floor. She now had a special cushion that made its way through out the house. I'd had it covered with an Afghan rug Ursula found for us. As I opened the envelope, she put her head and one arm on my lap. She was feeling a little blue. I played with her hair as I read out loud.

Dear Mom,

It's late tonight and I can't sleep. Everything is fine but I miss you, I miss Saadia, and God I miss Jake. This is only the beginning of the second week. At night if I do not have a lot of homework, there is a void and this is one of those! I miss both of you.

Don't worry; I am fine, just feeling empty right now. I am meeting lots of wonderful people, the classes are fabulous, but food around here, not so good... I like this place but I cannot yet get it through my head that I will be here for four or more years. Mom, I want to come home for Thanksgiving, PLEASE.

I met a new friend, she is from Algeria, speaks fluent French and English too. You know my French is not so bad! She is a 'Musulmane' she says—an activist.

It appears that a lot is going on in Algeria. I never gave any thought to this region of the world, yet they have their own and similar struggles to those Islamic patriarchal societies seem to develop. If I understand her correctly, soon after the French left Algeria, varied degrees of fundamentalism began to erupt. And according to Yasmine (that is her name, nice hey!), the country began to change. Of course, she was not around during the French period, but she has lots of stories from her parents. She said there were some good times and some very bad times, too. What was a quasi-French society disappeared. Those who wanted to retain a semblance of French culture were beaten for 'punishable crimes.' Lives were taken by those on a mission to re-Islamize Algeria.

Mom, there is so much I know nothing about. How is Saadia doing? Does she miss me? I miss her a lot, but don't tell her. I miss talking to her. She makes so much sense always. You can tell her that Kazim was asking about her. Ali introduced me to his girlfriend. She is from Rhode Island, small world.

Yasmine told me about many people called . . . I don't remember, but she said something about dispensing the ruling orders. Women could no longer wear their western clothes, and like in rural Iran or Afghanistan, they could not go around town alone. If one did, she was promptly dealt with. Beatings and people disappearing became a new norm. Yasmine went to high school in Wisconsin, lived with her aunt and uncle. She did not

271

talk to me about her mom and dad—only that her father was killed because some people did not like the idea that his daughter went to school, and in a foreign country no less. Her mother was whipped in a public square to teach other mothers a lesson. I don't know what happened next. Can you imagine this! Somehow, I never gave Algeria any thought. I never read a thing about them.

I think I know what the problems were and possibly are in that country. Anger! If I understand her correctly, since the mid 1800s, one million French made life very difficult for the inhabitants of the country. Violence about race and violence for and against colonization was what young people knew. I am finding out so much. There was a movement established by intellectuals, way back during the time of the existentialists. She said they wrote letters, I am not sure I know what she means. We talk a lot, so there is a lot to absorb.

Did you know Jean-Paul Sartre visited Algeria many times? Regardless of what was going on in that place, some people had a blast! At the same time, changes were occurring, people were getting angrier, and the fundamentalists were getting stronger. Same story, different country.

Mom, one thing is for sure, the more people I meet here, the more I realize I have many lifetimes of studies to do. Again and again, I am seeing that, once a man makes a ruling, the women of certain regions just bend their heads and obey. Muslim women are groomed to obey. I pray that I am wrong, but somehow my understanding of societal workings and behavior is not something for the faint to take on. I have a huge task ahead. It is exhilarating, yet since I am but one person, I will stay with the two countries I know something about. I know what I experienced, including sexual abuse, which seems to be pretty global.

This fundamentalist thing is a circle that grows larger every day. I am learning, surely, in patriarchal and tribal societies the identity of girls and women is not recognized. No wonder they do not want them educated — they do not exist. There is something pretty scary about educated women. They become emancipated, and they teach their children a different set of values. I know how lucky Saadia and I are.

Mom, so much I must learn, read, and understand. It is hard and it is fun all at once. I am meeting wonderful people here. They are from every single state and some from foreign countries. Sometimes I feel like a way station, and my knowledge of the world is limited. Tell Saadia to do well in school; she will enjoy college very much. Tell her to focus on what she really wants to do. Mom, I miss her a lot.

I miss you too, Mom. It is not even November, and I know I will like this place more and more, but don't forget I want to come home for Thanksgiving. For me, it is the best holiday there is, and I have a truckload of things to be grateful about. I am also realizing my ideas and ideals have not changed, but the road I must take is going to be an arduous one.

I am going to meet a teacher here, Yasmine is going to introduce me to her. She is from Algeria. More on that another time because I have no details, just that I will meet her. I am also meeting some American girls and boys, too. They are all nice and so, so bright. Not what I left in high school!

I love and miss you very much.

Tell Saadia a long letter to her will be mailed in a day or two. I miss my sister. There is no one here to wake up in the middle of the night and talk with.

I love my Mom, I love my sister.

L (Oh, I like signing my name just ' L' now, pronouncement of Elle ... I like!)

Please, remember Thanksgiving.

L

CHAPTER 39

Interlude

Saadia and I did not have much to say after the letter and her comment about Thanksgiving. We likely were contemplating our own feelings about the course Leila's new life was taking. From where she had planted herself at my feet, Saadia got up, kissed me on the forehead, and went to the kitchen.

"So, Mom, how many people are we having here for Thanksgiving? You think we will be able to get aunt Ursula from the care place? I don't like that place at all. Mom, there is not one cookie in this house, I am so hungry. Can we go get some? Better yet, I am going to make cookies."

Smiling, I said yes, realizing it was not cookies she wanted but the void around us needed to be filled before heading to the grocery store for the mysterious things she needed. I called the veterinarian. I felt one trip out would be all I could do.

"Saadia, do you want your new dog tonight?"

"Now. Let's go. What are you saying, 'my dog'?"

Since I was on the phone, I told him we could be right over. He was about to close the clinic, so we made arrangements to meet at a halfway point—the grocery store. I would pay the fees for this new dog in the morning.

In a matter of seconds, we were in the car and very exited. Neither of us knew what we were going to get. While in California, I had called the vet to tell him I wanted a dog. As providence would have it, a female and her six puppies were left at his door. They were Labradors. He told me one of them would be perfect for us.

It took only a few minutes and we were united with our new dog. Saadia explained to him that her mom would not allow her to get a dog in California, and now she knew why. Doggy did not care. I knew he preferred being the only alpha in the house. Judging by the size of his feet, I knew we were now the owners of a dog that would be very large.

We got back home, and before closing the garage door and after marking his new territory, Doggy marched all over the house. The look he gave us was perplexed. He must have smelled Jake.

"How do you explain to a dog that his sister went away to school and his brother Jake is gone?"

"You do not. He will get used to not having her around until Thanksgiving. We all will."

"And after that?"

"Saadia, I have no idea. This is new for all of us, including our dog. Just know that we will all survive. Do you have a name for him?"

"This is so cute—look, Doggy is looking out the window. I know he is looking for Leila! He can smell her. This reminds me when I was a kid living just outside of Kabul. All the windows had to be painted black. We could not see out, and no one could see in. Now, I so enjoy looking out at the harbor from my room. This simple little thing is huge for people like me, and Leila, too. We value many aspects of freedom most people do not even realize they have. Actually, I feel most people have no idea what freedom is. Going on the radio and screaming at the government is far from what freedom means to me."

"Why were the windows painted black?"

"At the time, I did not know. You grow up with something, and you think it must be like that all over the world, even if you do not exactly have a concept of the world. It turns out that the various moral police (ignorant boys and men) were appointed by the Taliban to make sure girls and women were not seen. According to them, we were evil, so all windows were to be blackened.

"All new rulings were according to the Taliban. I am not sure when these things happened, but they pronounced themselves the enforcers of the voice of God. What they said and did from that point on were edicts directly from the mouth of Allah. They knew, period! Yet, those same men of virtue could walk in somebody's home, take a girl or a mother, if she was to their liking, and make sex slaves out of them. Those with such preferences did the same to young boys, too.

"Regardless of what went on, no one questioned, because they would be killed if they did. When I think of it all, it is not different from my father marrying me off for what he could get. It is the same—a man or many men dictating what will happen to girls and women—not a bit of difference.

"You know, Mom, I do not believe a man taking nine years old girl is listening to the voice of any god. The laws of civilized countries punish pedophilia. I read the social and medical definitions, and I also understand that, in many Islamic societies, there are customs that permit and promote such behavior. No one in an Islamic society would dare say a thing about it all because of fear and because people are made to believe that a man who declares himself a patriarch has absolute power over others. That's what keeps the females of some societies oppressed.

"The sadness of all this is that men and women are simply fearful and do nothing to change their way of life. Women pass on to their children the only thing they know: being abused. And because of their acceptance, they show their sons how to become the abusers!

"Mom, we need a small doggy door and an enclosure for Cooper. He looks like a Cooper."

"Cooper it is! Saadia, my love, it is a wonder that you were able to find the strength and the courage to forgive and go forward. Though I hear passion from you, I do not hear pain, anger, or distress of any kind. You are not consumed by your circumstances of birth. I applaud and admire you."

"Mom, I am not sure how, but I think it is your openness that permitted both Leila and myself not to be consumed. I must also say, at the beginning, we did not have the emotional development or understanding that would have given us the tools to feel much of anything. We had become or were groomed, at a very young age, to be closed, and numbness had overtaken us. I don't know if this is the way it is for all people in similar circumstances, but that is the way it was for me. We did not understand that we had been abused, because all around us, that was all we saw and what we experienced. We had not been exposed to anything else. We each felt some degree of pain, but without understanding, there is a sort of paralysis that sets in. What emotions we felt did not come with a recognizable perspective.

"I think things like that can potentially destroy the spirit. We were lucky. You provided the countermeasures to change and support. Without apparent effort, you provided us with the ground to walk away untainted. Today, I can say I remember the damages done to me, but it does not define who I am. I can assure you, this is something that would not have been acceptable where we came from. By the time we could have understood that we had been damaged, our thoughts had been liberated. I give you full credit for that. The only sadness is that many girls in the same circumstances do not have a Julienne Fairchild as an ally. You are comfortable with yourself, and we learned from that.

"When you told us the stories about your mother, Suzannah, your dad, and also his brother—actually your father—we did not hear anger or pain. When you told stories you had heard about WWII, again we heard the facts as you understood them, but we did not hear anger. We knew you missed some aspects of each member of your family, and we still know, when you look at a piece of cheese, it takes you to a different place. You are funny about that! You did not lose who you were, but you are not paralyzed by any of your past life experiences. I think all these things opened doors for our psyche to see light where there was mostly darkness. You did, Mom! Remember, *remarkable*! I love you, Mom."

After a wonderful hug that had become something she did often, I told her if she ever felt the need to talk about emotions she could not cope with, she was to let me know. If not from me, we could find a good psychologist.

"Have you ever been to a psychologist?" she asked.

"No, I have not. I gave it some consideration after Frank died, but allowing my self to love what was no longer with me and remembering the little things I had taken for granted eased the pain. No psychologist could have given me any relief for any of that. I think moving to New England was also a key factor to my recovery. I had no choice but to cope with this old house. It was desperately in need of repairs. I knew no one and needed all sorts of people to do work for me.

"I was lucky the day I received a newspaper by mistake and it had some advertisements. In no time, I began to make phone calls. It was hilarious. With my broken English, I think some of the repair people felt sorry for me. Amazingly, when they could not fix something, most of them were able to suggest other people. I was very engrossed in being at the center of something different and, before you know it, the house became my home. During this process, I redefined who I was. Missing Frank was no longer consuming. I came to miss him for reasons I did not know before. Like you, I can remember, but the memories do not define me. I cannot exactly explain it."

"Well there you have it! In our case, we had to be consumed with learning our language and making an attempt at understanding your jabber. We knew somehow we had to understand you. Crazy woman, we did not know what to think, when you were going around the house touching things and saying words we could not pronounce. That was not fun, you know! You made us laugh and cry.

"I remember one evening a light bulb from the chandelier went to heck. You pointed to it, said something ridiculous we could not understand, and you kept pointing to the ceiling. We could not understand, and the light bulb was not a problem to us. Neither one of us ever had a chandelier, and the fact that one bulb was not on meant nothing to us. We were not sure if you were pointing to the chandelier or the ceiling. We could not figure out whatever you were teaching us. Come to think of it, what *were* you teaching us? You went to get the broom and I think, at that time, we lost it. When you started sweeping and showing 'ceiling, ceiling' you were so funny—a broom in your hand, sweeping a ceiling. We thought you had lost your mind. The teaching of that day was extreme laughter."

"I no longer remember the details, but obviously that day you learned ceiling, light bulb, broom. Lesson accomplished."

"And, like you, in the process, we redefined who we were. Mom, you gave us a gift most birth mothers never have the ability to give. I also speak for Leila. The people who moved into your home—two damaged, scared girls—were made to find themselves. Based on my observation of parents, I see that they attempt to control and define who and what their children need to be. Somehow you made sure that the reverse happened. We found the core of who we were and what we were meant to become. Once we were able to speak with you and express the things that scared us and the things that pleased us, we were no longer victims. I did not represent the country called Afghanistan, nor did I represent the people of that country. The people who grew from your guidance are portraits of the new people we now see in the mirror. The place and the circumstances of our birth can no longer imprison us.

"Being here, I learned a great deal. One thing is for sure—I came to understand the experiences of one, or in this case, two individuals, who could not define for others what an entire country was about because, ultimately, each experience of life is different, even if circumstances are similar. Unfortunately, circumstances and stories set prejudices in action. People do not necessarily trust people from the region were they came from. While no single individual represents the misdeeds of the land of his or her birth, they remind others of things unpleasant, things they could not face. I am not sure I will ever understand the behavior of people. My experience with blind faith has not been a pretty picture."

"Sweetheart, it is such a pleasure to hear you and be exposed to the expansion of your mind. I love it. I am privileged. Thank you, Saadia. You make me proud of you."

"Cooper needs to go out. The vet said he was trained, but he did not tell us the signs. I think he needs to go. When I come back, let's have tea." And with that, out she went.

CHAPTER 40

One Hundred Years on Earth

It took awhile, but when they returned, Cooper was happy and went straight to his bowl—Jake's old one, until we got new ones. He did not seem to mind. That dog could drink gallons. This four-month-old puppy was also in need of lots of food. The idea of a temporary enclosure for him was still to be handled. Once Saadia showed him the dog door, he understood, but we could not let him go out alone.

"Mom, are you going to have a party for your aunt? I saw the hideous cakes they serve at the health care place. I know we can't bake like she did, but there must be something we could do to celebrate her 100 years on earth. It is amazing that her mind is still so swift. I love talking to her. She told me a great deal about World War II. She told about Germany and what she remembers of her little sister. They were courageous girls, your mother and your aunt. I hope one day I can be as strong as they. I am going to ask her for her most favorite cake, get the recipe, and make it. What do you think? You know I admire her so much, she is such a courageous woman. I want to be like her."

"Saadia, I am not a baker. Her cakes did not come out of a box from the grocery store — she made them from scratch. I am not sure we would be able to approximate what she did."

"Mom, she will know we made it. Will you pick me up tomorrow right after school? We can visit her and right after go get the different ingredients."

Saadia had a special admiration for Ursula. This child of mine chose her friends with care. She had few, but they were all distinct in personality and age.

So went our days, one after the other. My very dear aunt Ursula died soon after her 100th birthday. In our small town, few knew she was a Holocaust survivor. My children did and drew wisdom and strength from her stories. She left her bakery to the gal who had worked with her since she was 15. Natalie was now the proud owner of the bakery, and she continued the practice of providing us with all the breads and cookies we could ever want.

Between the shelves containing the most delicious cakes, she began something new: once a year she showed Saadia's art, the sales of which went to various charities. Ursula left me her home to be sold, the proceeds of which were to be divided between Leila and Saadia. She left me a silver spoon, she had a jeweler make it into a key holder. In a letter given to me by the lawyer handling her affairs I was told the silver spoon had belonged to Suzannah when she was a little girl. The letter did not say who the person was but the workmanship was exquisite, he gave a bend to the handle and added an attachment with a clasp to hold the keys. A spoon my mother ate with when she was an infant now holds my keys together.

Holding this gift close to my heart allowed my mind to wonder, and the harbor breeze put punctuations to my wondering mind.

New people walked into our lives, some lingered a bit, and some did not stay. Saadia and I became closer. Soon enough, as the days progressed she too will go away to further be educated. Not having Leila to speak with in the middle of the night, I often see the light from under her door as she paints the night away. Missing a loved one, in this case her sister is difficult. When the brush does not call her, she often climbs in bed with me.

Her paintings continue to reflect the maturity of her artistry. She was born a master. To think of the stones ready to be thrown at her would have taken that talent away from the world enrages me. The sales of her landscapes, seascapes, and her architectural drawings expanded to enormous collections. Mr. Jackson, the small gallery owner, now her agent, sells her work throughout the eastern coast of the U.S., often talking to her about yet another agent for disbursement of work in Europe. Saadia's earnings go to her bank account. Some of her earnings are used to shower Leila and me with presents. She also gives to various philanthropies dealing with children welfare. Saadia is not the type of soul one sees every day.

Leila's first Thanksgiving as a collegiate was spent at home with us. The next one we spent in California with her. Her Christmas and New Year's vacations were spent with us, at home.

With each passing day, as I realized my children had become independent people, we grew closer as three adult women. Their ideals had not changed much, and the modification around us was mostly within me. I accepted the fact that they would not always be at arm's reach. The rest of my life, I would have to accept this. Their wings escaped being cut, and they learned how to fly. I nurtured my the eaglets, and now I was watching them soar.

About two months before her graduation, Saadia began to receive letters from colleges and universities. Two or three days apart, the mailman delivered large envelopes. The one from Columbia University and also the one from Stanford were left unopened. Her grades permitted her any choice.

She only talked about medicine in relation to children' health issues, she excelled in biology and took extra classes in the chemistry lab. She helped in the children's ward at the local hospital. Cooper our dog even became a regular there. Her favorite sketches continued to be of buildings, sea- and landscapes. The content of each envelope puzzled me. For reasons I did not know, she said nothing. I decided there was a choice between the two establishments, and the grand opening would happen when Leila was home. My children were the teachers of patience I needed.

We were getting ready for Leila to arrive for Saadia's graduation. Two years had gone by, and we were well adjusted to our individual stations in life. All was fine, except again soon this house would only hear the sounds of my feet and those of Cooper.

My bedroom door opened. Saadia came in from a walk with jet-black Cooper, who came in first. I was writing a letter to Leila, but at that moment, I realized Saadia needed attention.

"Mom, we need to talk. I suppose you saw the envelopes?"

"If you are talking about the ones you did not open, yes, I saw them."

"See, I love to paint, I will do that for the rest of my life, but only as I paint today. I love architecture, and that, too, I could do for the rest of my life. My real calling, however, is taking care of people. Working in the hospital stirred something within me. I decided medicine is what I need to do. I will serve people, but most of all I will be satisfied with myself. What do you think? Oh, one more thing—I went to the bank. I now have $42,906.50 saved! How do you like them apples?"

"Wow . . . I had no idea you had saved so much. You have enough money to travel far, and for a long time. Ultimately sweetheart, only you can decide what you want to do with your life. I think, since you are passionate about more than one career, I would do three things, if I were you. First, talk to a guidance counselor, and second, after that conversation, examine the reasons for your choice and go with your heart. The third is keeping the door of art and architecture open. At anytime in your life, you can go back to school and prepare for a new career. I am so proud of you for so many things."

"I will follow your advice, and, no—the money is not traveling money. It is for renovating aunt Ursula's house. Leila and I talked about it. The house has not sold, and to us it is an omen. We want to make it into a combination art gallery and a small bed and breakfast place. My God, that house has six bedrooms and seven bathrooms. Do you know why she got such a large house? We have not yet gotten the logistics of the operation straight, but that will come. What do you think of our idea?"

Hugging her, I could not help the free-flowing tears. "Ursula always thought her sister and her family would end up here. Both of you are such remarkable young woman. You bring so much pride in my life. I love you."

"Do you remember when I did not know what 'granted' meant, and you spent half a day explaining the concept to me? I did not understand then, but I do now. I love you, Mom, and I do not take you for granted, not ever!"

There is something that happens inside when one feels such deep emotions. I had not felt like that before this time. Now, looking at my life, I felt it was both complete and also beginning anew. It was joyful and sorrowful. "Completely complete," Ursula said many times; now I understood that.

Two weeks after Leila came back, Saadia declared Columbia University would afford her the program she wanted. Leila asked if they could travel to New York and find out firsthand how that school would fare.

Now a pro in matters of schools, she took it upon herself to evaluate Columbia University. Ultimately, I felt she wanted her sister to be in California but respected her choice. We decided New York would be a great place to visit again. Cooper was not too sure about the suitcases. Saadia explained to him that she would return, like Leila. Somehow that dog knew that something was about to change.

That afternoon, Leila spent in her garden. She had seeds of California poppies that I did not think would grow here. Without hesitation, she reminded me that we all must take chances and give chances. She was giving the seeds in her hands a chance to grow in her garden.

"Mom, imagine, if they grow, you will have a multitude of yellow-orange flowers for your table and a canvas or two. Most of all, the seeds will know they had been given a chance to grow. You did just that with us. You had no guarantees that we would grow. It is the same with my seeds."

Something brilliant and fluid flowed, as I looked at both of them. Two accomplished young women on their way to full lives. Who knew all this would happen to two rescued girls who were meant to be killed?

Smiling, I went back inside. It was many hours later, when I realized Leila was still outside. Saadia was finishing a huge canvas for a show. I went out to check on Leila.

Her back was to me, hunkered down, holding her legs against her chest. This was not a typical Leila pose. She turned her head and began to cry as she had years before. I knew immediately the tears had to do with her past. I walked to her and lowered myself to my knees. I never could squat as they did.

"What is going on?"

"Oh, Mom, sometimes I think I have it all handled, and other times I am not so sure."

"What is it that is not handled? How can I help you?"

"Do you know why I planted this beautiful rose bush facing east?"

"When we got the rose, it was much smaller and covered with scented roses, like it is now. Tell me why the eastern exposure? I did not pay attention to this detail, and I am not sure what the scent meant to you, either."

"Remember, when we went to the nursery, when I saw this bush in its diminutive magnificence, I don't know why, but I thought of my daughter. That is why I asked you to get it for me. You see, when I buried my daughter in the garden, a very similar rose bush was next to her. When I planted this one here, I felt the bush was symbolically planting my daughter all over again. To me, at the time, I was planting her, not burying her.

"I cried that day, too, but you and Saadia were making cookies, and you did not see me. I am glad, because you probably would have taken me to the nearest psychologist. It is not that I miss my daughter—she was in my life only two days. Her life was taken from her and me. For some reason, today, when I saw all the flowers, I thought about her all over again. She would have been a little over fourteen years old now. If she had lived, she would most probably have been raped hundreds of times by her husband and would probably be the mother of more than one child. I was thinking of all that misery. Looking at the bush, I felt gratitude because she was dead and did not get to know the pain awaiting her. I also feel bad because she was killed by the action of her own father. I think I am trying to make sense of my feelings. Mom, it is not easy right now. I never had a memorial for her, so this rose bush, planted to the east, is that memorial."

I stayed with her not knowing what to say or do. Saadia arrived awhile later with Cooper, her shadow, always at her side. She took one look at us and asked what was going on. We told her, and she managed to find space between us. Arms around us, she started singing a song in Pashto. We said nothing at all for a long while.

"Leila, I am not a singer, but I think the words will find your daughter's soul and the many other souls who have been lost to abuse and violence. Every time we are here to water the bush, we will honor her and you, too. We will honor our sisters who have been abused, killed, and maimed. We will honor all our sisters whose skin can't resonate with the sounds of their hearts."

She wiped her mouth because her lips were wet from tears and kissed each of us.

"You and I will go forth and be all that they attempted to break. We will show and teach others that, no matter what the wound, we do not have to be victims."

"Thank you, Saadia, and thank you, Mom. I love you both so much. We all have a place in the world, and today my daughter has one, too."

I was filled with gratitude. Despite the adversities they had suffered, my children chose not to spend the rest of their lives as victims. In their individual ways, they each had chosen to help humanity and, ultimately, help themselves.

I was still a widow, now a woman over fifty years of age. At times I had also walked on difficult terrain, but no one I knew had journeyed the road my children traveled and conquered. I felt good about them and myself. By some miracles, I had made a difference in two lives. Reflecting on these things, I gave homage with thanks to all those who had made the difference in my life. They were essential influences that created the person I am today.

Knowing we all have boulders to climb or go around, if we choose to, I knew it was the choices we made that allowed our stories merge into something glorious.

There were many long pauses that sunny afternoon, when Leila, Saadia, our new dog, now a swimmer, and I went for walks on the beach.

About the Author

Eveline Horelle Dailey is quick to laughter and tears. Taking life to heart, she responds to a volcano within. She unearths the stories she must tell. She has a passion for the human spirit and its potential.

Educated overseas and in the U.S.A., Eveline's readers find French, her first language, influences and delivers texture to her prose. Design and art bring structure to her composition. She writes from the center of her emotions. When not writing, she can be found weaving, painting, or reading.

She is author of *Lessons from the Lakeside—A Journey Toward Self Discovery* and *The Canvas—A Secret from the Holocaust.* Along with her books, Eveline's essays and articles are read internationally.

Residing in Arizona, Eveline is a member of many writers groups and several not-for-profit organizations.

Made in the USA
San Bernardino, CA
14 November 2015